The Rancher of Willow Creek

(Willow Creek Series Book 3)

by

Casey Dawes

Mountain Vines Publishing

Book cover design by GetCovers
Edited by Amy Ewing

Published by Mountain Vines Publishing
Missoula, MT

Chapter One

Michael Quinn's feet hit his cool bedroom floor. The sun was streaming through the window, giving him hope that the late September weather was going to hold to its moderate temperatures. Slipping his feet into his house loafers, he got up to start his day.

A half hour later, he poured himself a cup of coffee.

Was it warm enough to go outside and drink it?

Temperate days were on the wane; he may as well enjoy them while he could.

He put on a jacket and went outside to sit on his front porch and take in the beauty of his ranchlands and the valley that surrounded them.

After settling into the rocker that had been on the porch since his uncle owned the place, he stared out at the land around him and sipped his coffee. The cottonwoods that lined the Yellowstone River were a brighter tangerine hue this year than they'd been in a while. Beyond them dark green pines marched up the mountains, interspersed with groves of marigold-leafed aspens and the orange-yellow needles of tamaracks.

The wind must have been just right, because the sound of chainsaws carried over the valley. People were preparing for the inevitability of the long winter ahead.

Closer to him, a few horses nibbled in a corral, the occasional whinny reaching his ears. A magpie flew by on its striking white and blue-black wings, not deigning to give him the time of day. In the distance some of his cattle grazed peacefully.

It was a great day to be alive.

But there was something missing, as uncomfortable as the pea beneath the princess on her mattress.

Maybe it was Laura and Jake's wedding a few weeks ago in Iowa. He'd been Jake's best man. It was an honor, and he was happy for his friend, but …

But what, exactly?

It had been a picture perfect Midwestern wedding—all blue skies and cornfields. A big red barn as a backdrop and tables groaning with hearty dishes for the reception. Everyone was friendly. And when it got to be too much, he had hung out with Jake and Caleb to plan their next fishing trip. Quinn wanted to get a few more good-sized trout to cover him over the winter.

Ice-fishing had never appealed to him.

Jake and Laura had stayed a few days in Iowa after the event, then gone on to Hollywood for a more glamorous reception, finally returning home where the locals had hosted a party at the Buckhorn Bar and Grill the previous weekend.

Anna Wells, the owner of the establishment, had done her usual stellar job. She liked to claim that the other women in town, led by the never-take-no-for-an-answer Heather Daley, were really the ones responsible. Quinn could give Heather and her crew their due, but he knew Anna was excellent with details and had standards he could only aspire to have.

Little Anna Wells, all grown up. He'd hoped for the best for her when they were kids. She was running her own establishment and seemed to like it, but sometimes during the reception, she'd leaned against the wall and the joy had skittered away from her face. Her eyes had dimmed, and her skin had sagged a bit. He didn't know all of what had happened between the time they were in high school in Butte until now, but it looked like she had a lot of emotional scars.

Scars he'd do anything to make go away.

When footsteps sounded on the back steps leading up to the porch, Quinn turned his head and saw "Young Ted" O'Shay coming toward him.

Young Ted was in his late forties, but old-timers still used the moniker to distinguish him from his father, Ted, who had been Quinn's uncle's ranch manager before turning the job over to his son.

"Howdy," Ted said.

Quinn gestured for him to take a seat in a second rocking chair next to him.

"Beautiful day," Quinn said.

"Sure is."

The two of them let silence linger as they rocked like they did every morning when Ted came over to discuss the day ahead.

"Weatherman says we're going to get snow early this year," Ted said.

"They say that every year."

"Yup."

Quinn drank more coffee.

"There's other signs, too." Ted pointed toward the cottonwoods. "Color like that means a harsh winter." He reached into a pocket and pulled out an acorn. "Feel this shell. Thicker than normal. Another sign."

Quinn took the shell and examined it, more for Ted than anything else. He had no idea how to tell an acorn shell was thicker than usual.

"So when do you think we should bring the herd down?" he asked.

"I was talking to Ralph Daley yesterday," Ted said. "He's thinking we should aim for mid-October and not any later."

Quinn and the Daleys had agreed to share the upper reaches of their land during the summer to make it easier for the cattle to have access to nearby forest service land they leased from the government. It meant separating the cattle in the winter, but gave the cows more territory to range the other seasons. So far, it had worked out well, and they had a well-fed group of expectant mamas, as well as steers designated for market.

"Probably a good idea to get them down before hunting season really begins. We're getting more and more tourists, but there's less and less accessible land for them to get to."

"You going to keep the right of way open for forest service land?" Ted asked.

"Yep. It's the way Jed always did it. He claimed it was what made the state what it was. Easy access to forest service land gave a person a chance to feed their family, and increase state income from out-of-state hunters."

Ted nodded. "Your uncle was good people. Not like some of them ..." He gestured to the southern end of the valley where business people and Hollywood types had homes, most of them second ones. "Helena's making it easier for them to shut people out."

Quinn nodded. He had his opinions on the subject, but until the state government changed its current course, there wasn't much to be said about it.

"Mid-October sounds good," he said. "You'll get the people we need to make it happen and coordinate with Ralph?"

"Sure thing, boss." Ted rose, placed his cowboy hat back on his head, and added, "See ya," before walking back the way he'd come.

Quinn continued to rock and star at the cottonwoods.

If it was going to be an early winter, it was going to be a long one. Best to take a ride today and see if he could figure out what was bothering him the most—the weather or the woman.

~ ~ ~

An hour later, Quinn put on a jacket, saddled up his horse Champion, and headed for the higher elevations of the Rocking Q Ranch. The quarter horse was retired from rodeo work, and his previous owner had been forced to sell after some bad investments. Quinn had renamed the animal Champion, after Gene Autry's horse, and turned him into a trail animal.

How he'd enjoyed all those old westerns as a kid, not only Autry, but the Lone Ranger and Roy Rogers. The era had seemed so simple back then. The bad guys got what they deserved, the good guys were heroes, and people were genuinely nice to each other ... except when they got drunk. It was only later that he'd realized how stereotyped all the characters were, especially Native Americans.

Even as a teen, he'd watch and drift back into a world that never was. Sometimes when she was at their house, Anna had found him, sat down, and watched with him.

Quinn frowned as he left the wide fields that dominated the valley portion of the ranch and started to ascend. Anna had been close friends with his sister, Mary. It seemed like they were always at his house, never at Anna's. He'd never questioned it at the time, but now he wondered why.

Grassland gave way to sagebrush, its potent aroma surrounding him. Here and there he noted places where cheat grass had taken over. The invasive was a problem in the sagebrush, as it took over the territory and was more prone to fire. He'd have to contact someone to see the best way of getting rid of it before the snowfall. Although it wasn't ideal to run a large amount of cattle on the sagebrush, it was a matter of proportion.

He crossed one of the creek beds on the trail, pleased to see there was still water running. The sun's warmth made him remove his jacket and tie it behind the saddle.

His uncle sure had an amazing spread. When he'd inherited it, he'd been surprised at how many acres there actually were, over half of them unused. He'd asked the lawyer to explain it.

All he got was a shrug and a few words that sounded exactly like his uncle.

"Jed figured if he had enough there was no sense in taking it from the other critters we shared the earth with."

For all his live and let live ideas, Jed had been an astute businessman. If he managed the ranch conservatively, Quinn had enough for the rest of his life and something to leave his two children.

He'd married Amy, his buddy's sister-in-law, after returning from his last tour in the Middle East. His buddy had convinced him his hometown city of Detroit needed men like him on the police force. Quinn had liked the city, fallen in love with the woman, and found purpose in becoming a cop.

Unfortunately, Amy hadn't liked the reality of being a cop's wife. They broke up as amicably as it could happen, and he put his heart into his career until his retirement a few years back. He'd been as good a father as he could be, but his kids were living lives of their own and had no interest in an existence that included cows.

"Whoa," he told Champion.

The horse stopped, and Quinn looked around him.

He should be satisfied. Why wasn't he?

Was it just because his two buddies, Caleb and Jake, had found women with whom to share their lives? Once he'd divorced, he'd become okay with being single. There had been some long-term girlfriends, but he'd never had the urge to take the plunge again.

Anna Wells came to mind again. She wasn't like any of the women he'd ever dated, far stronger and opinionated that any of them. But the women he'd dated had been up front about what they wanted and why they wanted it with him. Anna's desires and secrets were like a deep cave where only a few people knew how to find.

If anyone could.

Maybe Anna wasn't the problem. They had a good friendship going, and that was enough.

Jed had left him a ranch that ran almost too well. Quinn had the usual problems of competition and price-fixing that everyone denied happened, but somehow Jed had established a niche brand for Rocking Q beef that kept them in business from one economic lurch to the next.

He'd risen to the rank of lieutenant on the Detroit Police Force and had used his position not only to aggressively go after criminals of all stripes, but to mentor new recruits who showed promise, no matter what their background. He looked for cops who didn't quite fit the norm but solved a lot of cases, and taught them the basics of playing the game. Often, those were the people who cracked cases, just because they looked at things in a different way.

That's what he needed now: someone to help him look at his own life with new eyes, a sounding board. Anna had always been a good listener. Maybe she'd have some insight into his life.

Chapter Two

Anna Wells placed the round dough for the sourdough bread onto the parchment-covered cookie sheet. After misting the top of the soon-to-be bread, she slid the sheet into the oven. She had thirty minutes before she had to turn it so it cooked evenly. Enough time to check the garden for anything that had survived the last few frosty nights.

She grabbed a basket and walked out the kitchen door of the modest cabin she had purchased a few years ago when the Buckhorn Bar and Grill started making a profit. Before that, she'd lived over the bar like the previous owners. Now she had a tenant and was able to spend at least some time away from her business.

This property was a sanctuary. She never invited anyone here.

No one would be able to disturb the peace and security she had craved since she was a child. Back then, there had been only two places she'd really felt safe: at her grandmother's house and with the Quinn family.

The breeze carried the aroma of the not too distant pines, and butterflies flitted through the wildflowers she'd seeded on the property instead of attempting the evenly grown grass of her childhood home. It may look untidy to some, but she loved being greeted by bobbing heads of color whenever she pulled into her driveway.

She opened the gate to the small garden, grateful they hadn't been hit by a hard frost yet. Montana's growing season was short enough.

Several medium sized pumpkins nestled among large leaves. They'd be handy to help decorate the bar. One or two she'd pick early to make a pumpkin pie and maybe some bread. They could wait a few days. She pulled a few carrots, cut spinach and lettuce, and checked to see how the acorn squash was doing.

The heavy work of gardening—dealing with all the produce in August—was behind her. Jars of zucchini relish were ready to hand out as gifts, and her freezer was stacked with sealed bags of vegetables. Jars of pickles and tomatoes waited in the root cellar next to braids of garlic and onions.

Just like it had been when she was a child helping her grandmother preserve summer's bounty for winter's chill.

About halfway back to the cabin, she stopped to survey her small corner of paradise. The cabin didn't have a view of the valley, but the mountains rose high enough that she could see the hard granite poking at the sky. She took in a heavy helping of fall air, savoring its chill edge.

Willow Creek was a good place to live. The community was strong and appreciative of the support from her business. If she was ever in trouble, she had friends who would come to her aid, but those same friends knew better than to try to get too close.

Anna Wells kept people at arm's length. Her life had taught her there was too much risk to trusting people. Nor was she to be trusted. She'd failed the one person who had the right to demand the most from her.

She started walking again before she went down that path. This time of year was always difficult. No sense in inviting it in early.

After stashing the vegetables in the refrigerator and retrieving the bread from the oven to cool, she plucked her car keys from the hook and headed to the Buckhorn to open up for business.

~ ~ ~

Around eleven, Anna unlocked the door to the establishment she owned. In the center, the U-shaped bar gleamed. Most of the tables and booths, along with a raised stage, were on the right hand side. To the left, there were more seating areas and a pool table. The walls were decorated with a mishmash of things: neon bar signs, deer, elk, and moose heads, and some local artwork.

Anna walked behind the bar, distributed cash in the register drawer, and made a note in the ledger she kept on a shelf in the bar. Although it was old-fashioned, she always kept a paper trail where money was concerned. She'd emptied the register the night before and dropped the deposit in the small branch of Stockman Bank that served Willow Creek, keeping a small portion in change to seed the register for Friday's business.

Her cook, Paul Tudor, arrived as she was starting to pull chairs off of table tops to set on the floor.

Paul had a checkered past, including a few stints in Deer Lodge for running scams and Ponzi schemes as well as being a well-paid sous chef in a few fancy restaurants. By the time he'd gotten to her establishment, he'd had a clean record for over a decade. All he'd asked for was a job doing what he'd come to love—cooking on a grill—and a chance to experiment with some different types of burgers and other sandwiches.

Since being a short-order cook wasn't high on her list of things she liked, and she believed in giving people second chances, she'd hired him. So far it had been a good decision. The suggestions he'd made to the short lunch and dinner menu had been good, and he was always supportive of her and her decisions. The customers loved his warm, open smile.

"Let me help with that," he said, putting down his car keys and a book.

Whenever things got quiet and the work was done, he'd find a corner and read. The books tended toward philosophical ramblings, something he'd told her he'd started reading during his last stint in prison.

Whatever got a person through the day.

"I've got it," she said, the rhythm of the task soothing her. "It's one of the last weekends before Yellowstone concessions shut down. People are going to take off work early and head down. It will probably be a later lunch crowd, but they'll get here. You're better off getting the prep done."

"On it," he said, picking up his stuff and heading back to the small kitchen area.

Once the chairs were down, she cleaned the tables. They'd been done the night before, but she always felt better knowing they were freshly clean when a customer sat down. She was on the last three when Olivia, the waitress she'd had the longest, came into the bar, a big grin on her face.

"He finally asked!" Olivia exclaimed.

"About time," Anna said, straightening up. Zach and Olivia had been dating for close to two years. It was past time he put a ring on that finger. "Show me."

Olivia thrust out her left hand. On it was a decent-sized diamond, the kind a man like Zach—who worked at the local feed store—could afford.

"Beautiful," she told Olivia. She was surprised as an unexpected and painful memory popped up in the back of her mind. She quickly brushed it aside.

"Thank you. I'll get the setups started."

"Good." Olivia walked toward the back.

As soon as she finished with the tables, Anna went back behind the long bar. Glassware already gleamed because that's how she'd left it the night before. Pulling out a few limes and lemons, she sliced up the fruit and put them in their respective containers.

If she concentrated on work, her mind couldn't wander to the memory of the large diamond that had once graced her left hand.

She should have known Brandon couldn't afford it ... not legitimately, anyway.

The door opened and a couple with a girl around the age of eight came into the bar. The girl was shifting from one foot to the other. They rapidly walked to the bar.

"Is it okay for her to be here?" the mother asked.

"Sure."

"Thank you. And do you have a bathroom she could use?"

"Absolutely." Anna came around from the bar and crouched next to the girl. She pointed in the direction of the restroom. "Can you see it? It's right over there."

The girl nodded and took off at a quick trot.

"Do you have a menu?" the man asked.

Anna grabbed three menus from her stack. "Why don't you take any seat you like? Can I get you something to drink?"

"I'd love a beer, but since I'm driving, a cola will do," the man said.

"Iced tea," the woman said. "And a cola for my daughter as well."

"Coming right up."

Anna returned to the bar and got the orders ready. By the time she was done, the little girl had returned to her parents, and Olivia had come out to take over the waitress duties.

Paul came out of the kitchen. "All ready back there to start cooking." He nodded at the customers. "Looks like you were right. Of course, you're always right being the boss and all."

"As it should be," Anna said.

"You should hire another bartender," Paul said. "Someone who can open and close. That way you don't have to be here all the time."

"I *like* being here."

"Or maybe close one day a week. Mondays are slow. That way, some of us could spend a whole day fishing instead of getting up early."

"You'd still get up early. That's when the fish bite," she said.

"There's dusk, too. Sitting by the river, pole in the water, beer at your side. You should try it sometime. It might relax you."

"I'm perfectly relaxed."

"If you say so. But seriously, think about hiring someone. You could use a break."

"Uh-huh."

Olivia came up with the orders, and Paul went back to the kitchen.

The door opened again, letting in a couple of locals. They gave a wave and went to their usual booth.

Just like kids in school, everyone took the same places whenever they came into the bar. Human beings were definitely creatures of habit.

The traffic picked up as the day went on. By dinner they had a pretty full house. Unfortunately, the new waitress she'd hired a few weeks ago on a trial basis didn't show, so Anna did double duty with Olivia.

A singer-songwriter set up on the small stage at eight which made people linger until she left at nine-thirty. Paul started shutting down the grill while Olivia wiped down whatever tables she could. Anna escorted the stragglers out at ten.

When she'd first opened the bar, she kept the place open later, but soon realized the people who stayed later were the drinkers and partiers, two groups who were prone to overindulging and rubbing each other the wrong way. She shifted more toward the grill side of the business, and only kept the bar open for a band or special occasion.

It had saved her mornings.

Once Paul and Olivia had gone, she counted up the money for a deposit and the start of the next day's business.

Maybe she should shut down one day a week. She wasn't the only one here seven days a week. For months now she'd been trying to hire a second waitress. Three had come and gone, allowing them to survive the summer traffic.

If it weren't for the holiday season, she'd stop looking. But the Buckhorn had turned into the town's social gathering place. For the last two years, she'd had a Halloween event. Every year she hosted a bring-your-own-family Thanksgiving—invitation only. Whatever holiday plan she didn't come up with, Heather Daley, or someone like her, would invent.

They even had a weekly group of knitters who came in every Tuesday afternoon to sip chardonnay in between stitches.

No, she liked it busy during the fall. If she took too much time off, the memories and the searing pain that went with them, would be only too happy to haunt her.

Chapter Three

Quinn finished his morning chores and walked through the barn to make sure the stalls had been mucked and the horses turned out to graze. His ranch manager had told him two of the horses needed reshoeing, and he'd made a note to schedule a blacksmith visit.

He liked horses. His uncle, as well as many of the hard-core ranchers in the area, considered them an outdated waste of feed. Most ranch chores could be done with an ATV or a pickup truck these days.

To Quinn, a ranch was incomplete without them.

He and the Daleys were still weeks away from moving the herd from the mountain pastures back down to the valley. Ted, the manager, and Ned, the new hand he'd hired on barrel-racing trainer Bridget Browdy's recommendation, were scheduled to start inspecting fences on the winter fields, fixing any that needed it.

Kevin Cooper, who had come to the ranch as part of a witness protection program and stayed for the summer, was off to continue his law studies at the university in Missoula.

Everyone had something to do except Quinn.

Even his paperwork was up-to-date.

He leaned on the railing and watched the horses graze. After a lifetime in the Detroit Police Department, inheriting his uncle's ranch was a dream come true. Convincing his two closest friends to move out here with him had only made his life better.

Jake was still on his honeymoon with his new wife, Laura, but maybe Caleb would be up for some fly fishing. If not, Quinn could take a ride down to Yellowstone National Park and take a hike or fish in one of their rivers. The park was only a half hour's drive away. It was a clear, crisp autumn day, perfect for either activity.

If he drove up to Caleb's, he could see how the mare he'd

rescued from her abusive owner was doing. Caleb had transformed himself from a police captain to a horse trainer and had been instrumental in convincing the horse that all humans weren't abusive. He'd told Quinn the mare would never make a good cow pony, but he'd offered to buy her as a trail horse.

Knowing the mare would have a good home, Quinn had sold him the horse for a fair price.

Quinn went back into the house, cleaned up, and grabbed his keys. His fishing gear was always in the truck, just in case the opportunity arose to throw a line in one of Montana's pristine streams. Fishing always relaxed him, and it was a long time since he'd enjoyed the simple pleasure.

His hands were tight on the steering wheel as he drove the short distance to Caleb's place, a parcel carved from the land Quinn's uncle had left him.

If Caleb wasn't free, he'd stop by Greenbriar's General Store, pick up a sandwich, and head south. Even if he only made it as far as Gardiner, there were plenty of spots outside the town to drop a line into the Yellowstone River both inside and outside the park.

Yep, he'd have a good day.

Caleb's truck was parked over by the new barn he'd built—with some help from Quinn and Jake—on the southern end of his property. The outside had been up for a few months, but Caleb's business had picked up enough that he was still working on the inside.

Quinn parked and walked over to the barn. Once inside, he saw Caleb in the dim light working on one of the four stalls he'd planned for the barn. Each was a good size, giving a horse room to move around if it wanted.

"Oh, good," Caleb said, straightening up. "You're the answer to a prayer. Can you hold up this door so I can set the screws on the hinge correctly?"

"Sure." Quinn lifted the door by the crosspiece until Caleb told him to stop.

The whirr of an electric drill whined in the quiet space. Then Caleb changed the bits and rapidly put in the screws.

"Up for another?" Caleb asked.

"Sure thing."

Once they repeated the process, Caleb nodded. "Thanks. I would have been here all day if you hadn't happened along."

"Glad to oblige."

Caleb walked to a cooler and pulled out a couple of waters, handing one to Quinn. "I'm hoping to get the stalls finished soon. I've got one horse to bring here to train, and I need one for the mare. If Bridget and Destiny can come to terms, I hope to get Elsa here, too."

"How's that going?"

Destiny Cooper had been Caleb's love in Detroit before he became a cop. Almost twenty-five years later she and her son had shown up on his doorstep as part of a witness protection program. One thing led to another, and she'd moved to Willow Creek over the summer to give them a second chance.

"Slow," Caleb said. "But then I figured it would. It took a lot for her to take the risk to move here. We've been out a few times, done a few trail rides, but she's keeping her distance." He shrugged. "It's only been a few months. She's still settling in."

"I'm sure it will work out eventually," Quinn said.

"Yes. I just hope eventually comes before I'm ready for assisted living," Caleb said with a laugh.

"Got anything planned besides this for the rest of the day?" Quinn asked. "I'm going fishing and thought you might like to come along."

"Gee, it's been a long time. I wish I could, but I promised to go riding with Destiny once she's done talking with the mayor about her new assignment. I've got to get the mare in the trailer, pick up her horse, Elsa, at Bridget's, then meet Destiny over by the river."

"You two go there a lot."

"It's one of our favorite rides. You should try it sometime." Caleb grinned. "I can usually coax a kiss out of her, too."

Quinn was sure it was a beautiful ride, but a trail ride by himself didn't have the appeal that standing in a trout stream alone did. He shuffled his feet, disappointed his friend wouldn't be able to go with him.

"Anything else wrong?" Caleb asked.

"No." Quinn reconsidered. He'd been off kilter all day. "Yes.

I don't know."

"I think you've covered all the bases. What is it?"

"I'm not sure how to describe it. I've got everything I've always wanted. I loved coming to Uncle Jed's ranch as a kid. When he left it to me, I was over the moon. I thought I was set."

"And now?"

"I still think I'm one of the luckiest men on the planet. The ranch is going well. We'll be in the black again this year, which can be tricky with a small-sized operation. There will even be enough to do some much-needed repairs. Anytime I want, I can hop on a horse or ATV and look over the land I own. I've got good friends and a strong community. What do I have to be unhappy about?"

"You're lonely?" Caleb suggested.

"I've been alone a good chunk of my life. Amy and I divorced decades ago. The kids are grown and have their own lives. I see my brother and sister on occasion. I even go to church now and again. Lonely? That can't be it."

"Right. I never realized how alone I was until Destiny came back into my life."

"Are you suggesting I need a *woman*?"

Caleb shrugged.

"I don't feel that way about anyone," Quinn said.

"Not even Anna?"

Quinn stepped from one foot to the other uneasily.

"Anna Wells? We're old friends that's all. She used to hang out with my sister, Mary. She was over our house practically all the time. Sometimes she came out here to the ranch with us." Quinn shook his head. "I don't need a woman in my life." *Especially not Anna Wells.* "That would complicate things. I like my independence."

"Okay, then. Why are you so restless?"

Quinn finished off his water as he contemplated the question.

"I think I need a passion project," he finally said. "Jake has his part-time deputy job, you've got your horses. The ranch pretty much runs itself, especially with an experienced manager."

"Could be," Caleb said. "Any ideas what that would be?"

Quinn shook his head. "Maybe I'll figure something out by

standing in a river."

Caleb nodded. "Want to see the mare before you leave?"

"Sure thing."

Caleb reached into the cooler and pulled out a carrot.

"She's become very demanding," he said, heading out of the barn to the corral that ran behind the building.

The mare lifted her head as soon as she spotted them. With a toss of her mane, she cantered over and stopped in front of Caleb. With a close eye on Quinn, she put her head over the rail and nudged Caleb.

"You're incorrigible," Caleb said and gave her the carrot.

She munched away. When it was gone, she looked at him expectantly.

"One is all you get," Caleb said.

"Have you come up with a name for her yet?" Quinn asked.

"I want to call her Dolly, but Destiny hates it. She'd rather call her Lady."

"What's it going to be?"

"I'll hold out a little longer, but I know I'll give in eventually."

"Yep," Quinn said. "Exactly what I figured. It's the problem with women. Once you fall in love with them, you want to give them the moon, the stars, and everything else they could possibly want."

"You've got that right," Caleb said with a grin. "Listen, I've got to get going. I'll go fishing with you some other time."

"Sounds good."

They walked back toward the house together, and Quinn split off when they got to his truck. He got in, put it in gear, and headed back down the drive with a wave.

He stopped at Greenbriar's to get a ham and swiss on rye as well as something to wash it down, then got on Highway 540 south.

During the entire drive, his mind nudged at Caleb's suggestion that he needed a woman. He'd been fine for decades without one.

And Anna?

Ridiculous!

She'd been like a kid sister to him, nothing more. They'd teased each other like siblings did. There was nothing flirty about it.

Until those last few years before he'd enlisted. Although nothing was said, there'd been a subtle change, as if they both recognized the enormity of what he was about to do.

After high school, he'd joined the army and served his time. A close friendship with a fellow soldier who'd gotten killed during the last few days of his tour had led him to Detroit and the woman he'd eventually married. He'd taken the courses he needed to become a police officer, a job that appealed to him after his time in the army. The organization and rules echoed the military, giving him a sense of security.

He'd lost track of Anna over the years, but had heard she'd gotten married. Rumors were there'd been a child. The woman he'd met when he returned to Willow Creek had hard edges that hadn't been there when they were kids. Beyond a curt, "We're divorced," she'd never said anything about the intervening years or a child, and he'd learned not to ask.

Caleb was barking up the wrong tree. If Quinn ever hooked up with a woman, it certainly wasn't going to be Anna Wells.

Chapter Four

Anna poured herself another glass of club soda and added a lime. The dinner rush still had another hour to go, but then it would quiet down. There'd be a few couples or lingering tourists … a few businesspeople and ranch hands who thought their night wasn't complete without a good buzz.

Those were the ones she watched. Most of the time they had sense enough to get a ride back to wherever with a friend, but every once in a while she had to get an acquaintance involved. If that failed, she'd call the one Uber in town. Except it wasn't really Uber, it was Jim, also known as The Willow Creek Uber, who took people home for a small fee.

In extreme cases, she'd call on the sheriff's department.

She had a reputation to uphold. The Buckhorn Bar and Grill was a family place, somewhere for the community to gather without being harassed by drunks. Most people knew her reputation and abided by the rules. For that, she was grateful.

Buying a bar and grill had been a risky proposition for her, but she'd made it work. Fortunately, she'd developed a deaf ear to the siren song of gleaming liquor bottles a few decades ago. Club soda was her drink of choice, followed by a non-alcoholic beer or two as she closed up. Fortunately, the world had evolved beyond the somewhat watery taste of early versions.

As she wiped down the bar, she automatically observed the customers to make sure they were getting the service they needed. Olivia was on top of the service in her section. The new young woman, Kiara Running Rabbit, wasn't as good, but she was getting better every day.

Satisfied, Anna let her gaze move to the three former cops at their regular table. Jake had returned from his honeymoon with Laura a few days earlier. Caleb was talking about something that had the others grinning. Her attention lingered on Michael Quinn, the one everyone called by his last name.

But she'd known him first as Michael, her best friend's older brother, the one she'd had a massive crush on when she was a teen. Although he hadn't often appeared to notice her, he'd been kind to her when he did. The men in her friend's family had given her the first demonstration that all men weren't the drunken abuser her father was.

She'd made a pact with herself that once she'd grown up, she'd attract Michael's attention and get him to marry her so she could live happily ever after. When he went into the army, she'd figured she'd have enough time to make that dream come true.

But then he'd moved to Detroit and married someone else.

She forced her gaze away. It was all water under the bridge.

After glancing at the counter that held dishes waiting to be picked up, she threw the bar rag into the sink and crossed to it. Things were stacking up. As she suspected, they were Kiara's dishes. With a sigh, Anna picked up a couple of plated burgers and took them to the tourists who were eagerly waiting for them.

Once the deliveries were caught up, she made sure to cruise through Kiara's section, refilling water glasses and chatting up customers. A solitary drinker sat at the bar. No one she knew, which meant he was driving somewhere. Her service to him could be a little slow.

By nine o'clock, almost all the diners had gone. Only Quinn's group was left, but soon they rose as well. Caleb and Jake walked out the door, but Quinn came over to the bar and took a seat.

"Can I get a cup of coffee, please?" he asked.

"Sure." Without glancing at the drinker, she went to the kitchen and poured him a cup of coffee.

Strange. He'd never stayed after the others had gone before. Was there something on his mind?

As a bartender, she was used to hearing out people's tales of woes. Between them, she and Maribel, owner of Silver Clips, the local hair salon, knew every bit of gossip the small town held. When appropriate, they passed along their knowledge to Heather Daley, who ran a group called Women Help. The group gathered donations for people in need and celebrated the recipient at a monthly meeting at the bar and grill.

She slid the cup of coffee in front of Quinn.

Before giving the drinker a refill, she poured herself another glass of club soda and tossed in a lemon wedge.

"Here you go," she said to the drinker. "Are you staying in town for the night?"

"I thought my buddy was going to meet me," the man said. "But he just texted and said his wife is ill. There's no way I can stay with him tonight. And your one-horse town doesn't have any hotels."

"We have a small inn and a bed and breakfast. Want me to make some calls to see if anyone has a room?"

"You'd do that?"

"Sure."

"I'd be grateful." He smiled and raised his glass. "Thank you."

She pulled her phone from the back pocket of her jeans, and called the inn. Fortunately, they had a room. While they were still on the line, she got the man's name and credit card information.

"Thanks again," he said, pushing the half-filled glass back toward her. "I'd better have some coffee, too, before I head out."

She poured him a glass of water. "Drink this first. It'll help more than the coffee."

He nodded.

After getting him a cup, she retrieved the coffee pot from the back. She poured his cup and then refilled Quinn's. Once both men were taken care of, she helped Kiara wipe down her tables, then said she could leave for the night. Olivia would stay a half hour longer. By ten, Anna could start to close up.

She sighed. She was tired. Maybe Paul was right. It was time to start thinking about closing one night a week. Mondays made the most sense. It was their slowest night, although Tuesdays weren't much better. Maybe she could experiment with closing earlier on Tuesday nights as well as shutting down on Mondays.

The few tourists they got could continue on to Livingston, and most locals cooked at home during the week.

She'd run the numbers and make her final decision.

The man she'd helped find a room gave her a wave as he left. When she returned to the bar, she wasn't surprised that he'd left her a healthy tip. Treating people well had always paid off. Plus, it made for a much more pleasant environment.

After helping Olivia finish off her tables, she told the waitress she'd see her tomorrow.

That left only Quinn.

"More coffee?" she asked.

"No, I think I'm done," he said.

"Okay." She checked the time on the clock that had been on the wall behind the bar since she'd bought the place. It was set five minutes fast, but customers didn't need to know that.

The face registered ten o'clock.

"Well, it's about time for me to close up," she said.

"Sure," he said, but didn't move.

"Something on your mind?"

He looked up at her as if he was surprised at the question. His blue eyes were as vibrant as they'd been as a teen, but there was a weariness there of a man who'd seen too much of the bad side of life.

Her eyes probably reflected the same thing.

"Yeah," he said, a hint of red showing in his cheeks. "I'm a little rusty at this … but here goes. Would you come riding with me some day?"

"Riding?"

"Yeah, you know. Getting on a horse and going somewhere. I seem to remember you know how."

"You want me to go riding with you?" she asked. Of all the things she'd expected him to say, that wasn't one of them.

She felt an unusual flutter in her chest.

"As a friend," he horridly added. "That's all."

Of course. Fairy tales never did come true.

So friends it was.

He twisted the coffee cup around in its saucer. "It gets lonely riding by myself, that's all."

Or else he just wanted what every other man wanted from a woman when he was "lonely."

For a moment she was tempted. She'd been lonely a long time, too.

But she couldn't have that type of relationship with Quinn or any other man, ever again. It left her too vulnerable.

"I'll pass," she said.

"Really?"

"Yep. I don't have time for trail rides. I've got a business to run. Unlike you, I don't have a manager."

"You should get more help," he said. "Take some time off. You work too hard."

"That's what Paul keeps saying."

"He's right." Quinn pushed the empty cup toward her. "I can help you close up. Get you out of here earlier."

"It's okay. Paul's still here. All I need to do is close down the register and put up the chairs."

"I'd like to help." He reached toward his back pocket.

"Never mind," she said. "Coffee's on me."

"Thanks."

"I'll walk you to the door so I can lock it behind you."

"I don't mind staying."

"Out, Quinn," she said. He was still trying break out of the friendship zone he'd claimed he wanted. She needed him out of there, now.

"Tell me you'll think about it," he said, easing himself off the stool.

"Will it make you leave more quickly?"

"Sure," he said.

"Okay, I'll think about it." She would, for the nanosecond it would take her to tell him no again.

"Good. I'll call you tomorrow for your answer."

The man was determined.

She came out from behind the bar and walked toward the front door.

He got the hint, but paused at the door. "Just friends," he said again. "Nothing more. Neither one of us wants that."

"Nope." She opened the door.

"See you," he said, an anxious smile on his face.

She locked the door behind her. Once she heard his truck start up, she walked to the bar and shut off the outside lights.

Just friends or not, it was a ridiculous idea. The sooner she shut it down the better.

She opened the register and began the tedious task of

reconciling transactions to credit card receipts and cash. This was her life. She'd had her chance and had proven to be a bad wife and worse mother.

Happiness with another person wasn't something she deserved.

Especially if that person was someone as innately good as Michael Quinn.

Chapter Five

Anna's sleep had been dream-filled. Memories of life with her parents and siblings had morphed into dragons, orcs, and other fearful creatures. The only knight trying to protect her wore Michael Quinn's face.

She must have flailed about during the night, because her sheets and blankets were twisted around her feet and absent from her shoulders. Her body felt overheated. She hadn't dreamed like that in a long time.

Her father had been dead for over a decade, his decision to drive drunk once too often costing him his life. Fortunately, no one else had been involved in the deadly collision. But even gone, his mark had stayed vibrant on every member of the family.

She'd tried to be there for her younger siblings, but for her own sanity, she'd needed the safety of Michael's family. Her closest friend, Mary, had been free with her invitations. Mary's parents, as if sensing the pain in the girl's life, had treated Anna as one of their own.

Despite their care, she'd already drifted too close to the flame. Her own drinking was borderline alcoholic and, to add insult to injury, she'd married an out and out alcoholic and emotional abuser.

Her siblings hadn't fared much better. Bethany, the next child, was a housewife with a controlling husband who lived in Billings; Richard had escaped to become a programmer in Silicon Valley, and never came back to Montana. The youngest, Sophia, had been in and out of rehab most of her life. When she was out, she lived with their mother in their childhood home in Butte.

After her husband's death, Anna's mother had seemed to shrink further into herself. It was as if the physical abuse she'd lived with all her life had given her a reason to live, and now she had none. She'd never acknowledged the horror they'd grown up with, maintaining the lie that their father had loved them all, and they were too blind to see it.

Anna shoved the covers aside. She had things to do before going to the bar. The first was to take a shower and try to put the night behind her.

After getting dressed and seeing her diminishing stack of underwear, she threw a load of laundry into the washer. Like dishes and dust, the laundry could always be counted on as a chore that needed doing. With only herself to care for, it took a lot less time than when she'd had a husband and a child.

She slammed the door on those memories.

Instead, she thought of things that needed tending in the small cabin she owned. It wasn't too far from the bar and grill, but tucked away in the woods enough to make her feel like she was all alone.

She liked it that way, not even feeling an urge to get a pet of any kind.

Once her bacon and eggs were cooking, she pulled out the stuff she needed to make a salad to eat later. She may serve burgers and steaks to her customers, but she needed a different diet. She'd need to make more soup this weekend. A Thermos of that served her well for dinner, when she had the time to sit down and enjoy it. Unfortunately, too many nights, she asked Paul to make her a burger, and she'd snarf that down between customers.

Sometimes she longed for the luxury of time she'd once had, time read a book … or maybe take a horseback ride. The only problem with the idea was she'd have more time to herself, more time for the memories to come barreling in.

It was coming up on six years since it happened.

She needed to keep busy.

~ ~ ~

By eleven o'clock Anna was at the bar and grill. Paul came in minutes behind her. Olivia wasn't scheduled until noon when the place actually opened; Kiara would come in at five. That gave Anna an hour to take stock and add to her weekly list of things that needed doing.

Sometimes they actually got done.

She began in the storage room, updating the inventory and noting what needed reordering. She'd originally tried to do this once a week, but found a nagging fear of running out of something left her more unsettled than if she was sure she was going to run low. Crazy, the way her mind worked.

Then she walked the restaurant, noting lights that were out, unsteady tables, and the perpetual squeak in one of the ceiling fans. She'd had multiple people out to look at it. Each had declared it fixed, but within hours the thing started squeaking again.

Chloe, who owned the thrift store and who was known to embrace new-age beliefs, had suggested the bar had a resident ghost.

It was as good an explanation as any.

She had just finished checking the liquor bottles to see if she needed backups when someone banged at the door. As tempted as she was to scream that they weren't open, she knew the person on the other side of the heavy door wouldn't hear her.

With rapid steps, she strode to the door and opened it.

"Heather," she said. "You know we don't open until noon."

"I know. I wanted to catch you before you did."

"Well, come in then. You'll have to talk while I work."

"Got it," Heather said and followed her into the space.

"What can I do for you?" Anna asked as she stepped behind the bar to finish her setup.

"If you remember, we were planning to do a donation drive for Dot Albertson over the summer, but her sister became ill so she delayed coming back to Willow Creek."

"Yes, I remember."

"Well, she's given us a date for her return, and I want to make sure you have us on your schedule."

"You could have called for that," Anna said, sliding money into the till.

"I know, but I was passing by, and it's been a while since I've seen you."

"Here I am, as usual," Anna said, remembering to smile at the last minute.

"You work too hard."

"That seems to be the theme of the week." She slammed the

drawer closed.

"We'd all be fine if you closed one day a week," Heather said. "Then you could have some fun, go riding or something."

Anna stilled. The statement hadn't come out of nowhere.

"Who have you been talking to?" she asked.

"No one except my husband."

"And Ralph's been talking to Quinn."

"Well, our spreads are right next to each other, and we do merge our herds for summer grazing. Ralph went to talk to him about the plan for moving the cattle off of forest service land and back down the mountain. Quinn might have mentioned that he'd asked you to go riding."

"Then you'll also know I turned him down flat."

"That's not what Quinn says," Heather said. "He thinks you've left the door open."

"I only said I'd consider it to be polite. I'm not going on a ride with anyone, especially not Quinn."

"I thought you two were old friends."

"Emphasis on 'old.'" Anna sliced through a lime, narrowly missing her fingers. "My best friend in Butte was Quinn's sister. He was several years older and barely noticed me."

"Rumor is that he sure is noticing you now."

There was that flutter again. *Down, girl.*

"You need to help squash that rumor. I chat those boys up when they're here for their Wednesday dinner, but I do that with all my customers." With a few more quick cuts, the lime was in wedges.

"Uh-huh."

Anna set the knife down and leaned across the bar to glare at Heather.

"You can tell Ralph to tell Quinn I have no interest in riding down the river trail or hanging out in the Greenbriar's grove with him or anyone else."

"Who said anything about Greenbriar's grove?"

Darn. Anna hadn't meant to mention the brief fantasy she'd had about kissing Michael in that grove.

She forced herself to look stern. At least she hoped it was stern.

"People are always talking about that magic grove. It's hogwash. I've been married and have the tee-shirt already. I'm done with all of that."

Heather took a step back. "Got it."

Anna picked up her knife and another lime. This time the rapid slice didn't threaten to cut off her fingertip. She'd made her point clear.

"Can I get Dot's party on the schedule?" Heather asked quietly.

"Oh, sure." Wiping her hands on a towel, Anna dug out the paper calendar she used for scheduling. It was old-fashioned, but it worked. Everyone could see when something was coming up and plan accordingly.

She wrote the information down in the date Heather requested, then glanced at the clock. Almost noon.

"The lunch crowd will be arriving soon," she told Heather. "Can you leave the door unlocked on your way out?"

"Sure," Heather said.

As she watched the woman leave, Anna knew she was being rude. But she simply didn't like people mucking around in her business.

What would it be like to take a ride with Michael? Could they keep it a friendly ride as he'd suggested? There was nothing about their relationship that said he wanted anything more. They didn't have that kind of connection.

Maybe it would be fine. Maybe he was lonely.

Maybe she should have her head examined.

She finished slicing the limes and went on to the lemons. There were more of these because she went through a lot of them over the time she was at the bar and grill.

If she could talk herself into hiring a manager to run the place when she wasn't there, she'd have more time to spend on things she enjoyed. As a kid, she'd enjoyed riding, and had gone through a horse-crazy period like everyone else in her school.

But after high school, there wasn't money for college. She'd tried to work and go to community college, but it had proved to be more than she was capable of doing, especially after she'd fallen in with a heavy drinking crowd of friends. Her job as a waitress in a local restaurant had taught her some basic skills: how to serve quickly with a smile, how to soothe over trouble, and how to avoid a man's wandering hands.

But it hadn't taught her about the lies men tell.

She'd given up her dream of going to college and becoming a nurse or a teacher. Instead, she devoted her brain to learning more about the restaurant business. She studied her bosses, moving on from a neighborhood establishment to a trendy fern bar, grasping knowledge like a thirsty person glugs water. She'd put all her lessons in a notebook, a journal she'd kept well-hidden, even after she'd married.

Especially after that.

She picked up her phone to text Quinn that she wouldn't go riding with him, but before she could do it, the door was flung open and a dozen people walked in.

"Are you open?" one of them called out.

"Sure am," she said. "Take a seat anywhere, and I'll be right with you."

She'd handle Michael Quinn later.

Chapter Six

Quinn heaved a saddle onto Champion's back. It had been two days since he'd asked Anna to come riding with him. She'd told him she'd get back to him, but so far he'd heard nothing. He'd probably been an idiot to suggest it. Too much, too soon. Anyone could tell Anna would need gentle gestures. She'd had a relationship bad enough to divorce, but exactly how bad had it been?

He tightened the cinch.

She'd always been underfoot at their house. For a long time, he'd regarded her as an annoying younger sister, like Mary. About the time he was a senior in high school, she'd begun to blossom into something more. Not only had her beauty begun to shine, but her wit had gotten sharper and her will more determined. She'd started becoming a truly interesting person.

After she and Mary graduated, Mary had lost touch with Anna. His life had gone into overdrive and he'd put her out of his mind until he'd arrived back in Willow Creek and found her running the bar and grill. When he'd asked about the intervening years, she'd put him off with a practiced line of it being the usual boring story: she got married. It didn't last. Yada, yada, yada.

No mention of the rumored child.

He put the sandwiches he'd prepared in the saddlebag and hitched his canteen to the pommel. Then he slid the halter off Champion, immediately replacing it with a bridle.

The soothing clop of the horse's hooves followed him out of the barn. He spotted his ranch manager, Ted, and waved. Ted walked toward him.

"You going to be gone long?" Ted asked.

"Most of the day," Quinn said. "I'm heading up to the summer pasture to check on conditions."

"One of us could have done that," Ted said.

"I need the ride."

"Got it. Being on the back of a horse is one of the best ways to get some thinking done, 'specially if it involves a woman."

There were times Quinn hated living in a small town where everyone knew his business.

"Maybe I should be thinking about replacing nosy ranch managers," Quinn said with a grin.

"Nah," Ted said. "Then you'd actually have to do some real work."

"Right," Quinn said. "Definitely got to think about personnel issues."

"Have a good ride," Ted said. "Ned and I are going to continue to ride the fence lines for the winter pasture."

"Good. See you." Quinn put his foot in the stirrup and swung into the saddle. Then he headed to the trail that would lead up out of the valley floor to the joint range he shared with the Daleys. If he made good time, he'd see how many cattle he could see on forest service land and what it would take to round them main herd and the strays up and get them back on their land.

The deal he had with the Daleys was working out well. They both had small-sized herds. By opening their ranges to the other they were able to take full advantage of the mountainous pasture. Jointly leasing the connected forest service land for grazing made it a cheaper option as well.

He made his way through the winter pasture to the large gate they'd use when they brought the herd down after the roundup. Then they'd go through the task of separating the herds and help Ralph and Heather move their cattle back up the road to their winter grazing area.

There were still a few more weeks of warm fall weather to go. It was Quinn's favorite season. Summer playtime was over. Locals laughingly referred to autumn as the season of getting ready for winter. The noise of a chainsaw was always going someplace. Local hunters were gearing up to restock their larders. Kitchens were busy with people canning and freezing the last bits of their gardens. Shorts and light shirts were put away in favor of flannel and woolen sweaters.

Even the air smelled different. There was a tang that hadn't been there before the leaves started changing. Aspen groves displayed a rich marigold color, easily visible against the dark green of pines. Here and there, orange-yellow needled tamaracks provided a bright spot in the mountains which were beginning to regain some snow on their granite tips.

He was heading toward the fall of his own life, and he'd been alone for a good chunk of it. Was his angst because he was lonely? Or was it something more?

His life was exactly how he'd planned it before he retired. No sense in mucking it up with attempting a relationship, especially with a woman who was so adept at hiding her secrets. Besides, he might want some friendship … maybe a little more … but if Anna wasn't ready, he didn't want to hurt her by asking for more than she was able to give.

He had no doubt she had secrets. He'd seen the pain in her eyes, no matter how hard she tried to hide it. He should leave it alone. If she wanted to keep her secrets to herself, that was her right.

The screech of a hawk echoed around him. Looking up, he spotted an osprey with a fish in its talons. From the effort the bird was putting in its wings, the catch must be good-sized.

The osprey swooped lower and landed on a branch. Positioning the still-flapping fish between its feet, it began to feed. Quinn watched, mesmerized, for a few moments, then turned away.

It was a long way from the river. Had the osprey caught the fish in one of the streams that descended the mountain? Unusual, but not impossible. There were places on his land where the streams pooled, and he'd caught a trout now and again. In fact, it was one of the larger streams that ran through the summer range and not too far from where he was.

The Nature Conservancy had been lobbying him and other ranchers to work with them on their effort to reclaim creeks and streams from overgrown vegetation and cattle that fouled river banks as they drank. While it could be expensive, there were grants to be had.

Maybe it was time to seriously look at that. If he was going to support the effort to stop gold mining at the southern end of the valley because it fouled the water, it was time to clean up his own act.

He headed Champion to the stream. It was a good a place as any to sit and have half a sandwich and let the horse drink.

As he rode toward the water, he saw clusters of cattle scattered across the range. There was satisfaction in seeing animals he was raising grazing on the sturdy meadow grass. His uncle had left him a solid legacy, and he was determined to keep it that way. Like Jed, he wasn't going to be able to leave it to his own children—neither was interested in coming out to the ranch, much less owning it. But one of Mary's kids had expressed an interest lately. He'd have to get the boy out for the round-up. Heck, he should invite Mary's whole family.

Thinking of his sister brought Anna back to mind. For the most part when she'd hung around their house as a kid, she'd been quiet and respectful. But every once in a while she'd crack some jokes and the whole family would be laughing.

He'd also known at some level that his sister's friend was tough. No matter what was actually going on at her house—and he kicked himself for not being more aware—Anna had always been put together, kind, and helpful. He now recognized that as the inner strength that had enabled her to get through whatever had happened to her. It had also helped her create a business and a place that was beloved in the Willow Creek community.

He was also barely in the "friend zone" as far as she was concerned.

Could he change that without hurting her?

No way of knowing unless he tried.

But he could stress her out simply by trying.

He shook his head and urged Champion on.

Once he reached the water, he rode upstream for a while. Even to his untrained eye, he could see the problem. Some of the flow had been reduced to a trickle because it was overgrown with vegetation. Other places, where the cattle tended to congregate, were muddied by the churn on the banks. Deep pools were crowded with something that looked like algae.

Trout would be struggling in those conditions. And the water, which helped supply the town, wouldn't be drinkable without some kind of processing, unlike the pure water that came from his own well.

He reached a spot where the stream tumbled between a few boulders, churned over a number of good-sized rocks, then settled into a deep pool before taking a sharp bend to snake through the meadow. Pulling one of his sandwiches from the saddlebag and grabbing the canteen, he perched on a rock. Released from his duties, Champion took a long drink before beginning to graze on the tufts of grass that had struggled through the rocks.

Although he couldn't see the valley below, his view encompassed the tops of the peaks on the other side of the valley, as well as the stream as it rushed off below him.

This was the life he'd always wanted, peaceful and calm. He'd done his duty, first as a soldier, then as a cop, but the longing for this land had never gone away. Out of Montana he felt like a piece of his soul was missing; in it, he was complete.

Except …

Maybe it was more than simply being about a woman—as if that were simple. Maybe he needed a purpose. He no longer made his community safe for the people who lived there, but the urge to protect was still strong. When he'd seen the abused horse berated by the man who owned it, he'd wanted to deck the man on the spot. Instead, he'd bought the horse and turned him over to Caleb to restore as much of the animal's trust as he could.

The animal shied away from humans for a long time, but had slowly regained its footing. In some ways, Anna was a lot like that horse.

Except that she had tenacity, dedication to hard work, and the ability to speak her mind. She'd be a good person to explore ideas with, if he could ever get her out of the bar.

He finished the sandwich and stuffed the plastic container back into the saddlebag. He mounted Champion, took a last swig of water, and hung the canteen on the horn before turning Champion toward forest service land to see how many cattle were still up there.

Should he press Anna one more time for an answer? Or take her silence as a no?

She'd almost been a part of his family. She even came along on vacations sometimes. Her parents never took her anywhere, not even on a camping trip. Poor kid.

If the rumors were true, her adult life hadn't been any easier.

But he wasn't a shrink, and that was probably what she needed, not some retired ex-cop who wanted a sounding board.

He wouldn't ask Anna again. There were too many risks that he'd hurt a woman he cared a great deal about.

Being friends was enough.

Chapter Seven

It was one of the few days every year that Anna closed down the bar and grill until evening. The sign on the door said, "Closed, Personal Reasons." Townspeople had stopped asking why the bar was closed for the afternoon on that particular day.

Each year, on September twenty-first, she put on her black jeans and matching shirt and drove to Butte. Today was no exception.

The sky suited her mood. The clouds were low overhead, dumping snow on the upper reaches of the mountains. Occasionally, a shower was let loose on the lower elevations. Wind whipped down the valley. The two major passes between Livingston and Butte weren't going to be fun.

Her pickup truck was old, but it came with four-wheel drive and a CD player. She'd purchased new tires the year before. She'd grown up in this weather and knew how to drive in it.

When she reached Livingston, she threaded her way through town to get on Highway 90 closer to the pass. Ironically, it was the corridor right before the road started climbing that caused the most accidents. Wind blasted down the eastern side of the mountains, capable of broadsiding unsuspecting RV drivers and toppling the occasional semi. If it became too much of a problem, the highway patrol routed the traffic through the center of town and back onto the highway. It wasn't an ideal solution for Livingston or the drivers, but it kept everyone safer.

Once on the highway, she guided the truck steadily up the mountain pass, grateful that she had to focus on the road, not where she was going. As she neared the top of the pass, precipitation hit her windshield. First it was rain, then it changed to snow at the highest elevations. The broad fields of the ranchers who chose to live up here were already covered with a thick layer of white.

By the time she descended to the Bozeman side of the pass,

the weather had cleared, providing the big sky views Montana was famous for. She pulled off at a rest stop, took care of business, then switched out the CDs for the next part of the drive. As she went through the river valley of Three Forks, she concentrated on the scenery, scanning for birds as she crossed the Madison and Jefferson Rivers. Once those two rivers joined with the Gallatin, it became the official beginning of the Missouri River. The three rivers gave the town its name.

The road rose again to go through the Tobacco Root Mountains. Sometimes golden eagles perched on fence posts along the road, but there were none this trip. The drive was familiar but it had been a while since she'd taken it. She rarely felt a need to see her mother, especially since Sophia was living with her in Butte. Sober or not, her sister could be a nightmare to deal with. She tended to blame anyone and everyone for her problems, never taking responsibility for her own part in her misery.

The road began to climb toward the Homestead Pass, forcing her to pay attention to the sharp curves of switchbacks and the actions of lumbering trucks. Like the Bozeman Pass, this one had snow at its highest reaches. Relief flooded her as she started down the other side toward the city of Butte.

After passing the open pit mine, she took the exit for Montana Street and made her way to St. Patrick's Cemetery. Her heart began to beat faster as she drove.

It took so much out of her to come here every year, but she felt it was her duty, her last one as a mother.

She parked as close as she could to the grave, then made her way past the familiar stones to the one she sought. There was always a moment of disbelief as she read her daughter's name, Madison Mallet. Once she'd divorced Madison's father, Anna had gone back to her maiden name, but let her daughter keep the one she was born with.

Her throat caught as she read the rest of the familiar words, the years of her birth and death, her age of twenty-five. Under Maddy's age was carved, "May you rest in peace." An angel perched at the top of the stone, Anna's one nod to her own religious upbringing, a faith that had died with Madison.

Truthfully, it had substantially eroded a long time before.

Anna could never understand why God had tortured her and her daughter so much when there were so many people who obviously deserved it more.

She bent and placed the flowers she'd brought with her from home on the grave. Then she touched her hand on the cold stone, hoping for some connection.

"I'm sorry," she said, just like she did every time she visited her daughter. There were so many mistakes she'd made that had led her here. Anna was never sure which one was the most critical sin. Was it because she'd chosen an alcoholic as Madison's father? That she'd raised her as a single mother who was dealing with her own addiction to alcohol? For not having enough money to buy her new clothes so the other girls wouldn't tease her? For not protecting her enough? For not sending her to a program when Madison was a teen with drug problems? For not finding the right therapist?

For not being a better mother?

There were so many things she'd done wrong.

"I did the best I could," she told her daughter. "But it wasn't enough, was it?"

Madison's problems began when she was only twelve and started experimenting with marijuana. Her grades tanked, and she had minor skirmishes with the law. Anna had tried an alternative high school. At first Madison seemed to take to that, but she'd fallen back in with kids who were never going to make it out of the addiction spiral.

At sixteen she'd run away from home, never to really return.

Anna's heart ached thinking about it.

"I love you, Madison. I always will."

She moved away from the stone and sank, cross-legged, to the grass. There she stayed for about a half hour, remembering her daughter from happier times. Tears slipped down her cheeks, but she barely noticed them.

Finally, she rose and with a final pat to the stone, turned to walk away.

Her steps back to the truck were heavy with grief, but she knew she had to put all her emotions back into their boxes before seeing Sophia and her mother. She toyed with the idea of skipping out and heading back home, but her mother had called a few days before to confirm she would be in Butte for the anniversary.

So she drove to her mother's home, the same house she'd grown up in.

When she arrived, she noted Sophia's car in the driveway. Her mother's car, which she rarely used, was parked in the garage of the faded salmon-colored house.

She slid the truck next to the curb and turned it off. With a deep breath, she picked up the pie she'd gotten at Greenbriars' and climbed the walkway and stairs to the front door.

Sophia answered Anna's ring.

"Oh, here you are!" her sister said as she pushed open the screen door. "We were beginning to think you weren't coming."

Sophia's eyes were too bright and her speech too rapid. Whatever program she'd been through last hadn't worked, but their mother hadn't noticed yet.

"Mmm, pie. I love pie." Sophia took the box from Anna's hands and walked to the tiny kitchen in the back.

Anna walked to the couch where her mother rose to greet her. Anna hugged her mother, noting the physical changes that were coming more and more to her seventy-plus-year-old body.

"We saved some lunch for you," her mother said.

"That was nice." Anna allowed herself to be led to the dining room, and her mother brought out a plate of cold cuts, a loaf of bread, and a bowl of potato salad.

"Look, Mom," Sophia said. "Anna brought us pie!" She'd unboxed the dessert and put it on a plate. She placed that on the table along with a knife and serving utensil.

"That looks wonderful," her mother said. "Could you get us some plates?"

"Sure, Mom."

Anna made herself a sandwich and took some potato salad. To do anything else would create more discussion than she could deal with.

"It's so sad that we always see you on this day," Sophia said when she brought back the plates. "It must be so hard for you. I can't imagine what you go through. How do you bear it year after year?"

Anna kept her head down so she didn't glare at her sister.

"I just do. And that's all I want to say about it. How's life been treating you? Got a new job?"

"I'm looking, Anna. I know you don't think I try, but I do." There was an edge to Sophia's voice. "They just want so much from an employee these days. Even McDonald's wouldn't hire me because I have a record. And it's for stupid stuff. So what if I wrote some bad checks. It's not like the people I wrote them to couldn't afford it."

Anna bit her tongue.

"I'm sure you'll find something," their mother said, her voice placating. It was the same way she'd talked to her husband, even after he'd backhanded her.

He didn't mean to do it. I made him angry. It was my fault.

Her sandwich threatened to make a reappearance.

"Why don't you guys start in on the pie?" she asked. "I'm not sure I'll have any. I need to get back to open the bar. It's a long drive."

"Only two hours," Sophia said. "And you never come to see Mom. She misses you. I'm the only one who cares. Bethany is too busy with her life in Billings. And we never hear from Richard."

"I'm busy," Anna said. "I work every day."

"Except today."

"That's right."

"Your dead daughter is more important than your living relatives," Sophia said, her lips twisting in a sneer.

"Oh, Sophia, you don't mean that," Mom said.

"It's true."

"Look," Anna said, dropping her half-eaten sandwich on the plate. "I live my life as I see fit. I need to make a profit from my business. It's the only income I have. If it takes being open every day, that's what it takes."

"You don't even come home for Thanksgiving."

"That's because I have a gathering at the bar. A gathering to which I've invited both of you every year." Anna had always felt safe in offering the invitation, sure she'd never be taken up on it. "This is a dumb discussion. I don't have time for it." She stood up. "Love you, Mom. Enjoy the pie."

After giving her mother another brief hug and glaring at her sister, she walked out the front door. This was how it always ended when Sophia was around.

But she still felt like a heel when she left.

She just wasn't made for any type of relationship at all.

Chapter Eight

Scenery made no impression as she went back over the pass by Butte and drove east toward Bozeman. The only image in her mind was the placating look on her mother's face, the same one she'd seen all her life. It was the expression her mother had worn trying to de-escalate her father, to keep him from erupting into loud cursing … or worse. As Anna's brother, Richard, had grown older, he'd pushed back when their father started tearing into everyone's self-esteem.

Their mother would try to interrupt, all too often taking the brunt of the two men's anger. Like Anna, her sister, Bethany, had found a friend's house for escape. Sophia had found relief in finishing off their father's beer bottles and whisky glasses when he wasn't looking.

It was a sad, too familiar story, one her mother and Sophia were still acting out.

But Anna wasn't in a position to judge. She had her own story.

She hated the way she let Sophia push her buttons. She should have stayed, ignored her sister. Today was the wrong day for that. She didn't have the strength, not after visiting Madison's grave.

Madison had been the perfect little girl, sweet and playful. Even Brandon's heart had been captivated by his daughter, at least for a while. Everyone had loved Madison, until, somewhere along the way, they'd lost her.

Anna couldn't think about that anymore. Not now. Now she had to pull herself together to open the bar. If profits were good this month, she'd send her mother some money, directly depositing it in her bank account so Sophia couldn't get her hands on it.

Maybe the next time her sister decided to try rehab again or was caught up in the legal system, Anna could convince her mother to go into some sort of assisted living facility.

But where would the money for that come from? She was

making enough from the bar to maintain her own life, but there wasn't a lot left over.

She drove back over the Jefferson and Madison Rivers, only this time she didn't check for wild birds.

What Paul had suggested was ridiculous. She couldn't close the bar for one day. She had to keep working. Otherwise she'd lose revenue … and likely her mind.

Once she'd given up the alcohol, only hard, constant work kept the demons at bay.

Her logical mind informed her keeping up this pace wasn't sustainable.

She was approaching the half-century mark. Her body wasn't going to be able to keep up with the demands of running a business unless she started to take care of it. She hadn't had a drink in years, but her diet leaned too much toward red meat, and her exercise consisted of pulling beer taps and putting up chairs in the evening.

A horseback ride would be lovely.

She'd loved riding as a young teen when she was lucky enough to be able to go to the ranch with the Quinns. The feel of being in control of a thousand-pound animal that obeyed her every wish had given her confidence. The no-questions-asked inclusion into the family had given her a taste of what love was really like.

Once she and Mary had left high school, she'd never ridden again. In fact, her friendship with Mary had faded away, especially once Anna met Brandon.

With Bozeman left behind her, she drove up and around lumbering trucks to the top of the pass. The wind hadn't abated, and she could see tracks where cars had gone off the road. Fortunately, the precipitation had quit and sand trucks had salted and sanded the highway. The wind had dried the moisture, but her truck still accumulated dirt kicked up by the traffic around her.

She'd wash it in the morning before work.

Once again she threaded her way through Livingston and headed south toward Willow Creek. There was no point in going home. She'd make herself a burger before getting to work.

A half hour later she pulled into her normal parking spot at the bar and grill. She let herself in and locked the door behind her. For a few moments, she stopped and looked around her.

This was *her* place. She'd bought it with every penny she'd squirreled away, saving money when it meant doing without things, pushing her vehicles to their limits, buying the cheapest things she could find at the grocery store. She'd paid for it with her aching back, a single-minded focus, and her grief at the turns her life had taken.

When she'd bought it, the grill part of the bar and grill had long ceased operation, and it was a place where people came to get drunk. It was a familiar scene. When she and Brandon had gotten together, her other friends hadn't seemed quite as important as the ones they partied with every chance they got. There was lots of laughter, more than a little flirtation, and the blissful oblivion of alcohol.

All too often, the happy nights were followed by recriminations and fights. Twice he'd hit her, but she was her mother's daughter. Until she got sober, she'd blamed herself for the abuse.

Once she'd given up the alcohol, their fights became about her sobriety and his drinking. But her eyes were clearer, and she no longer put up with the abuse. She had Maddie to consider. Eventually, she'd told him to leave and begun to rebuild her life.

Over the years since she'd bought the bar and grill, she'd turned it into what it was now: a family-friendly place where locals could gather to hear a band and dance, or listen to an up-and-coming singer-songwriter. The furniture may be worn, but it was repaired and upgraded as needed. Dusty neon signs no longer covered the walls. She'd eliminated some, polished the rest, and she'd cleaned and kept the mounted animal heads.

It was Montana after all.

With a sigh, she shook off her reverie and went to make herself a burger. By the time she finished it, Paul and Olivia had arrived.

"Taking over my job?" Paul asked with a grin.

"I was hungry," she said without a smile. She wasn't in the mood to joke with her employees.

"Okay. I'll get things prepped." Paul disappeared into the kitchen area.

Olivia started taking down chairs while Anna went about her

chores. They were about fifteen minutes into the routine when someone knocked at the door.

With a frown, Anna walked to the door to tell whoever it was they weren't open yet.

A young woman with a guitar stood outside.

"Hi," she said. "I'm Rachel, your entertainment for the night."

Anna had totally forgotten. Entertainment meant the bar would be busier than she really wanted. Nonetheless, she smiled. "Welcome. Let me show you where to set up."

As soon as she got Rachel set, she called Kiara and asked her to come in.

~ ~ ~

By eight o'clock the place was pretty full. Rachel turned out to be an accomplished performer, engaging the audience in between songs. People were happy, ordering drinks and enough snack food and desserts to keep Paul busy. Both waitresses were constantly moving.

It would be a good night, revenue wise, but Anna couldn't wait until it was over. Her mind and soul were weary beyond exhaustion. Her nerves were stretched as tight as piano wire.

There was a lull at the bar when Paul came out from the kitchen. "I'm out of French fries," he told her. "Can you let Olivia and Kiara know?"

"How did that happen?" Anna asked. "You're supposed to keep track of inventory. Or am I supposed to do everything around here?"

"It was a higher demand than I anticipated."

"Well, you should have anticipated it. You knew we had entertainment tonight. Come in early tomorrow and do a *thorough* inventory. Got it?"

"Yes, ma'am," he said and turned away.

She immediately wanted to call him back. Paul was her most loyal employee. And she was the one who'd forgotten about the entertainment.

Cleaning off the glasses and coasters from two customers who'd departed, she swiped the bar with her rag and checked the levels of limes and lemons. Occasionally someone wanted a fancy drink that required small onions, olives, or cherries, but those were few and far between. She'd refused to have a blender at the bar. Too much noise.

Around nine o'clock, Quinn came in and took a seat at the bar.

He was going to want an answer. She'd never gotten around to texting him her final refusal.

"What can I get you?" she asked.

"Beer," he said. "The usual. And a bag of potato chips, please." He looked around. "Nice crowd."

"Yep." She went to get his order.

Once she set the chips and beer in front of him, she started checking on customers, beginning with the other end of the bar.

What would be the harm of a ride? She desperately needed something to straighten her head out. She shouldn't have treated Paul like that. It would take a few days for her to shake off the grief she renewed every year on this date.

People had told her it would get easier.

So far it hadn't.

She also needed to mend fences with her mother. Mom was an enabler, but not the perpetrator. She'd done the best she could. Anna would call her soon and make arrangements to see her before the snow took hold. This time, if Sophia was there, she wouldn't let her sister rile her.

"You doing okay?" she asked Quinn when she got back to him, noting he'd finished the chips but was nursing his beer.

"Yeah, thanks. How was your day?"

She shrugged.

"Nothing you want to talk about," he said.

"No."

"Okay." He took a sip. "She's good." He nodded toward Rachel.

"Yes. I'll bring her back in the spring. She said she sticks to Bozeman in the winter. She doesn't trust the pass."

"Smart woman." He grinned at Anna. "Like someone else I know."

"Huh," Anna said, scanning the crowd which was thankfully

beginning to thin. Then she looked at him. "About the ride."

He shrugged. "I figured when I didn't hear from you, the answer was no."

She opened her mouth to tell him he was right.

"I don't know," she said instead. "It would be nice to ride again."

He put down his beer.

"Really?"

"I said nice to ride. Not nice to ride with you."

"I'm afraid it's an entire package," he said with a grin. "With my horse, you get me." Then he looked at her seriously. "Just friends. Not a date. Not anything more than a ride between two old friends." The tone of his voice reassured her that he meant what he'd said.

No romance.

Her heart ached for the girl she'd once been, the one with hopes and dreams, one of which was a marriage just like Michael Quinn's parents.

Take a chance.

"Yes," she said. "I'll go riding with you."

Chapter Nine

Anna didn't get to wash her truck on Monday. When she looked at her phone first thing that morning, she realized she had a meeting, something she'd desperately tried to get out of.

But Heather wouldn't hear of it. Anna really needed to be there since a number of the fall events were going to take place at the Buckhorn.

Additionally, since the meeting was taking place at ten a.m. at the bar and grill, she needed to be there to open up.

With a groan, Anna heaved herself out of bed and started her preparations for the day. She was tired, emotionally hungover, and berating herself for agreeing to go on a ride with Quinn. True, they hadn't set a date, but she'd said she'd go. As tempted as she was to never let him know when she was free, she wasn't that type of person.

Brandon had been an expert at passive-aggressive behavior, and she'd hated every minute of it.

~ ~ ~

By eleven, the members of the Fall Planning Committee, as it liked to call itself, were assembled in some chairs they'd pushed around a table. There were only four other women: Heather, Riley, Destiny, and Chloe. Riley owned the local coffee shop, Morning Glory. Destiny was a new transplant to Willow Creek, taking a second shot at love with Quinn's friend, Caleb.

They all looked a lot more put together than Anna ever achieved on her best day. Riley emphasized her red hair with a dark green blouse and long beige skirt. Chloe, who dressed herself from her thrift store, still managed to achieve the charm that went with her waif-like appearance. Destiny's wardrobe was city-focused, but her canary shell and khaki pants fit her body perfectly and amplified the glow of her dark skin.

Heather's approach to dress—a nice blouse, blue jeans, and cowboy boots—approximated Anna's, but Heather had taken time to put on earrings and makeup, something Anna rarely did.

What would it be like to take even a few more moments to pay attention to her appearance? She should at least put in earrings before going riding with Quinn.

"There's a lot of work to do," Heather said.

Anna snapped her attention back to the matter at hand.

"But I wanted to give you an update on Dot first," Heather continued. "Her house needs some repairs. Jose Diaz has promised to provide supplies for the repairs if we can find volunteers. I've already talked to Ralph about it. He's going to round up some people and get it done. I thought when they were done that we'd get a group together to paint the insides. You know, make it more cheerful."

"I don't know how she can go back into that house," Chloe said. "There must be so many bad memories."

"Dot's husband may have been abusive, but she raised her children in that house, so there are good memories, too," Heather said. "To add to that, she owns it outright. In today's housing market, that's worth a great deal."

"Makes sense," Riley said. "I'll help painting."

"Me too," Chloe said.

Destiny nodded, and they all looked at Anna.

"I have a business to run," she said. "I can't leave it."

"So do Chloe and I," Riley said. "And I've got two boys. You're closed mornings. Maybe you can help then."

"How do you manage to keep your business going when you're not there?" Anna asked. "Like now. Isn't it busy at Morning Glory?"

"I have a few trusted employees who step in," Riley said.

"I put up a sign," Chloe said. "It says when I'll be back. I don't really have busy times, so it works."

Anna shook her head. "I can't imagine doing either of those things."

"Maybe you should," Heather said. "Otherwise you're going to burn out."

Truth was, Anna was probably past burnout.

"Olivia could probably handle it," Riley suggested. "She's been with you a long time now."

"I'd probably need a third waitress, then."

"How's Kiara working out?" Chloe asked.

"She's getting there. She's a hard worker and quick learner. I just wish she could give me more hours. But she's a vet tech as well."

"Why is she working for you, then?" Heather asked.

"Usual story. She can't make ends meet on the minimum wage salary she's paid, even working thirty or forty hours a week."

"That's hard," Riley said. "She went to college for a degree, too."

The women were quiet for a moment, then Riley said, "I may know someone. She asked me for a job, but I didn't need anyone. She has a coffee shop background, and that means she's used to dealing with customers. I'll dig up her resume and send you her info."

"Thanks." An extra waitress would be good, but Anna wasn't sure leaving the bar and grill in Olivia's hands, even for a few hours, was the best idea. What did Olivia know about running a business?

About the same she had when she'd bought the bar.

She'd think about it later.

"Okay," Anna said. "I'll help out with the painting in the morning." The community had been good to her and giving back was what it was all about.

"Great," Heather said, making some notes in her notebook computer.

The woman was entirely too organized.

"First up," Heather continued, "is Halloween. The elementary school is organizing a trunk-or-treat that will run from five to seven."

Anna loved all the effort people put into decorating their cars for Halloween. They'd drive to the Buckhorn parking lot at the appointed time and give out candy and treats from their trunks or the back of their SUVs. It was a great tradition.

"Halloween is on Friday this year," Riley said. "Won't the parents want to party? Don't you usually decorate the bar and grill?"

"If I don't, there's a huge protest," Anna said. "One year they threatened to cover the place with cobwebs if I didn't get to it. I swear Halloween's become bigger than Christmas."

"Maybe for parents," Chloe said. "But not for kids."

"Good point," Heather said.

"I've got a band coming in that Friday night," Anna said. "And we're going to have some prizes for costumes and special drinks. I expect we'll get a good crowd."

"The babysitters better get ready," Riley said. "Taking care of kids on candy isn't going to be easy."

Madison had loved Halloween. She always wanted to be a princess.

"So that takes care of Halloween," Anna said. "The bar will be closed Thanksgiving afternoon for my annual gathering, but I'll open up again around seven. The young people like getting away from their parents."

"We need to do a food drive," Heather said.

"I can put a container in my store," Chloe said.

Riley and Anna concurred.

"I'll check with other businesses," Destiny said.

"Good. Now what about Christmas?"

"And Hanukah," Chloe said. "And any other gift giving holidays around then?"

"Quinn said he, Jake, and Caleb have been talking about it. They'd like to spearhead a toy drive for Christmas. They'd involve the sheriff's department and the volunteer firefighters."

"The school and library usually have a tree with names people can choose for gift donations. The paper also has the age of the child and idea of what they'd like for the holiday. That way a person can know what would be appreciated," Heather said.

"We could have a charity night here," Anna said, tentatively. "Something low-key to attract families. If they brought a package, I'd give them a discount of food items."

"Wouldn't that cost you a lot?" Destiny asked.

"I didn't say it would be a big discount," Anna said with a grin. "Besides, like most restaurants, we make most of our money on drinks."

"That would be amazingly kind of you," Heather said.

"Maybe we could arrange for some big, strong firefighters to come pick up the gifts," Riley said. "Sean's a volunteer firefighter. I'm sure he could get some guys to come along."

"Any of them single?" Heather asked. "We could raffle them off for the evening."

"That's crazy!" Riley exclaimed.

"I love it," Heather said. "If I weren't happily married, I wouldn't mind a date with some of them."

Laughter erupted around the table.

It felt good to laugh again. Anna didn't do nearly enough of it.

Once they finalized the donation plans, it was almost eleven. Heather assigned chores to everyone before they left.

The woman should have been a general. She managed to get people working together and getting things done. Willow Creek was lucky to have her, as annoying as she could sometimes be.

When the other three left around eleven, Destiny stayed behind.

"Can I help you with something?" Anna asked her.

"I wanted to spend a few moments getting to know you. If you have time, that is."

"If you don't mind talking over by the bar while I set up, no problem. How are you finding life in Willow Creek so far?"

Destiny perched on one of the bar stools.

"It's taking some getting used to. Even though I spent a few months here over the spring and summer, living here full time puts a different spin on things."

"I can understand that." Long practiced at keeping up a conversation while she worked behind the bar, Anna went through her daily rituals.

"At least I've been able to find more work as a consultant," Destiny said. "It seems every small town, and even Livingston, is dealing with some kind of housing crisis. It's not only the buildings, but the infrastructure needed to sustain them."

"Must be interesting."

"Can be." Destiny paused. "What's it like owning a place like this? It must be tiring being open seven days a week."

"I enjoy it." Anna leaned on the bar and looked at Destiny. "Why do you think it would be tiring?"

"Because you look exhausted," Destiny said.

"Oh?" Destiny's frankness startled Anna. "It's been a rough couple of days. I'll catch up on my sleep tonight and then everything will be right as rain. Can I get you something to drink? Club soda maybe?"

"Sure, that would be great."

"How are things with you and Caleb going?" Anna poured the soda and slid the glass to Destiny.

"Slow, but steady. We have history, but that was decades ago. People change, so we're getting to know each other all over again."

"I've found people may change on the outside, but most of the time their core values and personality stays the same," Anna said.

"That's almost true in this case," Destiny answered. "Caleb has the same values, but he's become a lot less driven and more present than when we knew each other before. I think some of it has to do with his work with horses. Speaking of horses, did you ever agree to go riding with Quinn?"

Anna should be used to the whole town knowing her business, but sometimes it still startled her.

"I did. We haven't set a time yet, though."

"Has it been a while since you've ridden?"

"Yep." Anna went back to work. "I figure all I'll have to show for it is a bunch of aches and pains in new places."

Destiny laughed. "You've got that right." She toyed with her glass. "But I've found riding to be a great way to clear my head and figure out what's important right now."

"Trust me," Anna said. "I know what's important to me—making enough from this business to cover my expenses and have some left over."

"Is that all there is?" Destiny asked.

"For me? Yes."

Destiny drained her glass.

"I don't know you very well," she said as she pushed the glass across the bar and stood. "But I think there's more to you than just work. I know something about how life can hurt you in ways you never anticipated. If you ever want to talk about it, I'd be happy to listen." She gestured at the glass. "Thanks for the soda. I'll see you at whatever meeting Heather calls next."

"Yeah, sure." Anna didn't know what else to say. She felt like the woman had looked directly into her soul and seen the truth about her.

Paul pushed open the door. "Got here early, boss. I'll check the inventory before I start the grill." He walked to the kitchen area.

"Thanks." There was another bridge she was going to have to mend.

With a wave, Destiny left the bar.

For a few moments Anna stared at the closed door, sensing her world shifting around her. She was powerless to stop it and fearful of what was going to come next.

Chapter Ten

Quinn let the four horses he owned out into the corral. They were all working cattle horses, including Champion. Three of them he'd gotten on a whim, not even knowing if they'd work out.

He'd been driving down one of the back roads of the valley when he'd seen a sign about horses for sale. The woman who was selling her father's ranch and all its contents had been eager to sell, but only if he took all three horses. After some dickering, they settled on a price that included a decent horse trailer.

The three had been Caleb's first project as a horse trainer. They hadn't needed much to make the transition to a new owner and new responsibilities.

For Quinn, it was more what the horses had represented than their usefulness. He'd been a sucker for old, sappy westerns where the good guys always won and often got the girl as well. The classics had always had smart horses, wild mustangs, and herds galloping across the vast expanse of the west. The movies represented freedom and a place where justice existed.

Unlike the real world.

His time in the Middle East had rocked his belief in the fairness of the world. Children were maimed or killed because they were in the wrong place at the wrong time. The same occurred with his fellow soldiers, some of whom were his friends.

Working in Detroit had driven the last bit of romanticism from him. People's wounds weren't always visible, but they were there nonetheless. It was the hidden pain that caused many people to fall into drug use which led to crimes to support the habit.

Quinn shook off the past and looked at the horses grazing. That life was over. He was back in a place that could reignite his belief that things would turn out all right in the end. The view in front of him of his land and livestock gave him a firm foundation. Beyond it, the majesty of the landscape, especially with her autumn finery, gave him a sense of something larger than himself, an existence that he would never fully comprehend.

All he could do was take the time to appreciate it and live his life the best he could.

"Hey, boss." Ted came from the barn and joined Quinn at the railing. "Beautiful day, isn't it?"

"Yep." At eight in the morning, the temperature still had a chill, but the sun's warmth promised a warm day. White puffy clouds floated across the cerulean sky, and the mountain peaks gleamed without a shadow of a storm.

"We've gotten halfway through fixing fences on the winter pasture," Ted said. "But we're going to need some more supplies after today. Do you want me to run up to Livingston?"

"No," Quinn said. "Let me take care of it. There's a few other things I need to get." Maybe the drive and lunch at a restaurant would help the restlessness that still hadn't eased. There was a new thriller he wanted to pick up as well. "Can you get me a list of what we need?"

"Sure." Ted pulled a scrap of paper from his pocket and handed it to Quinn.

Quinn scanned it, making sure he could read his ranch manager's chicken scratch. Then he nodded.

"I'll finish up my morning chores," Ted said. "Then Ned and I will pack a lunch and head back out. Have a good trip." With a finger to his Montana State Cats cap, Ted turned and walked back into the barn.

Quinn took one more look at his horses, then got ready to head out. He'd take the ranch pickup; Ted's list included barbed wire. No way was he scratching up his fairly new truck.

With a rumble, the ranch pickup started right up. Ted was a genius when it came to things mechanical, and he kept the pickup running in top form. It may look like a piece of junk from the outside, but it was top-notch where it mattered.

He liked the idea of keeping things running. Just because something was old or had a few dents didn't mean it should be discarded.

As he passed the Buckhorn Bar and Grill, Anna came to mind. She'd promised she'd go riding, but hadn't said when. He was going to have to text her to press her for a day.

Or should he drop it like he'd intended? Maybe she'd had second thoughts.

He'd never thought he'd be fixated on a woman ever again in his life, especially not Anna Wells. He remembered wishing she'd been older when she'd hung out at his house. If he was honest with himself, he'd also had deep feelings of wanting to protect her from whatever was hurting her. Sometimes the feelings were so strong, he wanted to seek out whoever had put that pain in her eyes and wipe the floor with him. His father would not have approved.

She'd been a big-eyed, raw-boned girl who hadn't quite come to terms with her body. He'd been aware how her eyes watched his every move. It was clear she'd had a massive crush on him.

What he hadn't realized at the time was how much he'd cared for her in return.

Mostly, he'd treated her like an annoyance, like his kid sister. But every once in a while, he'd find himself alone with Anna. She was a good listener—it was one of the things that made her a successful bar owner now—and he'd tell her all his plans for the future. At that time those plans hadn't included going into the army or relocating to Detroit. At times, he'd been tempted to ask her to wait for him to finish his studies, get established, and then they could live happily ever after.

But then he became aware of the wider world around him, and the need for everyone who was able to support their country to do so.

So he'd never indicated to Anna how he'd felt about her. He'd buried his emotions in a mental box and tucked it way back in the recesses of his mind.

None of his family had been thrilled when he'd enlisted, but they understood his need to do something for his country before living his own life.

When she'd found out, her jaw had sagged. He'd seen the tears pooling in her eyes before she turned away and fled the room.

That was about the last he'd seen of her until he'd run into her at the Buckhorn after he'd moved back to Willow Creek. The years in between remained a mystery. Since she was well-liked and had turned a sketchy bar into a family place, people let her secrets be. She was upbeat and pleasant most of the time, but he could see the haunted look in her eyes had turned permanent.

It was a look he wanted to erase.

But how could he get close enough to do that if she wouldn't even go riding with him?

As if cued by his thoughts, his phone buzzed.

Probably just another political text asking him for money. He'd check it when he stopped at Murdoch's.

~ ~ ~

He forgot about the text by the time he got to the farm and ranch store. Although he had a list, he had to walk up and down all the aisles like he always did. There were always new gadgets, or a warm pair of gloves that fit him just right. This time a bag of cherry apple horse treats and hand warmers wound up in his cart. A warm flannel shirt caught his eye. One could never have too many warm clothes to get through a Montana winter.

Into the cart it went.

He paused at some blouses in the women's section. There was one that would look great on Anna, if he knew her size and could be sure she wouldn't get bent out of shape by a gift.

That's when he finally remembered the text.

It was a single line: *Does Thursday morning work for you?*

Absolutely, he texted back. *I'll meet you at the trailhead at nine. Okay?*

Nothing.

She was probably busy.

But she'd set a time.

A smile lifted the corners of his lips, and his mood lightened.

Pulling out Ted's list, he got to work. By the time he was done, the bed of the pickup was loaded with heavy items, and he had several bags in the front seat.

~ ~ ~

Before finding a place for lunch, he stopped at Wheatgrass Books to browse. He'd discovered winters were a great time to sit in front of the fire with a good book and a cup of coffee. Like

Murdoch's, he went up and down every aisle, looking for anything that would keep him entertained. Mark Hume's *Reading the Water* caught his eye. Reading about fly fishing was almost as good as doing it.

He'd have to get down to the park before the cold weather really set in. Did Anna fly fish? Would she be willing to learn? And if he was to ask her, would she consider that a date?

Would he?

What was he planning on doing with Anna Wells?

He wasn't sure of the answer to that. All he knew was something was compelling him to get closer to her, to get to know her, and to find a way to wipe away the pain he'd always seen in her eyes. He had no idea how to go about doing that without scaring her away.

She was like a wounded horse, like the mare he'd rescued from her abusive owner.

Maybe she'd respond to the same treatment Caleb and Destiny had given the horse.

Ridiculous. He couldn't treat a woman like a horse.

Except maybe there was merit to the idea. He'd need to take it slow, let her come to him. He'd have to find things he could offer that would arouse her curiosity or was something she liked but denied herself.

He'd have to think about it some more.

His phone buzzed.

Anna had texted him that she'd meet him at nine.

That was a first step. All he had to do was not make an ass out of himself.

With a shake of his head, he continued browsing, paying particular attention to books centered around horses, cattle, and ranching. He pulled out a book called *Montana Sanctuary* and flipped through it. It was about a movement to provide a sanctuary for aging horses whose owners no longer wanted them.

Settling into a comfortable chair, he started reading. As he read, he became more excited. This was something he could do with his life. The cattle portion of the ranch practically ran itself. A horse sanctuary would be rewarding work, something that involved both the rescue work and advocacy for the organization.

Older horses would be the perfect companions for young children who wanted to learn to ride, kids with disabilities like Jose Diaz's daughter, and maybe even provide work for the juvenile offenders Jake sometimes arrested. Those kids often got community service. This would be a great way for them to give back.

Horses were incredible healers.

He stood and walked to the fiction section where he picked up a few thrillers. Satisfied with his purchases, he paid for them and walked to a nearby restaurant.

By the time he left Livingston an hour later, he felt lighter than he had in months.

Chapter Eleven

Anna pulled her truck into the parking area by the river trail. Her gaze brushed over the vibrant cottonwood leaves, crisp against the blue sky, and went straight to the man standing by the horse trailer.

For a few moments she was fourteen all over again. Michael Quinn was once again the center of her existence.

Then she brushed the sensation away. She was no longer that girl, hadn't been in a long, long time.

"Hey," Quinn said as she climbed out of her truck. He walked toward her. "Thanks for coming. It's a beautiful day for a ride."

"Yes. It is." Good grief. She sounded like a tongue-tied girl at her first dance. What had come over her today?

She knew the answer to that question. This ride was too much like a date.

"I brought along Rocky for you to ride," Quinn said. "He got his name because riding him is a little like sitting in a rocking chair. He's easy. I don't know when you've ridden last."

"It's been a while. In fact, I don't think I've been riding in decades." She'd tried to get Brandon to go on trail rides when they were together, but he wasn't interested. The few times she'd gone on her own, she'd returned to a sink overflowing with dishes, trash cans that were filled to the brim, and a husband who didn't really speak to her.

The pleasure she'd gotten from the rides hadn't been worth the punishment.

"I hope it isn't the idea of riding with me that's putting that scowl on your face," Quinn said.

"Oh, no. Not at all." She smiled at him. "Let's get going. I need to make sure I'm at the bar in time for opening."

"Sure thing."

They walked to the horses. She took Rocky to a nearby log and got on, her muscle memory kicking in as she mounted. Quinn got on his horse with ease and grace.

He wasn't eighteen anymore, but he was still in shape.

"I'd forgotten how much I'd enjoyed riding," he said. "I rarely did it from the time I left Montana to when my uncle left me the ranch."

"Was it hard?" she asked. "Being in the army?"

He was quiet for a bit, and she was afraid she'd already overstepped.

"There were parts that were good. Getting to know people from around the country, with different backgrounds and experiences, all working together to serve our country. But war is hell. It brings out the worst in human beings. And to see someone you consider a friend hurt, or worse, well …"

"I'm sorry. I shouldn't have asked."

"It's okay," he said. "It's the last memory you had of me when we were kids. I was around all the time, then I enlisted, and I was gone. Kind of abrupt."

"It was a big change. Your parents worried all the time." So had she. But when he came back and settled in Detroit instead of coming home, her young heart had broken.

"I know. Mom constantly reminded me to take care of myself. Dad didn't say much, just how proud he was of me. It was harder on them when I didn't come home after serving, but by then I'd met Amy and fallen in love. When my marriage fell apart, we had two kids, so I was committed to staying put."

Michael—he called himself by his last name now, but Michael had been the boy she'd crushed on as a teen, so that was the name that stuck in her heart— had always done the right thing, unlike Brandon. After experiencing her first crush on such a good man, how had she fallen for her ex?

"And your kids?"

"Tim is twenty-six, also a cop, much to his mother's dismay. He hasn't married yet. Women who have what it takes to be a cop's wife are hard to find. It isn't an easy life. My daughter, Kelly, is twenty-four. She's a teacher in Ann Arbor." He grinned. "She's going to make me a grandpa in March."

"Congratulations."

"Yeah. It's a milestone for sure. I'll have to get out there to see the baby as soon as she or he is born." He sounded almost boyish. "It will be good to see the kids. I keep trying to get them to come out to the ranch, but they're busy with their own lives. But maybe now that kids are on the way, coming to grandpa's ranch will be cool enough to get them here."

How different her life would have been if she'd married someone like Michael Quinn.

The conversation lagged for a little bit, but it wasn't strained. It was as if by mutual agreement, they'd decided to enjoy the sounds of nature and the warmth of the sun on their backs.

Rocky deserved his name. He had an easy gait that threatened to lull her to sleep. Her muscles relaxed and the spinning of the things she needed to do faded into the background of her thoughts. All that mattered was the gentle thud of her horse's hooves, the scattering of small birds in the brush, and the glimpse of a long-legged heron on the opposite bank of the river.

"It must be a challenge to own a business like the Buckhorn," he said. "I understand it was a pretty raucous place when you bought it."

"It was a run-down dump full of hard drinkers," she said.

"And you made it into what it is today. That took a lot of grit and determination. You must be pretty proud of what you've accomplished."

"I did what I needed to do."

"Oh, c'mon, it was more than that. You had a vision and made it a reality. That's an accomplishment." He shook his head. "That's the problem with people. We're quick to kick ourselves when we do something dumb, but reluctant to pat ourselves on the back for our accomplishments."

He had a point. She could recite all the things she'd ever done wrong at the drop of a hat, but had never taken a moment to savor things that she'd done right. In the beginning of her sobriety, AA had given her lots of reminders when she reached a milestone, but years had passed since her last meeting.

How many years had she stayed sober in spite of owning a bar?

"I've been thinking," he said a few minutes later. "I want to do more than run a cattle ranch."

"Isn't that a lot of work already?"

"Sometimes, but there's a lot of down time, too. I'm not used to being idle. For example, we're going to move the herd from the summer range. That will take a while. We have to drive them slowly so they don't lose weight. Then we'll have to separate our cattle from the Daley's herd. We'll send a bunch to market, but then it's just a matter of making sure the cattle that are left have enough feed in the winter. My ranch manager handles that. The next bit of excitement won't happen until February when calving begins."

The luxury of time. She'd forgotten what it was like to have that much time to herself.

"Sounds nice to have that many free hours."

"It is, but I'm beginning to realize it isn't enough." He stopped Champion and leaned back in his saddle. "I want to do something that involves horses. I got a book on horse sanctuaries the other day, and it seems interesting. These animals give us so much, and when their usefulness is over, too many people toss them away like they're rubbish." He patted Champion's neck.

"It's a nice idea," Anna said, trying to be positive. "But it would take a massive amount of work. And money. Do you even know where to begin?"

"Well," he said. "I have some ideas, but they're pretty undefined right now."

"Then that's your next step, isn't it?" she asked. "It's what I did when I was thinking about buying the bar. I made lists and crunched numbers for months until I was sure about what had to be done and how much it would cost."

He nodded. "I knew you'd be a good sounding board." He took a canteen off his saddle horn, and offered it to her. She took it, uncapped it, and drank. Quinn's well water was refreshing. After wiping off the neck of the canteen, she handed it back.

"You don't have anything I should know about?" he asked with a grin.

"I've had all the regular shots," she said with her own smile.

"Good." He drank deeply.

"You have good water on your place," she said.

He nodded. "And I want to keep it that way."

"Is there anything threatening your water supply?"

"Not really. The problem is running the cattle in the summer range. There's a number of small streams up there that feed down into the Yellowstone. The cattle trample the banks and contribute to the water warming. Warm water isn't good for trout. And as much as I love fly fishing ..." He grinned.

"What can you do about it?"

"I'm going to get the Nature Conservancy folks up here so they can advise me. I understand there are grants to be had to help with restoration and finding another way for cattle to get water."

"A big undertaking."

"Could be," he said. "But it will be worth it if we can protect the fish." He hung the canteen back on the saddle horn. "Have you ever fly fished?"

"No." When was she supposed to find time to fish?

"I'd love to teach you someday. It's fun ... and relaxing. You'd enjoy it."

She shook her head. "Not real high on my bucket list."

"I'll just have to convince you then."

"Uh-huh."

He laughed then urged his horse forward.

As they rode, they talked about what was going on in town: Dot's imminent return, Heather's ongoing passion to organize events, an empty storefront on the main street, the palpable loneliness of Robert, the manager of the hardware store now that Maribel, owner of Silver Clips, had broken up with him.

Eventually, they turned around and headed back so she could make it to the Buckhorn in time to get ready to open.

"Don't you ever take a day off?" he asked her.

"Nope. People expect me to be there. If I close, they'll stop coming by. I can't afford the loss of revenue."

"What about hiring a manager? It can't be good for you to be working all the time. You have no time for a life."

"I don't need a life," she said. Why was everyone on her case to have time to herself? A lack of things to do only gave her more time to think.

He was silent for a bit.

"It's none of my business," he said. "But it seems to me

you're really sad about something. Was the time between when you left Butte and now hard?"

"You're right. It's none of your business." She sounded like a shrew.

"Got it."

"Sorry," she said. "I don't like to talk about it. Let's just say I was married for a while, and it didn't go well."

"That's too bad. You always deserved the best."

Her throat closed up at his kind words. She wasn't used to people being sensitive to her feelings. In fact, she avoided people who might get past her barriers.

They didn't speak again until they arrived at the horse trailer.

"Thanks," she said as she slid off Rocky. "That was nice."

"It was. I enjoyed having company—having you—go riding with me."

His gaze was intent on her, his blue eyes full of concern and something else she couldn't quite identify.

And her? She hoped her eyes didn't betray the longing she suddenly felt, a desire to have a do-over with her life and spend it with Michael Quinn.

"Let's do it again sometime," he said. "Like next week?"

She shouldn't. It was too dangerous. He'd get past her defenses.

But the desire was too strong.

"I'd like that," she said. "I'll get back to you about when works for me."

He nodded.

"Go ahead," he said. "I know you need to get to work. I'll take care of the horse."

"Thanks," she said.

She got into her truck and slowly backed up to exit the parking area. Before she pulled out onto the main road, she looked over to where he stood.

He was staring at her.

She waved and pulled out onto the road.

What was she doing?

Chapter Twelve

True to her word, Riley called the woman who'd applied at the coffee shop. Sue Moorhead was a woman in her forties with a background working in coffee establishments. She was a solid looking woman with a friendly smile. She told Anna she'd taken some time off to care for a sick child and was looking for work now that the child was better.

"I can only give you some part-time work now," Anna told her. "Our busiest times are Friday and Saturday nights. Sometimes we have special events, and I'll need you then. Again, it's mostly late afternoons and evenings. Can you handle that?"

"Yes," Sue said. "My husband has an early shift at the post office so he's home when the kids get there after school. I expected the late hours, but it's a job. I appreciate the chance."

Anna's gut reaction was that Sue was going to be a great addition to the team, maybe someone she could train to be a manager. Olivia was a great waitress, but that was the work she enjoyed, not handling troublemakers or dealing with problems.

"Then it's settled," she told Sue. "Can you start on Friday? Come in about two?"

"Yes. I'll see you then."

Sue stuck around long enough to fill out the necessary paperwork then left with a friendly wave.

The Monday afternoon was quiet. There were long periods of time when there were no people. Anna had stopped having wait staff come in, handling any orders herself. At times, the only sound was the background music she played, primarily older country-western, the songs of cheating hearts and standing by your man.

With nothing much to do, Paul had gone home for the afternoon, leaving Anna with the sad tunes and her thoughts.

She'd enjoyed the ride with Quinn. It was good to be out in nature, and his company had been easier than she'd expected.

True, she'd experienced some of the same feelings she'd had as a teen, but those weren't real. They were merely a vestige of a long-ago memory when, even if everything in her life wasn't good, there were possibilities.

Riding with Quinn had evoked those hopes. She was too old now to believe in happily-ever-after, but maybe they could have a friendship based on a shared past. He'd already lived his life, gotten married and had his children. Even if he was single he was probably set in his ways, just like she was.

It would be okay to go riding with him again. Nothing was going to come of it. She'd text him a date next week. Agreeing to go with him this week would be too soon, would send a message she didn't want him to believe.

Gazing around the empty bar and grill, she wondered again if Paul was right. Even if she closed until the evening it would give her time off.

It was only one day. Surely she could survive one day without the memories overwhelming her.

She picked up her phone to text Quinn and make arrangements for the following week.

~ ~ ~

By the time Sue came in on Friday, the lunch crowd was thinning out. Anna introduced her to Olivia and Paul, and showed her how things worked. Sue asked a few questions, showing she was listening. As the traffic increased with the after-work crowd, she handled her tables easily, bestowing her smile on the customers.

Anna kept an eye on her, but as time went on, she became more confident in her new hire. It was a good thing because a man she'd had trouble with in the past arrived about three and began drinking steadily. He was the type of man who held onto a grudge so tightly it couldn't breathe. She hoped there was no one showing up who might have injured him, at least in his mind.

There wasn't a band that night, and she was grateful for that. For a week that had started out quietly, it had become problematic. Some of the supplies Paul had ordered had failed to show up, and a few bottles of liquor she should have according to her inventory had somehow disappeared.

Both Olivia and Paul, the only ones who had keys to the place besides herself, had been with her for years. While Kiara and Sue were new, they wouldn't have had time to filch any bottles.

She'd probably moved them and forgotten where she put them.

In addition to the problems, the tourists and locals seemed to have decided that the bar and grill was the perfect place to be this week. She'd been slammed from Tuesday on. The knitting group had come in on Tuesday, dealing more in gossip than stitches. Caleb, Jake, and Quinn had arrived on Wednesday for their weekly steak, but the place had been too busy for her to do more than give them a friendly chat halfway through their meal.

Now all she wanted to do was go home, pop open a non-alcoholic beer, and watch something mindless on TV.

It wouldn't be for a while, though.

~ ~ ~

The eruption happened a little after five.

Her ears immediately picked up the sound of male voices having a disagreement. So far they were keeping it low, but she looked around to identify the source. When she realized one of the men was the grudge-holder, she walked over to the booth where he stood. The man seated at the booth was another local she rarely saw.

"Problem, gentlemen?" she asked.

"Only if you call a back-stabber a problem," said the grudge-holder.

"You don't know what you're talking about," the other man said.

"Right. Tell me it wasn't you who reported me to the forest rangers."

"I didn't do it, but if you were shooting deer out of season like you always do, someone must have seen you."

"I have every right to shoot deer. It's a free country."

"That we all live in. There are rules. We all have to abide by them, even you." The man in the booth picked up his beer. "Now move on and let me enjoy my burger."

The grudge-holder stood there.

"I suggest you go back to your table," Anna said. "I don't want any trouble in here."

He looked at her like she was a fly who was annoying him.

She widened her stance and pulled back her shoulders. "You have ten seconds to go back to your table."

After a glare, he turned and walked away.

She breathed a sigh of relief. If he hadn't moved, she didn't have a good back-up plan. She walked back to the bar, stopping to say hello to people she knew, trying to reset the mood of the place.

Although she kept an eye on him, the grudge-holder stayed put.

People kept coming in until the place was nearly full. Tonight would certainly put a good amount of money into the bank.

"You had no right!" the man with the grudge shouted.

As she turned around she saw him tackle the other man and slam him to the floor, just missing a table where a couple of tourists had just been seated. The pair leapt up, knocking their chairs to the floor as they did so.

"Stop it!" she yelled as she ran over to the men who were rolling around on the floor, unsuccessfully trying to land punches.

She really needed a baseball bat under the bar.

How was she going to separate them?

Suddenly, Sue was by her side. "Paul's called the cops. But if you want, I can help you try to get them separated."

Anna nodded. "Arms?"

"Best bet. You grab one arm, I'll get the other."

They positioned themselves and yanked.

The man who'd started it all, who was still on top, wasn't ready for their assault and was pulled to his knees fairly easily.

The other man scrambled backwards, away from his attacker.

"I'm going to kill you!" the attacker yelled.

"Not in my bar, you're not." Anna crouched down to deliver the rest of the news. "You're barred from the Buckhorn for the rest of your life. Got it?"

"He deserved it."

Jake pushed open the door, his hand on the gun at his hip.

She really didn't need all this drama in her restaurant. How much would the reputation of being a family-friendly place suffer?

"Alright, Curtis, stand up," Jake said.

Neither she nor Sue let go of Curtis's arms as he struggled to his feet.

"Repeat offender?" she asked Jake.

"Let's just say he's been a guest of our facilities before. What started all this?"

She gave him a quick overview, then glanced around the restaurant. "Can you get this over with? People want to have a nice dinner."

"You going to press charges?"

"No, but he's banned from the place."

Jake nodded, then looked at the other man who'd managed to get himself up.

"How about you? Do you want to press charges?"

Curtis glared at him.

"No, that's okay. Misunderstanding. That's all."

"Your lucky day, Curtis," Jake said. "However, I'm still taking you in for disturbing the peace." He quickly placed handcuffs on the man and escorted him out of the Buckhorn, intoning the Miranda rights on his way.

"Okay, everyone," Anna said. "Show's over." She needed to do something to get back into everyone's good graces.

She helped the tourist couple set up their chairs and get settled. "Your dinner's on me," she told them. "I'm sorry that happened."

"That's the most excitement we've had in days," the woman said.

"I don't think I've ever seen a bar fight before," the man said. "But thank you. It's appreciated."

Anna didn't have the heart to tell him that the scuffle didn't come near to many bar fights she'd seen. She just smiled and went over to Sue. "Thanks for the help."

"No problem. I had a brother with a temper. I was always helping to pull him off someone."

"I appreciate it. I'm not sure I could have done it by myself."

"Have you considered a baseball bat?" Sue asked.

"I am now."

Sue chuckled.

"Please tell all the people you're waiting on they have one round of drinks on the house."

"Will do."

Anna went over and delivered the same message to Olivia.

Soon the waitresses were delivering smiles and reassuring people. By the time Kiara came in to help with the rest of the dinner rush, things had settled down.

The money she was anticipating was going to take a hit, but at least she had happy customers.

In a few hours she could go home, get some rest, and start all over again tomorrow.

Chapter Thirteen

The days of October were slipping by, as life tended to do especially as fifty approached. The drive to meet Quinn would take a little longer this morning. He wanted to do a trail on the west side of the valley, to get some perspective, he'd told Anna.

With some trepidation she'd told Paul she might be late and he should open up and start the set up. She'd be back before the place opened.

She'd make sure of that.

There were clouds this morning, but none that looked like they'd threaten rain, simply white puffs pushed along the sky to give a different experience from the unflinching blue of high summer. Light moved in patterns across the colorful cottonwood leaves, adding mystery to the day.

Her heart beat a little faster as she drove across the valley. She was actually looking forward to riding … or was it spending time with Quinn that was exciting her?

Probably it was just getting away from the bar for a while. Nothing out of the ordinary had happened since the previous Friday night's fight, but she was still hyperaware of everything going on around her. Rumors had flown around the town for a while, but they seemed to have settled down.

Much to her relief, the incident hadn't slowed any traffic. Montanans could feel the good weather slipping away and were doing everything they could to squeeze every ounce of joy from the time they had left before the cold and snow set in.

Following Quinn's directions, she pulled off onto a gravel road and found the trailhead. Like before, he was ready with both horses tacked up and out of the trailer. He gave her a big grin when she got out of the truck. It was the kind of expression designed to break down all barriers a woman might have.

She was stronger than that, although she could sense a softening of her resolve never to let another person close to her again. Was it risk worth taking?

"Hi," she said, once again feeling like the teenager she'd been.

"Ready to ride?"

"Sure am. It's another great day." She walked over to Rocky and fed him the apple quarters she'd brought.

"You're going to spoil him," Quinn said.

"He deserves it, don't you, boy?" She pet the horse's chin and was rewarded by a nudge.

It made her laugh, the sound unexpected in her ears. This was a joyful laugh, different from the times she laughed as an obligation.

"You seem in a good mood today," Quinn said. "Must be because of all that girl power taking down a nasty drunk."

"You heard."

"Everyone heard," he said as he swung into his saddle. "Small town. You know how that goes."

Exactly why she kept the details of her previous life to herself. Thankfully, social media hadn't been the full-blown monster it had become in the last few decades.

With a little bit of effort, she got herself onto Rocky's back.

"This way," Quinn said and led off.

Rocky automatically fell in line.

The trail led through grasslands turned brown by the summer sun. A breeze made waves through the stalks. Sagebrush dotted the area, allowing small birds to perch then flit to a nicer looking branch. Somewhere a Western meadowlark made its presence known.

Her shoulders relaxed as she swayed to the horse's rocking gait. As they rode, her mind released its hold on the list of things that needed to be done and decisions she was contemplating. She brought herself into the present, noting the warmth of the sun on her back, the hawk soaring high in the sky above her, and the strong back of the man in front of her.

When they reached the tree line, he pulled up.

She maneuvered Rocky so she was near enough to hear Quinn.

"The path is a little narrow at the beginning, but opens up into a series of mountain meadows. I'm told the upper meadows provide incredible views of the valley. We can stop there for a bit. I brought some chocolate chip cookies and coffee."

"Breakfast of champions," she said with a grin. "Didn't your dad love chocolate chip cookies?"

"Yep." His own grin was back. "And Mom gave me her recipe."

"You bake?"

"I'm a man of many talents," he said. "I can also iron my own shirts and sew on a button."

"Impressive."

"Thank you." He turned his horse and disappeared into the trees.

The aroma changed as soon as she was immersed in the shadows. Piney scents tickled her nose. The path was narrow, and the air seemed closer here. Occasionally, she had to duck under a branch as the path twisted its way through rocky switchbacks to gain altitude.

Rocky picked his way through the path without hesitation.

Soon they emerged from the trees into the sunlight of the meadow. Quinn was stopped with his horse and held up his hand. Once she'd come up beside him, he pointed.

A bull elk stood at the high point of the ridge in front of them. As they watched, he lifted his head, the heavy rack he carried seeming like nothing, and let out a bugle.

The high-pitched, strident sound echoed around them, then faded into silence. The elk waited a few moments, then repeated the challenge.

How long had it been since she'd seen an elk bugle? Later in the fall there would be herds in some of the lower valleys. Sometimes they were even visible from the road. But that was after rutting season, when all the females had been divided up by the strongest males.

"Magnificent," she whispered to Quinn.

He nodded, then moved on up the trail.

The elk gave them a glance, but didn't move. As they left the meadow to follow the path through a grove of aspens, he went back to the business at hand.

By the time they reached the upper meadow, the sun and rocking gait had lulled her to a half-asleep state. She hadn't been this relaxed in a long time, like she could lie down in this meadow and sleep for days.

"Oh my," she said when she stopped Rocky to take in the view. A stretch of the valley lay spread out before her, the Yellowstone River glinting in the sunlight, bordered by vibrant cottonwoods. Farms and ranches made a patchwork of colors below. Cows and horses seemed like toys she could pick up and move around if she wanted.

"You can even see Virginia's spread from here," Quinn said, pointing to the southern end of what they could see.

"That's a big place," Anna said.

"If you're one of the first people to get land in a valley, you can generally get a lot of it. She and her husband worked hard to build their various businesses. Even though he's gone, she's still working hard."

"It was cool to see her ride Blue in the Fourth of July parade."

"She's a neat lady, and really cares about the community. She's always donating to Heather's causes, and more than one person has gotten a helping hand from her. Not only cash, but a connection for a new job or advice on relationships."

"Really?"

"Sometimes you get it whether you like it or not."

She'd need to stay out of Virginia's way. If the woman ever heard she'd had two rides with Quinn, she'd have all kinds of things to say.

"How about we have our snacks over there?" Quinn pointed to a level spot that had a view of the mountains beyond the valley.

"Sure." She slid off Rocky, once again aware of her unused muscles. Too bad she didn't have a tub in her place.

Quinn pulled a blanket from one of his saddlebags and spread it out. From the other, he pulled a Thermos, two tin mugs, and a container of cookies. He gestured for her to sit down.

"This is luxury," she said as he handed her a mug. "I'm used to waiting on other people."

"You've certainly poured enough beer for me," he said, holding out the cookies.

She took one and bit into it.

"Oh my," she said. "These are delicious. They taste just like I remember them."

"Yeah, Mom could bake."

"And your dad grilled a mean steak," she said, remembering the flavorful meat Quinn's father had expertly seasoned.

"That he did. But I can grill up a good one, too. Sometime when you're not wrestling grown men to the floor, I'd love to cook one up for you."

"Please don't remind me. Then to have Jake show up and take him out of the place in handcuffs. I wish Paul hadn't called the sheriff. I could have handled it."

"You probably could have," Quinn said. "But Paul was looking out for you. You never were one to accept a hand willingly. I see that hasn't changed."

"Accepting help usually comes with conditions."

"Not always. I think you've been hanging out with the wrong people."

She shrugged.

"Accepting help is a skill we have to learn. Remember the person helping you also feels good."

"And I'll owe them."

"You're a hard nut to crack," he said with a shake of his head. "You weren't this bitter as a kid, even with whatever was going on at your house."

"Who said anything was wrong with my family?"

"No one. I figured since you were always with us, it can't have been too pleasant at home."

"It wasn't." That was as far as she was going to go. Since he'd already guessed it, she may as well acknowledge.

"Care to talk about it?" he asked.

"No."

"Okay." He held out the cookies again.

She snagged two.

"Did you ever contact the Nature Conservancy?" she asked.

"I did," he said. "They're coming out next week to take a look at everything and then write up some recommendations for improvements and help me through the grant process to pay for it.

Thanks for remembering."

"It comes with my job," she said, looking out across the valley. "Customers like it when I remember what's important to them."

"Most people do," he said. "But I don't think it's just your job. I think it's who you are. You genuinely care about others."

Something in his voice made her turn around.

He studied her, then pushed a hair behind her ear.

She wanted to kiss him when he looked at her like that. She'd always wanted to do that.

It would be the worst thing she could do.

She made a great show of getting out her phone and checking the time.

"I need to start back," she said. "I've got to get to the bar before it opens."

"Gotcha," he said and snapped the lid on the cookies. He held up the container. "I'll give these to you on one condition," he said.

"What's that?" They were really good cookies.

"You let me take you fly fishing."

"I don't know. It's a bad idea."

"Well, then." He stood and tossed the rest of his coffee on the grass.

Excellent cookies.

Why not? He was easy to be with, and she'd felt good after their rides. What's the worst that could happen? She'd get tangled in a bunch of fishing wire?

"Okay," she said. "I'll go. But don't expect much."

"You don't know how good a teacher I am," he said.

"You don't know how bad a student *I* am," she said.

They grinned at each other, and the moment was back.

No, the worst thing wasn't going to be the fishing line. The worst thing would be falling in love with Michael Quinn all over again.

Chapter Fourteen

"When is Laura getting back?" Caleb asked Jake as he passed him the pitcher of beer.

Quinn, Jake, and Caleb were having their regular Wednesday night dinner at the Buckhorn Bar and Grill.

"She's going to be back in time for the grand opening for the low-income housing," Jake said.

"That's this Saturday, isn't it?" Quinn asked.

"Yeah," Jake said, a sappy grin on his face. "She'll be home soon."

"It must be hard to be apart," Quinn said.

"Sometimes," Jake admitted. "But being on location with her is tough, too. I don't really fit in with a lot of those Hollywood people. And I don't have anything to do, so it makes it tedious. It's fun when we have time together, but even then she's focused on the role she's playing. She's insistent on going over her lines until they feel natural to her and talks about motivation all the time." Jake poured the beer into his glass. "I like it better when she's here."

"Here is a good place to be," Quinn admitted. "Although if I had a place in California, I'd definitely think about it when February rolled around."

"Way ahead of you on that one," Jake said. "Once the holidays are over, we're going to spend a month or so down there. We'll go to some museums. She's even threatening Disneyland."

"Disneyland would be fun," Caleb said. "Maybe Destiny and I could join you. Quinn can hold down the fort here."

"How are you all doing?" Anna said. She placed her hand on the back of Quinn's chair and stood close to him.

The air between them seemed to vibrate. If he moved a little, he'd be able to put his arm around her waist and pull her close, like he'd almost done when they were having coffee on the mountaintop.

It had been a bad idea then, and it was a bad idea now.

"We're good," Caleb said. "Destiny asked me to remind you that you're donating and pouring wine and beer at the housing celebration."

"Destiny can give Heather a run for her money," Anna said. "She's phoned me, texted me, and emailed me. Tell her I've got it well in hand."

"Who's going to run the bar while you're gone?" It was amazing to Quinn that she'd take the time off.

"I only promised a few hours," Anna said. "It's in the afternoon. Paul and Olivia can handle it."

"They sure got that housing up rapidly," Jake said.

"Jose was so excited to have his proposal turned into action, he worked his crew overtime to make it happen. The other developer, the one working on multi-unit housing, was happy to finally get to break ground. He'd been ready for months to get going with that project," Anna said.

"It's going to be a good thing for the community," Quinn said. "Nice that it will be ready before the winter months."

"Definitely something to celebrate," Jake said.

Anna took her hand off Quinn's chair. "Let me know if you need anything, although I expect Kiara will take good care of you."

"Thanks," Quinn said, turning to look up at her before she left. "I'm glad you're taking some time away from the bar."

"I'm still working," she reminded him.

"I know, but there's hope."

"You got fly fishing. Don't press your luck." She waved and walked toward another table.

"Okay, spill," Jake said. "What was that all about?"

"Nothing much."

"Define nothing much," Caleb said.

He should have kept his big mouth shut with his friends. But he genuinely liked Anna and wanted to talk about her. Okay, so maybe it was a little more than "like." She was still cautious around him, but was opening up more and more. He needed to be careful about pushing too fast and too hard. So far things were going well.

He didn't want to share all of that with his friends, though.

"We've had a couple of rides together, that's all. It gets lonely riding by yourself," he said.

"If that was the case," Jake said, "you could have asked one of us."

Quinn shrugged. No matter what he said, he would lose the argument.

"You like her," Caleb said.

"She's an old friend. She hung around my family as a kid. She's like a sister to me … nothing more," Quinn said.

"The way you look at her doesn't say 'sister,'" Jake said.

That was news to him.

"You're imagining things," Quinn said.

Fortunately for him, Kiara arrived to take their orders. That gave him enough time to think of a new topic.

"A couple of guys from the Nature Conservancy came by a few days ago," he said once Kiara departed. "We went up to the summer pasture. Met Ralph there. They've got some ideas for protecting the stream that runs through there from being damaged by cattle."

"Never knew you were a tree-hugger," Caleb said.

"Didn't think of myself that way either, but since my uncle left me the land, I've felt protective of it. I want to be a good steward and leave it in as good or better shape for the next generation. That stream feeds into Willow Creek before going into the Yellowstone. Lot of good trout fishing on Willow Creek."

"And cattle muck that up?" Caleb asked.

"Cattle, invasive vegetation, a number of things," Quinn said. "They've given me a plan to fix it, offered to get some volunteers to help, and pointed me to a grant I can access to pay for supplies."

"Wow," Jake said. "That's a lot."

"It's a good group," Quinn said. "They don't come in all high and mighty like they know everything. Instead, they listen to other people and reach consensus."

"Wish everything worked that way," Caleb said.

"Here's to that," Quinn said and raised his glass.

"How are the horses going?" Jake asked Caleb.

"I've got another one to train for Virginia," he replied. "One of the dude ranch horses started acting up. They think one of the guests may have treated it badly."

"What did they do to the guest?" Quinn asked. He hated anyone who mistreated animals.

"Barred him from riding and asked him not to come back," Caleb said.

"How's the training going?"

"Slow," Caleb said. "Like it was with the abused mare you bought."

"How's she doing?" Quinn had sold her to Caleb after his friend had trained her, but he'd always have a soft spot for that horse.

"Really well. She likes being a trail horse. We finally bought Elsa from Bridget, so now Destiny has her own horse. For two kids who spent all our lives in Detroit, we sure enjoy spending time riding."

"You haven't convinced her to try fly fishing yet?" Jake asked.

"Haven't asked. She's busy with her consulting business as she's getting a really good reputation for being able to dig in and solve housing problems for small to medium communities. She's been doing a lot of work for Livingston lately. And when she's not busy, she often goes up to Missoula to see her son at the university."

"Better be careful, or she'll turn into a Griz fan," Quinn said. Grizzlies were the mascot of the University of Montana which had its biggest rivalry with Montana State University, home of the Cats.

His parents had always been Cats fans, so everyone in his family became loyal to that team.

"Whatever works for her," Caleb said. "I'll join her, and we can start yelling at each other while we watch the Brawl of the Wild in November."

"Sounds like a good time," Jake said.

"You and Laura will have to pick a team," Caleb said.

"Can't we be neutral?"

"No!" Caleb and Quinn shouted at the same time.

Plates clanked on the table as Kiara delivered their meals with

Olivia's assist.

"Anyone need anything?" she asked.

"We're good," Jake said.

"I'll be back to check on you in a bit."

Quinn dug into his meal of steak and a potato slathered with butter, sour cream, and chives. He wasn't going to be able to eat like this forever, but it sure tasted good right now. He'd eat a bit of the salad that came with the meal to make himself feel more virtuous.

Once the three of them stopped chowing down, the conversation turned to community affairs. Quinn half paid attention, but he was aware of Anna every time she came into his view. What was he doing with her? He'd had his shot at love and blew it. Some people may find companionship later in life, but that wasn't him. He was fine the way he was. The loneliness he'd felt was an illusion. He simply needed to find something besides the ranch to sink his teeth into.

~ ~ ~

An hour later, Caleb looked at his phone and said, "It's time I headed home. I've got to take care of the horses before I settle in for the night."

Jake checked the time as well and nodded. "I've got an early shift tomorrow." He looked at Quinn. "You coming?"

"No, I think I'm going to get a cup of coffee before I head out."

"Right," Jake said. "And maybe do more chatting with the owner?"

"I'm sure she's too busy to talk to me. No, I just want a cup of coffee. That's all."

"Fine," Jake said, pulling some bills from his wallet. "Here's my share."

Caleb did the same.

Quinn knew there would be more than enough to cover two-thirds of the bill and leave a generous tip. "Have a good night," he told his friends.

Once they left, he added his own bills to the tray, then walked over to the bar and took a stool.

"Another beer?" Anna asked.

"Cup of coffee," he said.

"Sure." She disappeared into the kitchen and came back a few minutes later with a steaming mug of coffee. "I figured you'd prefer the mug."

"Thanks." He looked around. "Good night?"

"Yes. I keep thinking the tourist trade is going to drop off, but people are still coming down because the weather is holding. Not good for the snowpack melt next spring, but good for my business."

"I'm glad for you," he said.

She nodded and began to work the bar, starting from the far end to work back to where he was sitting.

He couldn't take his eyes off her. There was a still a resemblance to the girl he'd known as a teen, but there was sadness in her eyes and weariness in her shoulders. Life hadn't been kind to her. He wished he could wrap his arms around her and take the pain away. She didn't deserve it, whatever it was that had caused it.

By the time she got back to him, he'd finished his coffee.

"How's next Tuesday morning do for fly fishing?" he asked.

"How early?" she asked with a frown.

"The earlier we go, the better the chances of catching something," he said.

"I'm not sure I really need to catch anything."

"How about eight? Later than dawn, but early enough we may still get lucky."

"I'm not sure how you got me to agree to this, but fine. I'll be there at eight."

"Good," he said. "I'll bring some extra waders for you."

"How wet am I going to get?"

"Not too much. Unless you fall in, that is."

"I'm not planning on it," she said. "So make sure you don't do anything to make that happen."

"Would I do that?" he said with a grin.

She grinned back.

It was like they were teens again, teasing each other in his mother's kitchen.

"I'll be as good as I can," he said, standing and leaving a five on the bar. "See you Tuesday at the place I told you about on Willow Creek."

"I'll be there."

He nodded and walked out the door, badly whistling a happy tune.

Chapter Fifteen

Anna lugged the box of chardonnay and merlot to the table Destiny had set up for her at the new housing development.

"Let me take that for you," a polished-looking man said, practically wrestling the box from her before she could tell him she was fine.

"Where does it go?" he asked. He was the take-charge type, but she didn't recognize him as a local. His clothes suggested the type of Montanan who had money and was born out of state: blue jeans that hadn't seen any real dirt, a button-down shirt that still had faint creases where it had come out of its wrapper, and overly polished cowboy boots.

At least he'd left the hat at home.

"Over there." She pointed to the table.

"Got it." He easily carried the box to the table. "Any more?" he asked her.

As tempted as she was to tell him to find someone else to bug, having help would be nice.

"I've got a couple of coolers of beer," she said.

"Point the way." His smile was easy.

He wasn't bad looking, either, although probably a bunch of years younger than she was.

She led him to the truck.

He easily hefted one cooler.

She grabbed the other.

"I can come back for that," he said.

"I've got it," she replied, her voice firm. Time to establish that she could handle things on her own, thank you very much.

After they deposited the coolers behind the table, he held out his hand. "Len Drake," he said.

"Anna Wells."

"You run the Buckhorn."

"Yep."

"My firm built that building over there." He pointed to the two-story building at the far end of the lot. From that anchor, tiny homes fanned out on either side, leading to the multi-purpose building next to the playground where her table was set.

"You're a developer."

"Yes, ma'am." He chuckled. "At least you didn't say it like it left a bad taste in your mouth."

"Are you the one who was thinking about building on a floodplain?"

"A slight lapse in judgment."

"Hmm." She opened the carton with the wine bottles and pulled out a couple of the chardonnays. After uncorking one of them, she snuggled the two in the place she'd left for them in the ice chest.

"Don't hold it against me," he said.

"It was a dumb idea," she said. "Glad someone talked you out of it."

"Destiny can be very persuasive."

"Yes, she can" Anna put her hands on her hips. "The celebration doesn't start for a half hour, but if you'd like a beer or something?"

"Not yet," he said. "I've got to make some remarks. Better to do that sober, don't you think?"

It was better to do *everything* sober as far as she was concerned.

"Good luck," she said, putting the box of wine under the table. When people started arriving, she'd put out the two choices of wine and the same number of beer. Now he needed to leave so she could retrieve the rest of her supplies from the truck.

"There you are," Destiny said as she came up to them. Her cream blouse made her dark skin gleam, and her jeans hugged her figure until they disappeared into her signature blue boots. "I want to go over the opening one more time."

"It's not that hard," Len protested.

"Nonetheless, it will make me happy," she said.

"Anything to keep the lady happy," he said. "See you later."
Anna nodded

As soon as he was far enough away, she went back to her

truck to get the boxes of supplies and the cash box. While she could handle things herself, it had been nice to have a hand.

She could probably let people help her more. It never occurred to her to ask. Even when she was married, Brandon couldn't be counted on to help out, at least not without eye rolling that would rival a teenage girl's attempts. Or a loud slam of a door.

Even clicking the remote to turn off the television had an angry sound.

So she'd stopped asking.

Not all men were like that. She'd just been unlucky enough for her father and husband to share the same traits. It was probably why she'd chosen Brandon.

Well, she wasn't going to make the same mistake twice because she was never having another relationship.

Then what was she doing with Quinn?

He was like an older brother, she told herself as she set up plastic glasses and a few fall decorations on the table. Destiny had insisted on making up a sign for the table, so she attached it to the front. The sign looked a lot fancier than the Buckhorn would ever be.

Kind of like Len Drake. He was a fancy guy, nothing like her, or even Quinn.

Quinn was a real person. In spite of having a good rank in the police force and living in a city for most of his life, he'd settled back into his natural self as soon as he'd returned to Montana. Even if she hadn't known him since they were kids, she'd have known he was to be trusted, as much as she was willing to trust any man.

Their rides hadn't been as stressful as she thought they might be. He didn't press her to talk when she didn't want to. She liked to listen to him work out what was going on in his head. Sitting on a blanket looking over their valley had seemed like the most natural thing in the world.

Until that moment. The second when she looked into his eyes and felt the pull of attraction to him, the same desire she'd felt as a teen. He'd looked ready to kiss her.

She'd wanted him to kiss her.

Bad idea.

And now she was going fly-fishing with him. What would happen there?

Nothing. He'd offered her friendship. For all the people she knew in Willow Creek, she didn't have many friends. It would be nice to have one.

"May I have your attention please?" Destiny stood by the microphone in front of the multi-purpose center. "Thank you all for coming to celebrate the opening of this special housing area. We are proud that Willow Creek has been able to create this unique combination of tiny homes and a multi-family unit in such a short time. I'd like to introduce you to the two men who made it possible: Len Drake and Jose Diaz. Len would like to say a few words first."

With a gleaming smile, Len took his place at the microphone.

She wasn't really listening to what he said, but observing his composure speaking in front of the crowd. He wasn't a bad-looking man, if she was in the market for that kind of thing. He had the smoothness that reminded her why she'd been attracted to Brandon all those years ago. There was something very attractive about men who were sure of themselves. But Len had been considerate and helpful, something rare for her ex.

Len's remarks ended, and Jose took the microphone. He, too, thanked everyone and talked about the dream he'd had for the land since he'd bought it.

"Here," he said, "we have the beginnings of a small community within our town. Not only are these places people can afford, but they have some space around them. I'm looking forward to a time when each home will be a unique expression of its owner. The building behind me will offer classes, a place for community meetings, and offices for individual counseling or other kinds of support. There's even a kitchen so the community can cook meals together if they wish."

Anna could see the joy he had in the small village he'd built. He was a good man, always giving back to the town. In the crowd she could see his wife staring at him with love and pride.

What would it be like to experience that kind of love, the kind that lasted a lifetime?

Chloe came up to where she was standing as Jose was

wrapping up his speech.

"Pretty impressive, isn't it?" she said.

"Yes," Anna replied. "I'm glad to have this in our town. So many hard-working people can't afford a place to live."

Chloe nodded. "Traffic has increased in my thrift store as well," she said. "Lots of people are feeling a pinch."

"You have some nice stuff in your store."

"I have some good sources in Bozeman and Livingston, especially for kids' clothes."

"Can I get you anything?"

"Chardonnay would be nice."

Anna poured the glass. "That will be one dollar," she said. "All proceeds go to supporting the community center."

Chloe handed her a dollar. "Thanks."

Daniella Diaz rolled up in her wheelchair. "Hi, Anna! Hi, Chloe!" she said in a voice that didn't match her size. The girl often declared she was going to be an actress when she grew up. With her friendly manner and ability to have a conversation with just about anyone, she could also be a power in politics.

Jose and his wife, Elana, came to join their daughter, one of their four children.

"Great job," Anna told him. "It turned out beautifully."

"Thank you," he said. "It's nice to see a dream come into reality. And, much as I wasn't a fan in the beginning, the multi-unit building is a good addition. Len agreed to modify the outside so it fit more with the architecture of the tiny homes. And he's done a great job landscaping around the building. I'm sure there'll be some happy families there."

"Sure will. What can I get the two of you?"

"Two beers, thank you," Jose said, holding out a ten.

"I don't have change yet," Anna said.

"Keep it for the donations."

"Thank you."

Jose had contributed a lot to see his passion project get off the ground.

"So now that you are done with this, will you be home to take care of some of the things *I* need you to do?" Elana asked Jose.

"Yes, dear," he said with a smile full of affection. "My work is never done," he added as he took the two cans from Anna and handed one to his wife. "How about you? Are you getting time away from the bar? I hear you've been riding with Quinn."

Darn small towns.

"A couple of times. But you know what it's like to own your own business."

"You work too hard," Chloe said. "You need to learn to let go a little. Who's watching the Buckhorn now?"

"Olivia and Paul. But I'm still working." Anna gestured to the table in front of her.

Jose shook his head.

"You need to make time for yourself, for your friends and family. Otherwise you get to a point and can't remember what life is all about." He put an arm around Elana and a hand on Daniela's shoulder. "These two keep me grounded. If I start working too hard and not paying attention, they let me know about it."

"I like to play checkers with you, Papá," Daniela said. "Especially since I beat you all the time."

"She's vicious," Jose said with a laugh.

"There you are," Mayor Gloria Scott said as she came up to the small group. "There's a reporter from Livingston who wants to talk with you, me, and Len."

"Duty calls," Jose said, lifting his beer.

"I better find out what my other three kids are up to," Elana said.

"I'm coming, too," Daniella said. "I need a soda."

"You don't *need* a soda," her mother told her as they left. "You *want* a soda."

Anna chuckled. So like the conversations she used to have with Madison.

Pain pierced her heart.

She shoved all thoughts of her daughter aside and poured wine for the couple who came up to the table.

~ ~ ~

An hour later the festival started to wind down. She closed up and started bringing things back to the truck. When she returned to her table to get the box of wine bottles, she found Len standing there.

"I figured I'd help you out at this end," he said. "Did you have a good time?"

"Yes," she said. "Most of my supplies are gone. You'll find that a lot lighter." She shouldn't feel so grateful for his help, but she was tired and still had a night to go at the Buckhorn.

Poor planning.

He hefted the ice chest up and followed her to the truck.

They loaded the box and chest into the truck bed.

"I hear you provide a good steak dinner at the Buckhorn," he said.

"That's what people say."

"Good. As soon as I wrap up here, I'll stop by to see if the rumors are true."

"That would be nice," she said. "I'll make sure you get a good meal." Then she remembered. "We've got a band coming in tonight. It might be a bit crowded."

"Not a problem. Besides a band means music and dancing. Maybe I can persuade you to take a turn on the floor with me."

"I don't dance."

"I can be very persuasive."

She wanted to tell him to save it, but simply smiled.

The customer was always right.

"I'll go get the other ice chest," he said.

"No need," Quinn said as he thudded the second chest onto the truck bed. "I thought you might need some help," he said to Anna. His expression wasn't friendly, but she'd be hard-pressed to say exactly what it was.

"Thanks." She made the introductions and started moving toward the driver's side door. There was tension between the two men she didn't want to think about. "I've got to get going."

"See you later," Len said with a wave.

"Me too." Quinn didn't wave.

She hopped into her truck and backed it out of the parking space.

Men.

Chapter Sixteen

Who did this dude think he was?

Quinn fumed as he listened to Destiny chatter on about how successful the celebration had been. A lot of people had offered to lead classes at the community center, including cooking, painting, knitting, and gardening. Robert, the manager of the local hardware store, had offered to donate seeds and a few gardening tools. There was talk of helping residents set up some kind of child care arrangement so people could work or run errands.

It was a good town with a lot of good people.

Len Drake wasn't one of them. He was an outsider, probably lived in a pseudo-ranch house along one of the many rivers in the area, using horses as lawn ornaments.

Worst of all, he was encroaching on Quinn's territory.

Anna was skittish enough without having some high roller try to make nice with her.

Surely, she'd see right through him.

"Quinn, you paying attention?" Jake asked him. "We're helping Destiny clean up and then heading to the Buckhorn for dinner."

"And maybe do some dancing," Laura said with a smile. "Jake's been teaching me the two-step, and I'm eager to try it out."

"Since when do you know how to dance?" Quinn asked.

"Since I watched some videos. I was tired of being shown up by everyone else whenever there was a dance. You should try it."

"I don't need to impress anyone," Quinn said.

"Someone's a grump," Caleb observed. "Must have something to do with our new developer helping Anna with her stuff."

"Not at all. I'm tired of standing around listening to you guys talk. Let's get to work. Destiny, what do you need me to do?"

She pointed to the playground. "Can you and Caleb break down the tables and bring them into the community center? Laura,

Jake, and I will go in there and get it organized."

"Got it," Quinn said, relieved to have something constructive to do.

It took about an hour for them to get everything tidied up. Quinn climbed into his pickup with a sense of relief. He was probably over-reacting. Anna didn't want to date anyone. It had been hard enough to get her out to ride. She wasn't going to go out with Len.

At least he hoped she wouldn't.

When he got to the Buckhorn, it was difficult to find a place to park. Caleb pulled in next to him, and Jake a few minutes later.

"Place is packed," Jake observed.

"Sure is. I hope Anna has enough help," he said.

"Me too. I'm sure hungry enough tonight to eat one of those big steaks Paul cooks up."

They climbed the steps and went in. For a few moments they stood by the door trying to find a place that would fit all five of them. Quinn also took the opportunity to scan the room for Len Drake.

He didn't see him.

"Just sit anywhere," Olivia said as she rushed by with a trayful of food.

Caleb spotted a table and gestured toward it.

They sat down.

"Be with you shortly," Kiara said as she dashed to a table where a man had raised his hand to beckon her over.

"I'll go up to the bar and get the beer," Quinn said.

"Sounds good," Jake said.

Quinn positioned himself at an open spot at the bar and waited. Anna was steadily working her way to him, and he took a few moments to simply enjoy looking at her. She was an attractive woman with a few miles on her. Heck, they all had some baggage they were toting around.

More than anything else, he'd like to ease her burden, get her away from this business once in a while. Maybe while they were fly fishing, he'd see if he could convince her to come out to dinner with him. There were some nice places in Livingston.

Or would that be moving too fast?

The door opened and Len came in, making his way to one of the few open seats at the bar.

Quinn kept himself from muttering a curse.

"What can I get you?" Anna asked him.

"A pitcher of our regular beer," he said.

She looked down the bar where a man had shoved his glass forward for a refill. She raised a finger to indicate she'd be with him soon and grabbed a pitcher.

"You got enough help?" Quinn asked.

"I thought I did, but I had to press the new waitress, Sue, into helping Paul in the back. She's making salads and potatoes. I keep feeling like I'm getting farther and farther behind. Last thing I want is disappointed customers."

"I could help," Quinn said.

"How?"

"I tended bar for a while after I got divorced. It gave me something to do in the evening and come up with some extra cash to cover expenses."

"Well …" She placed the full pitcher on the table.

"Please. Let me help you." He leaned forward and looked into her eyes. "I want to. It would be fun."

Olivia came up and gave Anna a drink order.

Another glass was pushed forward on the bar.

"Okay fine. Go deliver your beer and get back here."

He grinned and did as he was told.

When he returned and slipped behind the bar, she said, "Keep them fed and watered. I'll run cards and cash every so often."

"Got it," he said.

She went out to work the floor, and he started checking on drink and food orders. When he refilled Len's glass, the man was watching Anna as she worked.

It took everything Quinn had not to drop the beer in Len's lap.

But he was here to help Anna, not make her life worse.

~ ~ ~

Around seven-thirty the band arrived and set up. The crowd had started to change from families having dinner to couples out for the evening. His friends were enjoying their meal. At some point Anna came back to the bar and told him to grab something to eat.

With less pressure on the kitchen, Sue was able to go back to waitressing. Soon everything was running more smoothly, so Quinn took a seat at the bar and ate his steak. He watched Anna's steady movements. She was so practiced and smart. She'd been sweet and vulnerable once, and probably still was. All he had to do was gently lift the hard shell she'd built around her.

He was protective. She was family of a sort. That's why it was his duty to keep guys like Len away from her. A sharp developer wouldn't understand the need to make sure Anna's needs were met before his own.

She gave Len a friendly smile. Was she flirting with him? Or being the friendly bartender she'd always been? Maybe Quinn was reading more into the situation than he should.

Except that Len was definitely interested. Quinn had spent too many years reading people to be unaware of what Len was after.

He finished his meal and bussed the plates himself, keeping an eye on Len the whole time.

The band had been going for a while, playing a number of tunes that had couples on the floor dancing a rhythmic two-step or some variation. Every once in a while they'd throw in a slow song. Destiny and Caleb were dancing with no air space between them during those songs.

After depositing his plates and cutlery into the bin, he turned around and saw Anna and Len in discussion at the end of the bar. The guy moved fast. Anna was shaking her head emphatically, and he was talking, his expression as eager as a boy asking a girl to prom.

Finally, he must have said the right thing because Anna followed him to the dance floor. Len was a polished dancer and glided Anna around with a practiced step.

Quinn felt a surge of anger

Down, boy.

It was only *one* dance.

But it was so out of character for Anna to do something like that with someone she hardly knew.

Slipping behind the bar again, he took care of the orders that a few of the people had, watching over Len and Anna the whole time.

Once the number was over, he expected Anna to return to the bar.

Instead, the band slid into a slow number, and the couple continued dancing.

Quinn wiped his hands on a towel and strode to the dance floor.

"Can I cut in?" he said to Len. Without waiting for an answer, he took Anna in his arms and guided her away from Len.

"What do you think you're doing?" she asked him.

"Dancing with you," he replied.

"I need to get back to the bar."

"Everyone's taken care of. Finish the dance with me. You were going to dance with Len, weren't you?"

She looked up at him. "You're jealous," she said with a trace of astonishment.

He shrugged his shoulders. No matter what he answered, it was going to get him in trouble.

"I told you I don't want a relationship."

"It's a dance, not a relationship," she said.

"It is on your side if you're jealous," she said.

"I'm fine," he said. "I just wanted to dance with you. Nothing wrong with that. Now, relax and enjoy it."

She narrowed her eyes and gave him one more inspection before allowing herself to relax into the motions as they moved slowly around the floor.

He could feel the heat of her body. It felt so good, so right, to hold her this close, like a puzzle piece that had been missing all his life.

Pushing aside his thoughts, he forced himself to be present and enjoy the dance.

This might be the last time she let him get this close.

Chapter Seventeen

Becky Orkland trudged up the steps of the Buckhorn Bar and Grill. It had been a tough week. She'd hoped Brad would back off from his demand for a child, but he'd only dug his heels in. Then she'd spent a week in Mississippi trying to figure out how to make unpermitted wastewater discharges more painful for the ag companies that were doing them. Up to this point, they'd considered the fines the state imposed as the cost of doing business.

She was going to need to go after the company citing federal law which would take some time to get through the state courts as Mississippi regarded anything the feds did as an encroachment on their state's rights.

Becky was an attorney for Climate Action, a group that sued corporations, states, or anyone else at all who was threatening the environment. The Mississippi case was her latest. She was just wrapping up the one she'd been working on for years in Montana.

The case had become her passion project. The young people of the state had joined with some of the people of the Willow Creek Valley to sue a gold mining company. The company had done exploration and obtained the rights to drill for gold in an environmentally sensitive area. The dirty results of gold mining threatened to foul the water in the valley. The plaintiffs were suing on the basis of the state constitution articles that guaranteed a clean environment to future generations.

Oral arguments were next week.

To get to Helena, where the local offices of Climate Action were located, she'd had to change planes three times. One plane was late, leading to a three-hour layover in Des Moines. When she'd finally gotten to Montana late Friday night, it had been to fall into bed at a motel and sleep fitfully on an uncomfortable mattress.

She'd spent the weekend working with her fellow attorneys

to bone up for oral arguments that were happening on Thursday.

But now she needed a break, and she could think of no better place to do it than the small town of Willow Creek.

"Hello," the woman behind the bar greeted her.

At two o'clock in the afternoon, the place was basically empty. The only sound came from a sound system playing background music. She was relieved. The last thing she needed right now was a crowded, noisy gathering of humanity.

"Hi," Becky said, approaching the bar.

"You can sit anywhere you want," the woman said with a smile.

"This will do," Becky said, hauling herself up onto a bar stool.

What was this woman's name? She'd met her a couple of times at Quinn's place, but couldn't recall the name. She must be more tired than she'd thought; she was generally good with names.

"Would it be possible to get a burger?" Becky asked. "And a Coke?"

"I can probably do both of those things," the bartender said. "Our cook's taking a break, but I know my way around a grill. You're the attorney, Becky, aren't you?"

"Yes."

"Thank you for what you're doing for us. We value our clean water around here, for drinking and trout fishing. I'm Anna Wells." Anna held out her hand, and Becky shook it. "Let me get you that soda, and then I'll get your burger started."

"Thanks."

Once she had her soda, Becky took out her phone. Before she could check her messages, "I Want You to Know" came on the sound system.

It had been her wedding song.

She turned away from the mirrored backdrop of the bar so she couldn't see the haunted look in her own eyes. As she listened, she gazed around the space, idly noting old neon beer signs, heads of deer, elk and antelope, and bold artwork that was probably local.

It was a very different place from the middle of Ohio. Radically different.

Yet she felt more at home here than she'd ever felt in the trim house she and Brad had purchased a year after their marriage.

People in the Midwestern town were cordial, but most had lived there all their lives, their friendships firmly cemented, their relatives nearby.

She and Brad were rarely home, weren't churchgoers, and didn't have children. All the paths to finding new friendships were closed to them.

Why did he think that bringing a child into such a fractured environment was a good idea?

The song ended, and memories released their grip on her.

Relieved, she turned her attention to her messages. The majority had to do with the case in the South. Everything that could be said about the Montana case had already been discussed over the weekend. Now her job was to conserve her energy and make sure she had her arguments ready for her court appearance on Thursday.

That's why she'd come to Willow Creek. There was no better place to find the peace she needed.

Anna emerged from the kitchen with a plate in her hand. The burger was substantial, a garnish of lettuce, tomato, and pickle on the side.

"The fryer isn't hot," she said, sliding the plate onto the bar. "Potato chips okay?" She put a container of ketchup, mustard, barbeque sauce, and napkins next to the plate, then added a bundle of cutlery wrapped in its own napkin.

"This will be fine," Becky said.

"Okay. Holler if you need anything else."

"Will do." Becky unwrapped the cutlery, then picked up the burger and took a bite. It was cooked to perfection, and she took her time savoring the taste.

She was used to eating alone, but for the first time in a long while, she felt the loneliness of it. Would she ever share a meal with her husband again? Their schedules would keep them apart for the next three weeks, and she'd promised him a final answer at that time.

How was she going to give him what he wanted when every fiber of her being said it was a bad idea?

Most likely the dinner in three weeks would be their last together. All the hopes she'd had for a long-term relationship based on shared values, friendship, and, yes, love, were seeping away a little more each day.

She took another bite of burger, but the taste was no longer savory. In fact, it tasted a bit like sawdust. Putting it down, she sipped her soda.

"Everything okay?" Anna asked. "The burger cooked right?"

"The burger is fine," Becky said. "I'm afraid it's me."

"I'm sorry to hear that," Anna said, picking up a glass and polishing it with a towel. "Personal or professional?"

"Personal." Becky was torn between wanting to keep everything to herself and wanting to spill out everything to the woman in front of her.

"Personal problems are the worst," Anna said. "Professional things can usually be worked out -- someone somewhere has had a similar problem. But no one can tell you anything about your own life because they haven't lived it."

"Exactly."

Anna put the polished glass on a shelf and picked up another.

"My life has had its challenges. While my ex wasn't physically abusive, he did a lot of things that damaged me … us … emotionally. If he'd ever hit me, it would have been clear I had to leave. But it was all words, and half the time I believed I was the one causing my own problems."

"Gaslighting," Becky said.

"I guess that's what you'd call it." Another glass went on the shelf, then Anna refilled Becky's soda glass without saying anything else.

It was her turn to speak.

"My husband wants a baby," she said. She picked up the burger, then put it back down.

"Do you?"

"Not really. No."

"That's a problem."

"Yeah. The thing is, we had an agreement. He's an environmental lawyer, like me. Our jobs require a lot of travel. It wasn't the right situation for children. He agreed with me before we married," Becky said, hearing the bitterness in her own voice.

"What's changed his mind?"

"Getting older. Realizing that he wouldn't have a chance to experience what being a father was like."

"But how would that work if you're both on the road?"

The woman should have been a therapist. But wasn't that what they said? Hairdressers and bartenders were the oldest therapists of all.

"He thinks I should take a more research-focused job so I could stay home more."

"Oh," Anna said.

"The thing is, I'm a good trial attorney. I enjoy the back and forth. Heck, I even like oral arguments, and they can be nerve-wracking." As she spoke, Becky realized why she'd been tormented by the suggestion that she give up trial work, work she loved.

Brad wanted the child, but he didn't suggest he be the one to give up trial work. She hadn't realized how old-fashioned he was, but she should have. His mother had been a stay-at-home mom for most of his life, only going back to work when the youngest of his siblings—five in all—entered high school.

No, she couldn't give up her passion to bring a child into this world, a child she didn't even want.

She picked up the burger and took a savage bite.

"I had a child once," Anna said softly. "They can be a lot of work and joy when they're little."

"But?"

"They get to a point when they develop their own opinions and lives. That's when you realize you have no control."

Becky wanted to ask more questions, but from the expression on Anna's face, she knew she'd be treading into a very painful place. Instead, she chewed her burger, then washed it down with another drink from her soda glass.

Anna was quiet, too.

The door opened and two young women walked into the bar and grill.

"Sit anywhere you like," Anna called out. "I'll be right with you." She looked over at Becky. "You need anything?"

"No, thanks. And thank you … for, you know … talking to me."

"No problem." Anna smiled. "You'll figure it out. You're one smart woman." She picked up a couple of menus and went to wait on the young women.

Becky ran the problem through her mind while she finished her burger. A child was a lot of work. Not only that, but there were many reasons not to bring a child into a world that was rapidly heating both in temperature and conflict.

But the biggest reason of all was the one the conversation with Anna had teased from her subconscious: she didn't want to give up her work.

~ ~ ~

Once Becky finished her meal and paid her check, she drove through town on a whim. It was a pleasant small town. Most of the people she'd met had been friendly. They hadn't offered to become best friends, but that was because she wasn't here that much. Still, she had more of a relationship with Quinn, Heather, Bridget, and their spouses than she had with anyone in Ohio.

After traveling through town, she took the road up to the Rocking Q Ranch.

It was good to be back. She'd get some rest, go over her arguments, then go to court and win clean water for the people of this valley.

Chapter Eighteen

Quinn waited under a gray sky at the fishing access point. The lack of sun didn't disappoint him. The fish bit more often under those conditions, where the dim light hid what was really happening. It would be nice to catch a big, fat trout for dinner and the freezer.

Would she show?

She'd barely talked to him after he'd cut in and danced with her on Saturday. He'd stuck around to make sure she didn't spend too much time with Len.

Even Quinn knew he'd been acting like a jealous lover, but he hadn't been able to stop himself. Len was all wrong for Anna.

The crunch of tires on the gravel road made his heart beat more quickly. Instead of Anna's aging RAM pickup though, a highly polished green Jeep Wrangler pulled into the lot. A man, dressed in gear he must have recently gotten at Yellow Dog Flyfishing in Bozeman, stepped out.

"How's the fishing?" the guy asked.

"Don't know. Waiting on someone."

"Guess I'll have to go find out myself."

"You going upstream or down?" Quinn asked.

"I haven't decided. This is the first time I've been to this access point."

Probably the first time he'd been to any access point.

"Okay. We'll be sure to stay away from you."

"I appreciate that. Have you been here before?"

"Yep," Quinn said.

"Any pointers?"

Quinn debated for a moment, then suggested the man go upstream. That would leave the shallower pools of the downstream for him to teach Anna. In truth, the fishing was good all along this spot.

The man nodded and left, unaware of the tag still dangling

from the back of his fishing vest.

Quinn chuckled.

Ten minutes later, Anna pulled into the parking lot.

"You're late," he said, taking in her freshly washed hair, long-sleeved shirt, and tight jeans.

"It's too early," she grumbled.

"Not for fish," he said.

"How can anyone enjoy anything that requires getting up at the crack of dawn?"

"It's not the crack of dawn," he said with a grin. "Although that's when the fishing is best. Watching the sun rise over the river and the meadow makes me feel part of something grand. It's awe-inspiring."

"I'll take your word for it. Now tell me what I need to do so we can get this over with."

"Not a morning person," he said as he walked to the pickup for the waders and fishing gear he'd brought with him for her use.

"Ya think?" she said, attempting a smile.

"Try these on," he said, handing the waders to her. "I think they'll fit."

"Can't I just stand on the bank?"

"You could, but it's easier if you get out where the line isn't going to get tangled in the trees."

With a sigh, she struggled into the waders and snapped the straps over her shoulders.

"Where'd you get these?" she asked. "I don't recall you had any women at the ranch."

"Uncle Jed kept them for his friends of the female persuasion," Quinn said.

"I seem to remember there was always some woman hanging around."

"The love of his life was Maribel, but they were too much alike. She bailed about a year before he died."

"The owner of Silver Clips?" Anna scrunched her face. "That seems like an odd combination. She's so flashy." She shrugged. "But now she's dating Robert, who's always struck me as a traditional, conservative guy."

"They broke up," Quinn said.

"Really? When?"

"About a week ago. I picked up some supplies at the hardware store last week, and Mary Clark was asking about it."

"Scooping up gossip for the newspaper?" Anna asked.

"Everyone reads her 'News and Notes' first. You know that."

"I do. Now where are these fish?"

"This way," he said. He led her down the path to the bank of the Yellowstone. Here the river was fairly shallow, especially this time of year. Rocks strewn in the riverbed—probably tossed there the last time the Yellowstone volcano exploded—created little waterfalls that produced quiet pools where the trout liked to hang out, particularly under the shadow of a tree.

As he'd hoped, the decked out fisherman had gone upstream, leaving some of his favorite spots to them.

Leaving his rod on the bank, he showed Anna how to pull the line, flip it backward, then settle it gently into the water.

"You want it to look like a fly landed on the water, and they don't make a big splash," he told her.

The first time she tried, the line flew back and landed in the water behind her. He patiently had her reel it back in and try again. The fourth time she managed to get the artificial fly to land in front of her.

"Now what?"

"Now we wait," he said.

"We just stand here?"

"Pretty much. You can play with the line a little, so the fish thinks the fly is moving, but don't overdo it. We want the fish to think he can catch it. After a while, pull the line back in and do it again."

She frowned. "That's it?"

"Pretty much."

"Sounds boring."

"Give it a chance," he said. "Think of it as meditation: you, the fly, and the fish. Feel the ripple of the water as it flows past. Concentrate on light and shadow. You don't have to do anything but be right here."

"I was never good at meditation," she said.

He laughed. "Somehow I can see that." He started to walk

toward the bank.

"Wait! Where are you going? You can't leave me here by myself."

"Calm down. I'm just getting my rod. You'll be fine. Just keep fishing."

He couldn't quite hear what she grumbled.

Once he retrieved his rod and hooked the net on his waders, he went to a spot that was far enough away from her that their lines didn't get tangled. He looked at the water for a bit, trying to figure where the fish might be hiding.

Trout for dinner would be really good. Maybe he could get Anna to come by and share, except that she never took a night off from that darn restaurant.

Somehow he had to persuade her that she deserved a life.

Which begged the question. Why did she drive herself so hard? What was she punishing herself for?

He cast his line and watched it play out before drifting through the air to land on the surface of the water. A gentle breeze ruffled his hair, and the river exerted a pressure against his legs as it flowed on its way to the mighty Mississippi. Birds fluttered in the trees, discussing important matters of the day.

Glancing to the right, he watched Anna as she prepared another cast. She had a look of determination on her face. Like the rest of life, she wasn't going to let fly fishing defeat her.

She looked cute in the waders, her wavy hair floating around her face like a halo. There were gray streaks in the auburn hair, and lines etched in her face, but to him she'd grown into the beauty that had been a strong suggestion when they were younger.

He'd been attracted to her even back then, even though he'd tried to deny it.

Now, though? There was no denying the longing he had to take her into his arms and find out how she felt there.

If she had been a little older …

What was that old saying? "If wishes were horses, then beggars might ride …"

No sense in going over what might have been. It was today. Anything they could possibly have between them would have to start now, if she would let him.

Maybe it was time to move on from the pretense of friendship. He'd thought he could contain himself to that, but even in the few times they'd ridden, he'd been hungry for more. His behavior on the dance floor made him aware of how much he wanted a chance with this woman.

"I got one!" Anna screamed. "I got one!" She was so excited she almost lost her footing, but managed to steady herself without falling into the river. "What do I do now?"

"Reel him in," Quinn said as he pulled his line back so he could come to her aid. "Not too fast. You don't want to lose him. Pull him in, let him go a little, then pull him in."

She did as he instructed.

"That's it," he said as he made his way over to her.

She was almost instinctive in handling the fish. When it got close enough, Quinn slipped the net under it and pulled it from the water. It was a decent-sized fish.

"Now what?" she asked.

"Do you want to let it go or have it for supper?" he asked.

"Oh, let it go. He'll get bigger, and *then* we can have him for supper," she said, sounding almost like the teen he'd once known.

Happiness filled him.

"You got it." He handed her his rod, then went to work to get the hook out of the fish's mouth and sent him on his way.

"That was exciting," she said with a grin. "I can see why you like this fly fishing thing."

"Let's see if you can catch another one." He took his rod back and walked back to his spot.

They spent the next half hour casting their lines. Occasionally, he spent a few minutes looking at her as she concentrated on the task at hand. He never caught her looking back.

Eventually, the position of the sun prompted him to walk back over to her.

"I'm glad you got your first fish." He pulled his baggy-enclosed phone from his pocket. "You said you wanted to get back to the bar by noon. I brought some coffee and muffins. Care to join me before you take off?"

"Okay," she said. "This fishing can be exhausting. All that

standing around and waiting followed by crazy adrenaline. Kind of like running a restaurant and bar."

He nodded, glad she'd agreed. Maybe during their conversation he could convince her to take a night off and go to dinner with him in Livingston. At the very least he could get her to go on another ride or come fishing again.

Maybe he'd get a rod just for her.

Probably not. She'd get all prickly about it, saying she could take care of herself.

Getting her to a point where he could do things for her was going to take a little while.

He stowed their rods and peeled off his waders. Once she'd done the same, her pair went into the truck as well.

Grabbing the muffins and coffee he'd brought, he led her to a picnic table on the edge of the parking lot.

Chapter Nineteen

Anna felt lighter than she had in a long time. Who knew that standing in a river in the early—well at least to her—morning hours could prompt such … such what? What was she feeling?

Joy? Happiness?

For once, the heavy weight of her daughter's death didn't weigh on her shoulders.

She glanced at the man across from her, carefully pouring coffee into two tin mugs. Michael Quinn had always been a good man. He said he wanted friendship, but she could tell from her own reaction to being around him that there was something more going on. In the year or so since he'd come back to Willow Creek for good, rumors hadn't indicated he'd been doing any long-term dating.

Yet he was finding ways to be with her. Nothing with too much pressure, but still time spent together. It was easy time, too. He wasn't asking her for anything more than spending some time doing activities he loved.

She liked being on a horse about as much as the next person. When he'd suggested fishing, she figured she'd indulge him once, then that would be that. But some part of the process had hooked her as much as the fish she'd caught. She could see the appeal of doing it alone, with only thoughts and observations to keep one company.

Unless someone had thoughts they didn't want to surface.

But sharing the time with Quinn had allowed her to simply be present, feeling safe with him nearby to help her if anything unexpected happened, like falling into the river and being swept downstream … or a bear appearing on the bank for his mid-morning snack.

Somehow, his presence had also protected her from the darker thoughts of her own mind.

"Riley's muffins?" she asked as he passed her a confection

studded with blueberries.

"Of course," he said.

She peeled off the paper and bit into the muffin. Sweet succulence exploded in her mouth.

"Oh my," she said after she'd swallowed.

"Totally agree," he said. "My ex used to make fantastic muffins, but I think these are even better."

"Was it a bad break-up?"

"Not really. We both knew it was coming, I think. We'd gotten together after I came back from the Middle East. I'd gone to Detroit to offer my condolences to my buddy's widow. Amy was her sister. Emotions were running high, one thing led to another, and we wound up married. It was good for a while, but my being a cop took its toll. I found a place not too far from the family and stayed involved in my kids' lives. They're all grown now with lives of their own."

"Have they come here to visit?"

"Not yet," he said. "I'm working on it, though. My daughter, Kelly, just had her first child. I'm going to pitch the ranch life to my grandkids and get them to help me persuade their parents to make the trek." He grinned at her.

"Underhanded."

"You do what you gotta do." He sipped his coffee. "How about you? You were married, weren't you?"

"Yes. I did food prep at Butte Community College," she said, intent on not answering the question he'd actually asked. "I figured I'd start at the bottom and eventually figure out how to have my own restaurant. I knew I didn't want to work for someone else forever."

"And you achieved your dream. Congratulations."

"The Buckhorn wasn't exactly what I had in mind, but it's mine, and that's what counts."

"Life takes twists and turns," he said. "It's how we adapt to those changes that matters."

She nodded. How much more should she tell him? She normally skimmed over the details, but opening up to Becky yesterday had produced a crack in her resolve. Maybe she didn't need to keep her life clutched to her chest.

"After I graduated, I worked at some restaurants in Butte, but I wanted to get away from everything I'd grown up with, see the world, or at least more of Montana. I made my way to Billings and had a good job there. I was starting to put away real money, and my skills as a chef were improving. The owner was friendly and knew my ultimate goal. We talked about all aspects of the business. She was great."

"Sounds like you had a good mentor," Quinn said.

"I did."

"What happened?"

She took another sip of coffee and ate a piece of muffin, drawing sustenance from the beauty of the river running through the meadow before she answered.

"Brandon happened. He was hired to run the bar." She looked over at Quinn. "Restaurant workers have high rates of addiction and alcoholism. There's a lot of pressure to get meals out on time, head chefs generally have short fuses, and alcohol is way too available from a friendly bartender."

Quinn nodded, but didn't say anything.

"Brandon and I started drinking while he closed up at night. He was charming, swore he was on his way to making it rich. Then he'd get me whatever my heart desired. Too bad I didn't realize his way to making it rich was running drugs."

"He get busted?"

She shook her head. "It would have been better if he had. No, he kept it a secret from me, and he was smart enough to avoid detection. We partied a lot—that's where he made a lot of his contacts. And we started sleeping together." She shifted in her seat. "I ... uh ... sometimes did things that made me uncomfortable just to please him. He'd flirt with other women, and I was desperate to keep him."

"I'm sorry." Quinn moved his hand toward hers, but stopped when she jerked hers away.

This was a story where physical contact wasn't needed.

"I know he slept with other women once or twice ... maybe more ... but I looked the other way. I loved him, I told myself. And love is forgiving. My mother taught me to stay with your man no matter what." Anna hadn't thought she'd absorbed her mother's lessons, but looking back on her time with Brandon, she could see she'd taken them in all too well.

"This went on for a few years," she continued, willing herself to get it all out. Once Quinn realized how compromised she was, he'd back off. "Then I wound up pregnant. We were both happy about it. He proposed, and we got married."

Her parents hadn't made it to the ceremony. Only Sophia and Bethany had managed to make it. Bethany had been sweet, but Anna had always been sure Brandon and Sophia had fooled around behind her back. Pregnancy had been rough, and she hadn't always been the willing partner Brandon demanded.

"I quit drinking when I found out I was pregnant," she said. "It was tough, and that was my first hint I may have had a problem."

She looked over at him.

His face was rapt with attention, and his body was still as he listened.

She couldn't remember the last time someone had listened so closely to her.

"Brandon continued to party while I was pregnant and after Madison was born. I tried going with him sometimes, but it had all become too much. I had a little girl to take care of. I wanted a better life for her than I'd had growing up. Brandon and I began to fight. He had all these passive-aggressive behaviors that let me know when he was annoyed with me. Stupid things like 'forgetting' to take out the garbage or leaving the toilet seat up when I was potty-training Maddie."

It took every fiber of strength in her not to burst into tears as she remembered the sweet little girl Madison had been. She'd had hugs and love for everyone. Anna had loved curling up with her on the couch while watching a favorite movie, even if it was for the fifth time.

Brandon was always absent.

She forced a shrug. "We finally agreed to go our separate ways, and he disappeared from our lives."

"He didn't pay child support? Come visit?"

"Oh, he'd pop in now and again to treat Madison to expensive presents, but even though he looked like he was making money, he never paid anything on a regular basis. On his visits, he'd leave me an envelope with a few hundred dollars, but that was about it."

"I'm sorry," Quinn said. "That must have been tough."

She nodded and picked up her coffee cup. Telling him had worn her out. She'd never told the story to anyone before. If there was going to be any relief from unburdening herself, it was apparently going to come later. Her insides were twisted into knots, and she felt like throwing up.

Quinn opened his mouth to ask a question, and she knew what it would be.

She shook her head. There was no way she was telling anyone what had happened to her daughter.

"Well, as fun as this has been," she said, standing up, "I need to get back to the bar."

"Come with me again sometime?"

"Are you sure you want to do that?" she asked him. She'd been so sure her story would have put him off.

"Absolutely." He cleared his throat. "We do the best we can at the time. I don't know the details, but I know you had a rough time when you were a kid. You weren't prepared for a manipulator like your ex to come along." He stood as well. "In fact, I'd like to take you to dinner sometime—if you'll let me, that is."

"I work every night," she said.

"That needs to change."

"So everyone keeps telling me, but I'm not sure how to do that right now."

"Got it. But if you ever see your way clear, the offer stands. Meanwhile, I'll text you so we can set up a time to go riding or fishing again."

"That would be nice." It would be. She almost gave him a hug, but settled for patting his arm. "Thanks for this. It was fun."

"I'm glad you enjoyed it." He picked up the muffin wrappers and napkins and placed them in the bag they'd come from before tossing the remains of their coffees in the bushes.

Together, they walked back to their vehicles.

As she left the parking lot, she gave him a wave.

It only took her a half hour to get to the Buckhorn and park in her usual place. Someone was sitting on the steps.

It felt like a stone dropped to the pit of her stomach.

When she got close to the step, he stood.

"Hello, Anna," he said.

All of her good feelings fled on the passing breeze.

"Hello, Brandon," she said. "What are you doing here?"

"I've come to make it up to you."

"Water under the bridge," she said, wondering how to get past him to get into the bar.

"There are things to say," he said. "I'm hoping you'll listen."

"I need to get the bar open."

"I'll help," he said.

She took the first few steps, her mind racing as to what to do next.

"I'm sober," he said. "I've been to rehab. I've got amends to make, and I hope you'll let me."

She shrugged. "I've got work to do. If you want to talk while I work, I'll listen."

"Fair enough."

He followed her into the bar.

Chapter Twenty

"Have a seat," Anna said, indicating a bar stool. "I'll be right back." She walked to the small office she kept in back, unlocked it, and dumped her purse. She picked up the banker's bag of cash she kept to open the till, locked the door, and returned to the front.

"What can I get you?" she asked. "Coke, seltzer water?"

"Coke will be great. Thanks."

She poured the soda in a glass and slid it across the bar to him. Then she began to check the liquor bottles for ones that needed backup. The process reminded her that she still hadn't figured out who was pilfering from the storage room. Although she kept it locked, the mechanism was flimsy.

There'd be time to think about that later. Right now, she had to figure out what the man behind her wanted. Sober or not, he probably hadn't changed. Brandon always wanted something.

"I'm sorry I rode you so hard after Madison died," he began. "I said some things I shouldn't have said."

She kept working. He wasn't getting off the hook that easily. After her daughter's death, he'd nearly broken her with his accusations and statements about her lack of competence as a mother and human being.

"I know I can't go back and fix the past," he said. "But I'm really, really sorry and would like a chance to make it up to you."

How could he ever make up for what he'd done? There wasn't a do-over for what had happened. She knew. She'd spent the last bunch of years waking up every morning hoping things could have been different.

But every morning her daughter was still dead.

Every fiber of her being anticipated his sigh before she heard it.

"I can see it's going to take a while for you to believe me," he said. "But I'm willing to work on it. I want to make sure you hear me. I don't need you to forgive me, but it would be nice."

Her grip on the pen in her hand made her knuckles whiten.

"After we split, I was okay for a while, but then I started drinking more. I got myself fired from several jobs for being drunk. No one gave me a second chance. Pretty soon I was working in dives. They were the only ones that would allow me behind a bar. Who cared if there was one more drunk in the place?"

Spare me the self-pity.

"My relationships didn't fare much better. The woman I was with when we broke up dumped me when I lost the second job. That's why I couldn't help you out with child support. I didn't have a steady job."

She finished up the bottle tally, including the wine bottles. "I'll be right back," she said. "You okay?" She pointed to his almost-empty glass.

"I'll get it." He reached across the bar, grabbed the correct nozzle, and refilled his glass.

She went to the supply room to get what she needed. When she returned, she noticed the banker's envelope wasn't where she'd left it on the shelf under the register. It was still on the shelf, but six inches away from where it had been.

When someone lived close to the edge of poverty their whole life, they tended to keep track of money.

She glanced at Brandon.

He gave her his practiced smile. "Anything I can help with?"

"Nope."

After she put the bottles where they belonged, she picked up the envelope and counted the money carefully into the register.

Nothing was missing. He must have decided stealing from her was too obvious.

What did he want from her? Other than to make himself feel better by confessing his sins?

She went to work cutting up lemons and limes.

"When I found myself waking up stinking every morning, often in a stranger's bed, I began to think maybe I had a problem," he said. "Still didn't do anything about it. Then I woke up in an alley with all my money missing. That's when I decided to get help."

"So you started going to meetings," she said.

"I am now, but I started with rehab."

Rehab costs money.

"You still doing your side business?"

"No. I gave that up a long time ago."

His answer was fast and practiced. Was it the truth? She'd never been able to totally read him which is why she'd thought she was head over heels in love with him.

She put the fruit in their containers.

"I did six months," he said. "It was really eye-opening. I saw how my parents' rigid rules made me want to rebel. And I felt I deserved the best of everything, but I didn't really know what that was." His face lost its animated expression. "Like you. I didn't realize how good you were for me, how much I loved you."

She tried to hide her snort.

"I don't expect you to believe me," he said. "But I know it's true. I've changed, Anna. I really have changed."

She stopped what she was doing and studied him. She'd loved him once, believed in him. She'd been as much of the problem in the beginning as he'd been. Most nights, she was partying right next to him. A vestige of the feelings she'd had for him still existed, but it wasn't ever going to be enough to trust him again.

"I'm glad for you," she said. Then she moved around from behind the bar to start putting chairs on the floor. Paul should be arriving soon to get the kitchen going. Olivia would be right behind.

As she began with the first chair, he got off the stool to help.

"I know we can never have what we once did, but I'm hoping we can be friends."

"Are you planning on sticking around Willow Creek?" Not something she wanted.

"I'm thinking about it. Or maybe Livingston. It's a nice area, especially with Yellowstone being so close. It's a lot better than the dusty small town I'm living in now." He was looking at her with that lazy smile she'd always loved. "And it would be good to get to know you again. I'm really impressed with all you've achieved." He gestured to the bar. "How'd you do it?"

"The owners of the Buckhorn hired me as a waitress when

Maddie was about sixteen. The place was rowdy, and they were looking for mature help. They were willing to give me a good base wage and a lead on a cheap place to live. I thought if I could get Maddie out of the old school, I could pull her off the path she was on Nothing he could do about that now before she did something stupid. She was running with the wrong crowd."

Anna picked at a cuticle. Her throat was tight.

"But it was too late," she said. "I was barely here a month when she dropped out of school altogether and ran away. I don't think people in town even noticed her before she was gone."

"Did you hear from her?"

"Every once in a while. She'd tell me she was working to get clean, or that she'd just gotten out of a program, or jail, or something … But she never came home again."

"I'm sorry I wasn't there to help."

"If you were still drinking a lot, I didn't need your help." She placed the chair on the floor with a little more energy than it needed.

"Ouch."

She shrugged.

"So how did you get from waitress to bar owner?" he asked.

"I worked really hard and saved my money. They made me manager, and when they retired they offered me the business. They hold the mortgage and gave me terms I can manage."

"Sweet deal."

"Still hard work."

"Yeah. You ever take any time off?" he asked.

"Nope. It's my business. I need to make it successful."

"You're going to burn out."

"Haven't yet." Another chair thudded to the floor.

The door opened, and Paul walked in.

"You're almost done," he said, then looked at Brandon.

"This is Brandon, an old friend," Anna said. "And this is Paul, our chef."

"Nice to meet you," Brandon said.

Paul looked between the two of them. "I'll get started in the back."

"Okay," she said.

Once Paul was out of earshot, she placed the last chair on the floor.

"Are we done here?" she asked. "I've got a business to run."

"Let me prove to you I've changed." He looked around. "You've built a good business, but you're running yourself into the ground. I know you, Anna. You work harder than anyone I've ever known. Let me help you. Hire me on as a bartender and manager. Then you could take some time off."

"Hire an alcoholic to run a bar?" She barked out a laugh.

"Rumor has it you don't drink, but you own a bar."

"I haven't had a drink since you walked out the door," she said.

"Not even when Maddie died?"

"Not even then." It had almost killed her. After they informed her of Maddie's death, all she'd wanted to do was crawl into a bottle and stay there for the rest of her life.

But that wouldn't have done a thing for Maddie. The only person she would hurt would be herself. So, she'd struggled through the first days, attended a meeting almost daily, and found herself again with the help of a therapist who'd given her a cut rate.

"I have all the help I need," she said.

"Can you at least consider it? You know I'm a good bartender."

"When you're sober."

"I'm sober now and determined to stay that way. I need someone who will give me a chance. This way, you could have some time off, too. You deserve that, Anna. You've worked too hard all your life."

"Like I said, I don't need anyone else."

"At least take my phone number. If you reconsider, you can call me."

If she took his phone number, maybe he'd leave.

"Fine. Tell me," she said.

"I can put it in your phone."

"Just give me the number." She glanced at the clock.

He complied.

"Let me have yours," he asked again. "That way I can check

in with you to see if I can help out."

Maybe he'd go away.

She rattled off the digits.

"We done?" she asked.

"Sure. I'll see you again sometime." The easy grin was back, as if he'd won some kind of victory.

"Have a good one."

Don't let the door hit you in the rear on your way out.

"No problem," he said and left.

Curious, she followed him to the front of the building. She hadn't seen a car when she'd pulled in.

He pulled out from the side of the building in a fairly new Toyota. How could he afford that?

No, he wasn't telling her everything.

There was no way she was hiring him, even if what he'd told her was right. He knew how to manage a bar and was good with people. When they'd first met, the owner of the restaurant where they worked had sung his praises. It was only when his drinking had gotten out of hand that she'd fired him.

It would be nice to have some time off, maybe take Quinn up on his offer to go to dinner.

How could she hire Brandon when her gut didn't trust him?

She pulled up the phone to delete his number. Her finger hovered over the button for a few moments, then she slid the phone in her pocket with his number still stored in her contacts.

Chapter Twenty-One

The sun was barely up when Quinn's crew started up the trail to the summer range. The leather on the saddle and bridle was stiff from the early morning chill, and breath from the horses' nostrils was visible.

Quinn was warm enough in his sheepskin lined coat and leather gloves. Even though his hat was pulled low on his head, his ears were cold, so he'd pulled the scarf he wore higher on his neck. By mid-morning they'd be sweating from the higher sun and work.

His ranch manager, Ted, was with him, as was Destiny's son, Kevin. The young man had volunteered to come back from Missoula where he was studying environmental law to help with the roundup.

Between the three of them and Ralph's crew, they had plenty of people to move the cows down off the mountain. Ralph and Ted had spent the previous week locating the cattle scattered around forest service land and herding them back into the fenced-in pasture on their land. Ralph's suggestion that they tear down the fence between their summer ranges to give their cattle more room to graze as well as the ability to access forest service land had paid off. The cows were able to find food more easily, increasing their weight over the summer months.

Now their job would be to ease the herd off of the mountain without losing too much of that weight.

The only sounds as they rode the trail up the mountain were the thud of the horse's hooves, the rubbing of saddle leather, and the caws of ravens and crows. Overhead, an eagle, identifiable by the sun glinting on its white head and tail feathers, was on a silent hunt.

Quinn took in a deep breath of mountain air. It was good to be alive on a morning like this. For once, his feeling that something was missing in his life was subdued. Right now, everything was as it should be.

It took them about an hour to reach the upper pasture where Ralph, Heather, and two of Ralph's part-time ranch hands were waiting.

"Morning," Ralph said. "Ready to do this?"

"Yep," Quinn replied. Because Ralph had more experience moving cattle, Quinn deferred to him. "Where do you want everybody?"

"Once we get them rounded up, I figured Heather and Ned …" Ralph pointed to one of the ranch hands. "They could ride in front. You and Kevin can ride the flanks. Ted, Maggie, and I will bring up the rear and chase stragglers."

Ned had done some work on Quinn's ranch, so he knew him. Maggie must be the other ranch hand. It was hard to judge her age; Montana sun could add lines around the eyes from squinting. She was wiry and looked capable of handling anything thrown her way.

"Sounds like a plan. Kevin, I'll take the far side. You can stay on this side."

"Okay, then," Ralph said. "Let's get this herd rounded up and on their way."

As they moved to the front to open the down slope gate, Heather and Ned helped bunch the cattle. Quinn went to work on his side, keeping an eye on Kevin as the young man maneuvered his horse to bring the cows on his side into the herd. It wasn't a smooth operation, but the cow horse he rode knew the drill and helped him along.

Soon they had a large group of mooing, disgruntled cattle headed in the right direction. Quinn eased into his saddle and settled into the rhythm of scanning his side of the herd from one end to the other, to make sure none of them decided to break rank.

At first he was simply present, enjoying the warmth as the sun progressed higher in the sky, and the iconic scene of cowhands moving a herd from one place to another. Champion's gait was easy, and the horse was as aware of the movements of the cattle as he was.

Every once in a while, a cow began to drift, and they'd quickly work their way to it and correct its adventurous spirit. On the whole, though, the herd was well-behaved.

As the morning wore on, he began to think about Anna. Her story about her ex had been painful to hear. She hadn't deserved that. He sensed there was more to the story, but hadn't pressed. She would tell him in her own time.

If he ever got his hands on the man who'd hurt her, he'd make him pay.

While women deserved to be treated equally and have the same opportunities as everyone else, a man needed to honor his commitments to the person he loved. Or said he loved. The love of another person was a precious gift and needed to be treated as such, even if it didn't stand the test of a lifetime.

It was how he'd always treated Amy, even after he became aware that their relationship probably wasn't going to last. He'd loved her, but some of his feelings had been a result of the war. He was ready for anyone who promised a safe haven.

They'd tried, even gone to counseling, but he was unwilling to give up being a cop, and she no longer had a desire to be a cop's wife. But even after they'd split up, he'd treated her with more respect than Anna's ex had treated her.

The story meant he needed to be careful with Anna's feelings. She'd been through so much that she didn't deserve to be rushed, even if she was willing to explore something deeper between them. When they'd been up in the meadow, he'd had such an urge to kiss her, he must have transmitted his feelings. There was a moment when he thought she'd leaned toward him.

Too quickly the moment had passed.

Then again, he'd felt close to her as they'd danced, but once it was over, she'd gone right back into business mode.

What did she really want? Should he try to take it further? Or deny his own wishes to give her the space she seemed to want.

She had the bar, and she was practically married to her business. He had the ranch and a half-baked idea of starting a horse sanctuary. Most of those ideas were inspired by the grit, determination, and dreams he saw in Anna. In spite of the torment she'd lived through, she still put her all into life.

Did he want them to ultimately end up together?

Yes. If he had something to say about it.

A young cow bolted away from the herd, and Quinn pursued him, putting an end to his rumination. The calf was followed by another, then a third. It was like schoolkids. When one of them got an idea in their head, they all seemed to have the same idea.

By the time he'd gotten them all back to where they belonged, they reached the meadow where they'd planned to have lunch. There was a fence that prevented the cows from going back up to the summer range. If they drifted down toward the ranch, they could simply pick them up as they moved the herd in that direction.

Quinn directed Champion to where the others were settling: a group of boulders near the stream that continued to trickle down from the upper pasture. He'd have to get the Nature Conservancy to make recommendations about this portion of the water as well as the one in the summer range. That would give him the winter to find grant money, make a plan, and be ready when the snow melted.

"How's it going?" he asked Kevin as he settled in next to him with the sandwiches and coffee he'd pulled from his saddlebags.

"My muscles are reminding me that I haven't done a whole lot of riding lately," he replied.

"Too much school?"

"Yeah. I thought undergraduate school was tough in a way, but graduate school is a whole other level. It's not only the law I have to learn, but to become an environmental lawyer, I have to have a sound understanding of earth science, something that is *not* my strong suit."

"I'm glad you're tackling it, though," Quinn said. "We need you to help save what we can from greed and inattention to what's been happening around us."

"I'm enjoying it because it stretches my mind. It makes me feel like I have a purpose in life."

Quinn nodded. "Your mom okay with your decision now?"

Kevin grinned. "Well, she can't complain I'm here now that she's moved in with Caleb."

"I'd heard that."

"No one can keep a secret in this town," Kevin said. "She'd still like it better if I was going into something stable like corporate law, but she understands this is what I want."

"I'm glad."

"Ned and Maggie are keeping watch over the herd," Ralph said as he, Heather, and Ted joined them. "Heather and I will go relieve them in a little bit."

"I brought brownies for everyone," Heather said, putting a plastic container on one of the rocks.

"How did you get so lucky?" Quinn said to Ralph. "Not only can your wife do makeup for the stars, she can ride a horse on a cattle drive and bake brownies." Before she'd married, she'd been a makeup artist in Hollywood, but she'd given up that career to marry a Montana rancher.

"I know. I sure lucked out," Ralph said, gazing at his wife.

"Except I gave up my makeup gig," Heather said.

"I thought Laura wanted you to do her makeup for this movie she has coming up," Ralph said.

"I turned her down. I'm done with Hollywood." She gave her husband a kiss on the cheek. "I've got everything I need right here."

Ralph's skin turned pink.

"Although I wouldn't mind a trip to Hawaii in February," Heather added. "It gets too darn cold here to be reasonable."

"Especially those first two weeks," Quinn said. "It always seems to go down below zero then."

Ralph nodded. "It's been that way as far back as I can remember."

"And what's with you and Anna?" Heather asked.

"Nothing. We've had a few rides, and I took her fly fishing. We're just friends, have been since we were kids in Butte."

"That's it?" Heather sounded disappointed. "That woman could use someone in her life. She works too hard."

"Everyone thinks that but her," Quinn said. "That's why I've been trying to get her to do other things."

"She'd need to hire a manager, or promote one of her staff," Ralph said.

"I don't think she trusts anyone that much," Heather said.

Ted cleared his throat.

Everyone turned to him.

"I was talking to Paul the other day," Ted said. "He told me there's a guy hanging around wanting to be her manager. Paul says he claims to be an old friend, but feels more like an ex."

"Her ex?" Quinn said, his arms tensing.

"That's what Paul said."

"Well, that doesn't sound good," Heather said. "I don't know exactly what happened—Anna's too close-mouthed. But you can tell by looking in her eyes it was bad."

"It's not good," Quinn said.

And if he had anything to say about it, the ex would be taking the road out of town and not coming back.

Chapter Twenty-Two

"That needs to go a little higher," Riley told Chloe.

Chloe was balancing on a ladder holding up one end of an orange and black sparkling streamer. "You just told me to lower it," she complained.

Anna hid a smile. Riley was a perfectionist when it came to decorating. That's why everyone stepped aside and let her do it. When the group of them were through, the Buckhorn would be the perfect place for their Halloween activities.

It was between the noon rush and the afternoon dinner hour on the day before Halloween.

The front of the establishment was already decorated with cobwebs and spiders, perfect for the trunk or treat that the school had been running in the Buckhorn parking lot for the past three years. She had one of the biggest parking lots in the area, and loved to see the creativity people used to decorate their cars so they could hand out candy from their trunks. In a community as spread out as this one was, the event was a safe and easy alternative to door to door knocking.

Once that was over, the doors would be opened for an adults-only party. There would be prizes for best costumes, raffles, and a buffet-style dinner created from dishes supplied by many of the townspeople. The tickets covered costs with some left over. All proceeds were going to be donated to the school for supplies so that those supplies didn't need to come out of the teachers' pockets. Anna always added to whatever was collected. In her mind, good education was essential for all children, no matter who their parents were.

Having hung one end of the streamer to Riley's satisfaction, Chloe climbed down the ladder. The two of them moved it to where Riley decided the other end should go, and Chloe once more ascended.

In another corner, Maribel, owner of Silver Clips, and Kari, who owned the local saddlery, fussed over flower arrangements. Most were built from straw flowers and other decorative branches from an online craft store. They would intersperse them with containers of live chrysanthemums in fall colors. Both arrangements would be raffled off at the end of the evening.

Destiny, Laura, and Heather were conferring over food at another table. Leaving Chloe and Riley to hash out the wall decorations, Anna joined them.

"How many people do you think will show up?" Heather asked her.

"In past years we've had forty or fifty show up. More people than that bought tickets because they want to support the school. This year we planned for sixty, so we should have plenty of food."

"We have commitments from about thirty people and most of them are reliable," Heather said. "Will that be enough?"

"I reached out to a caterer I've used in California," Laura said. "She gave me an estimate of how much food we'd need per person and gave me a way to estimate how much food is in each container."

"But we don't know the size of the containers," Destiny said. "Everyone will be bringing what they have from home."

"We can estimate from the size of the average home casserole," Heather said.

"That's a lot of math," Laura complained.

"I can figure it out," Anna said. "I'm used to estimating stuff like that." Her phone buzzed. "I need to take this."

She got up from the table and asked, "What's up Olivia?"

"I'm so sorry, Anna." Her waitress sounded terrible. "I know I said I would try to get in this afternoon, but I've just been to the doctor. I've got bronchitis. He wants me to stay home for at least three days so I don't give it to anyone else." Olivia gave a hacking cough.

"Well, I don't want you here either," Anna said. "You need to get better. You've got some sick days. It won't make up for the tips, but I can pay you the base rate."

"Thank you," Olivia said. "You're the best."

"Okay. Let me know Sunday how you're doing."

"But how are you going to handle the crowd tomorrow?"

"I'll figure something out," Anna said. "Don't worry about it. Just get better."

As she ended the call, she realized it wasn't going to be as easy as she'd indicated to Olivia. Sue was coming along, but she was still new. Kiara was on evening shift at her vet tech job this week, so she wasn't going to be available either. Because it was a buffet and all they had to take was drink orders, Anna had figured she could handle it with Olivia and Sue.

"Problems?" Laura asked when she sat down.

"Olivia's sick."

"That's going to leave you short-handed," Heather said.

"Yep."

"Maybe one of us could help out?"

Anna shook her head. "There's a rhythm to bartending and waitressing. If you don't have recent experience, it's hard to fit in. A new person can sometimes make it worse."

"What about Quinn?" Destiny asked. "Didn't he bartend for you once?"

Anna nodded. Quinn was a possibility, but she didn't want to owe him anything. After she'd told him about her ex, she'd thought she'd revealed too much. But he'd called her anyway, and they'd gone riding again. During the ride, he'd kept the conversation friendly, and she'd eased back into whatever the relationship was.

There was another possibility.

"I'll figure it out. Let's get this planning done and finish the decorations. People will start trickling in soon and without Olivia or Kiara, I'm going to need to pitch in."

It wouldn't be as busy as tomorrow, but it was still going to be tight.

Maybe she should give Brandon a trial run. He'd checked in with her by text during the week, but she'd told him she didn't have anything for him.

Having Brandon in her place would open her to a whole host of other problems, but what choice did she have?

As Heather gave them a list of who was bringing what, Anna began to relax. There would be plenty of food. She didn't need to crunch the final caterer's numbers to figure that out. There was even a good ratio of main dishes to desserts, which sometimes didn't happen.

"I can be in during trunk or treat to help set up the buffet table," Heather said. "There are benefits to not having children."

"So can I," Destiny said.

"Me too," Laura said.

"That would be very helpful," Anna said.

"Good, I think we're settled," Heather said.

"I just have one more question," Laura said. "What is up with you and Quinn? Jake says you've gone on a few dates."

"They aren't dates," Anna corrected. "We've gone for some rides together as friends. And he wanted to teach me fly fishing."

"How was it?" Destiny asked. "Caleb keeps trying to get me out on the river."

"It was fun, actually."

"I'm not sure Quinn thinks it's only a friendship," Heather said.

"Really?" Anna asked. "He's been clear to me that's all it is."

"He does that so you won't spook," Heather said. "We spent a bit of time together when we were moving the herd to the winter pastures. There's something in his eyes when he talks about you, an expression that doesn't indicate friendship, but something more."

"I hope not," Anna said. "Because that's all it can ever be."

"Why?" Destiny asked.

"I don't have time for a relationship," she said. "Not with the business. And I don't want to share my life with anyone. I tried that once, and it didn't work out."

"Quinn's a good man," Heather said.

"And everyone in town agrees you work too hard," Laura said.

"Everyone in town should mind their own business," Anna said.

The other three women laughed.

"In what century do you think that's going to happen?" Heather said. "We're worried about you. And some of it's self-motivated. You've made the Buckhorn into a great place. What are we going to do if you get sick and can't run it anymore?"

"I'll take care of myself. I promise," Anna said, touched by their concern.

Riley and Chloe came over to the table, followed by Maribel and Kari.

"We're done," Riley said.

Anna looked around. There were lots of streamers, cobwebs, spiders, ghosts, and witches with their cats, yet it wasn't overdone. "It's great!" she said.

"I'm glad you like it," Chloe said.

"I appreciate all the help. Anyone want a glass of wine before you go?"

Chloe, Maribel, Destiny, and Heather took her up on her offer, but the others left. Once she'd delivered the wine, Anna went back behind the bar to get ready for the next round of customers. Since she'd closed the place while they decorated, she'd given Paul some time off. He'd be back soon.

Tomorrow would be tough without extra help. The only way she'd know if Brandon would fit in would be if she gave him a trial run. Taking a deep a breath, she dialed the number he'd given her.

"I'm short two waitresses," she said after greeting him. "And tomorrow's a big party. Any chance you could come in tonight and tomorrow?"

"You're offering me a job?"

"On a temporary basis. And only as a bartender."

"It's something," he said. "Yeah, I can be there."

"How soon can you get here? I need to go over the set up with you."

"About an hour. I need to change and it takes a half hour to get there from where I'm staying outside Livingston."

"That would be great. I appreciate the help on such short notice."

"I'm grateful you're giving me the chance," he said. "You won't regret it."

They ended the call, and she went back to prepping. When she noticed the other women stirring, she walked to the table to pick up the glasses and say goodbye.

"Thanks for all your help," she said.

"Thanks for the wine," Maribel said. "It was a real treat. And remember, anytime you want to stop by the salon, I'm happy to give you a discount on a new haircut."

Anna smiled and nodded without any intention of taking Maribel up on the offer.

Heather lingered after the other women left.

"I know it's not my business," she said. "But I meant what I said about Quinn. I think he's a lot more invested in this than friendship."

"We've known each other a long time. That's it."

Heather shook her head. "I don't agree, but that's how I see it. You may be right. All I'm asking is that you think about giving him a chance." She looked directly at Anna. "I believe you've been terribly, terribly hurt, and you've handled it all on your own. You don't have to, you know. You have friends here who are willing to help with more than decorations."

"I'm fine," Anna said, hating the vulnerability that rose up inside her.

"Yeah, I know," Heather said. "If you ever decide you're not fine, we're here for you. So is Quinn. See you tomorrow." With a wave, she left the Buckhorn.

Anna swallowed back the tears that threatened to overflow. She had a job to do, and she needed to stiffen her spine and get it done.

Chapter Twenty-Three

The moon had cooperated fully with the spirit of Halloween, raising its bright orb over the valley, becoming more visible as the sun set over the horizon at six. Perfect for the kids and their trunk or treat.

Quinn reminisced about Halloweens he'd known growing up in Butte. He'd gone as a ghost, a pirate, and a clown before they'd garnered the reputation of pure evil. It was a family affair. Their parents helped with costumes, gave them strict instructions on where they could go, and how to be polite trick or treaters.

No toilet paper or eggs allowed.

He'd always been in charge of his younger siblings, and Anna when she'd come along with them.

One year, she'd come as one of Charlie's Angels—all glamor and attitude. He remembered that costume as clearly as if it were yesterday. It was the first inkling of the woman she would become.

It was also probably the first time he'd looked at her as someone other than a kid sister. The feeling had quickly faded though, as more girls his age took notice of him and started flirting.

Once again he cursed the age difference between them. Would he have been able to be her knight in shining armor, saving her from all the heartache she'd obviously endured?

Nothing he could do about that now, but if he was patient, he might be able to build something with her going forward. Would she want to do that? How could he convince her to open her eyes to something more than friendship?

He needed to keep his feelings to himself, at least for now. It was still too early.

Trunk or treat was still going on, so he pulled his truck into the far end of the parking lot. Walking back, he was impressed by the imagination people had shown in decorating their cars and pickups. Kids in all manner of dress, from the ghosts and witches that still made a regular appearance to creations based on popular movies, raced among the vehicles, their bags heavy with candy and other treats.

He didn't miss the sugar high of Halloween.

With a grin, he took the steps two at a time, eager to see Anna and offer his help for anything she needed during the evening. He'd dressed up as Bat Masterson, a gambler, sometimes lawman, and journalist who was known for his fancy suits, hat and cane. After taking a few moments to admire the decorations outside the door, he pushed it open.

The inside was as Halloween-inspired as the outside. Several people he knew were setting up casseroles and Crock-Pots on tables on one side of the restaurant space. The other side held what looked to be desserts. Urns for coffee and hot water stood guard next to the desserts.

Quinn had dropped off a Crock-Pot of beef stew earlier.

Even as he absorbed those details, he was aware of Anna, dressed in her traditional Annie Oakley costume, behind the bar talking to a man he didn't recognize. He was good-looking in a city kind of way: a lot of effort had gone into making himself look exactly as he wanted. Tonight he was a slick, old-fashioned bartender.

It was a look intended to attract females that immediately made Quinn suspicious.

Could this be the ex? If so, what was he doing behind Anna's bar?

Quinn strode across the room.

"Hey, Anna," he said when he reached the bar. "Place looks great. Is there anything you need help with?"

She looked up from whatever she was explaining to the man next to her. "Hi, Quinn. Thanks." She looked around. "No, I think we've got it."

"Hi," the man behind the bar said. "I'm Brandon. I'll be your bartender tonight. Can I get you anything?"

Torn between wanting a stiff shot of whiskey and asking for a glass of soda water, Quinn hesitated.

"Quinn usually has one of our local IPAs," Anna said, grabbing a glass and pouring the beer with a practiced hand. She pushed it across the bar to him.

He put his credit card on the bar. "I'll run a tab," he said.

"Perfect," she said. "I was just about to show Brandon my system for handling these." She turned back to the register.

Before he stepped over to follow what she was doing, Brandon gave Quinn a look that clearly marked his territory.

That's what you think.

Quinn took his glass and walked away. Now was not the time to confront the man who thought he was taking over Quinn's place in Anna's life. If Brandon was the ex, which he probably was, he'd had his chance and blown it. He was responsible for some of the pain in Anna's eyes.

If Quinn had anything to say about it, Brandon wouldn't be staying long. He'd have to be careful, though. Unlike the developer, who'd flirted with Anna and moved on to the next project, Brandon might be sticking around. If Quinn's instincts were right, the man would use every dirty trick at his disposal to keep Anna where he wanted her.

The guy made Quinn's skin crawl.

He made his way over to the serving table and asked Heather, dressed as an old-fashioned woman of questionable morals, if there was anything he could do.

"Manufacture electricity?" she asked him. "There aren't many outlets over here, and I'm afraid to plug too many things into one outlet."

"Where's the nearest empty one?" he asked.

She pointed.

"Extension cords?"

"I've already used all that Anna has," she said. "I think one more would do it. I tried to get Ralph to bring one of ours, but he's not answering his phone."

"Caleb and Destiny here yet?" he asked.

"No, she's on clean-up detail."

"Let me call him."

Quinn made the call and reached Caleb right before they were leaving the house. Caleb agreed to bring down a couple of extension cords.

"Problem solved," he told Heather with a grin.

"You're a life saver," she said.

"Remember to mention that to Anna."

"You need to get points with her?" Heather smiled. "I thought you were 'just friends.'"

"Even friends need help now and again." He glanced at Brandon.

Heather frowned. "I think that's her ex. Two of her waitresses are out tonight. I think she brought him in because she felt she had no other choice."

"I could have helped."

"We suggested that to her, but she went with him. I'm not sure why. It's almost like he has some kind of hold over her."

"Have you ever heard what her story is?" Quinn asked.

"No more than anyone else. She was married to him, they had a child, they got divorced. No one is sure where the child is. Alcohol must have had something to do with it because I've never known Anna to drink, in spite of owning a bar."

"Me either." He knew the story of Brandon, but it wasn't his to reveal. Like Heather, he had no idea what had happened to Anna's child, but he sensed it wasn't good.

The door opened and four people carrying instrument cases walked in, bringing with them the sound of cars starting up.

"Trunk or treat must be over," Quinn said. "And that looks like the band."

"Let the fun begin," Heather said.

~ ~ ~

The evening flowed smoothly. People had worked hard to come up with imaginative and striking costumes. Kari had made a jingle dress that provided music whenever she walked around. Laura had reincarnated as Glinda, the good witch of Oz. Men arrived as Captain America and other Marvel characters, woodsmen, and lawyers. There was even a devil.

But Chloe won the costume contest for her faerie costume. She'd combined a body suit with make-up to appear ethereal and constructed wings from lace and white wire. Her hair, crowned by a wreath of flowers, flowed freely. The effect was amazing.

Quinn spent most of the evening at a table with Caleb, Destiny, Jake, and Laura. Occasionally, Ralph and Heather joined them. When the band played, the couples danced. The women offered to dance with him, but he turned them down.

There was only one woman he wanted to dance with, and she was busy making sure people had drinks and were having a good time.

He couldn't take his eyes off her.

"You've got it bad," Jake said.

"What?" Quinn asked, turning to his friend.

"Anna."

"We're just—"

"Friends. I know. That's what I used to say. I've known you too long to be fooled by that, even if you are. Caleb sees it too. The question is, what are you going to do about it?"

"Take it slow," Quinn said. "She maintains she doesn't want another relationship, but I know sometimes she feels the same things I do. I know it in my bones." Quinn sipped his beer. "And now he's here." Quinn nodded at the bartender.

"Laura thinks he's the ex."

"That's the rumor." Quinn stared at Brandon.

The man seemed to sense Quinn's gaze because he looked over and gave him a slow, victorious smile.

Quinn continued to gaze in that direction until a customer asked Brandon for something, and he had to turn away.

"I don't trust him," Quinn said to Jake.

"Yeah. I get that. If I'd pulled him over, I would have run a background check."

"Why don't you do that?"

"Randomly doing a background check is frowned on," Jake said.

"Please. For Anna's sake."

"I'll see what I can do."

"Thanks, man."

"Anything for a friend. But it would be better if I had more. If you find out something else, get it to me right away."

"Will do."

Jake lifted his glass and clinked with Quinn.

~ ~ ~

A few hours later, the party started to wind down. Heather and her group of women started to clean up, making an announcement for everyone to pick up their casserole dishes and Crock-Pots. Jake, Caleb, Ralph, and Quinn pitched in, doing whatever Heather directed.

That woman matched any lieutenant Quinn had ever served under.

At some point he managed to get to where Anna was working.

"It was a great event," he told her.

"Thanks."

"How about we go fly fishing on Monday morning?" he asked. "It should be quiet then. You could even ask Paul to open up."

Anna was quiet. Then she said, "I'm not sure that's a good idea. Olivia is really sick. I'm not comfortable with Paul opening up." She glanced at Brandon. "I know everyone thinks I should take more time off, and I'm thinking about hiring a manager, but I'm not there yet."

Quinn's heart began to ache. Had he already lost to Brandon because he'd been too worried about spooking Anna? Had he gone too slow?

Should he make his feelings known now? Or was it too late? Or too soon?

The woman was twisting him in knots.

"Fly fishing takes a while," he acknowledged. "So maybe a quick ride some morning?"

She picked up the glasses from the table and put them in the bussing bin.

"I don't think that's a good idea, Quinn," she finally said. "The weather's getting cold and I can't afford to get sick. Plus … well … I …" She took a deep breath. "I don't want to get any more involved than we are right now."

"Does it have to do with him?" Quinn asked, gesturing toward the bar.

"No." Then she shrugged. "Well, maybe. Working with him

again reminded me why I'm happier being single. No offense. You're a good guy. I just don't want any kind of guy right now." She picked up the bin and carried it back to the kitchen.

Quinn stared after her for a few moments, then turned and left the Buckhorn.

Chapter Twenty-Four

Brandon had only been working for Anna for a few days and already he was messing with her head. He appeared to have changed, and he certainly knew how to work a bar, but she couldn't forget how he'd treated her when things had gotten bad between them.

Nor the cruel things he'd said to her after Madison had died.

Her internal walls, which had been softened by her time with Quinn, had slammed back into place. She still felt terrible about telling Quinn she didn't want to see him anymore, but also sorry for herself. She'd enjoyed their time together. For the first time in a long time, she'd been seen as a likable human being, not someone who'd messed up her life and her daughter's.

He would have turned away eventually, when she told him how Madison had died, as she inevitably would've had to. When he did, her heart would have been crushed. If she was honest with herself, she'd been falling for him.

Just as well she'd told him it was over.

But why did it hurt so much?

Her phone rang. Her sister. She'd been half-expecting this call.

She put the glass she'd been polishing down on the bar and answered.

"What's up?" she asked.

"Are you coming to Mom's birthday celebration tomorrow?" Sophia said. "She keeps asking if you'll be there. It's a big one, you know. She's turning seventy-five."

Her mother had only been nineteen when she'd gotten pregnant with Anna. She'd been forced to marry Anna's father and had had three more children in rapid succession, children neither she nor her alcoholic husband were capable of raising.

"I don't know."

"You have to be here. You're the only one she wants. She

doesn't care that I'm here, taking care of her every day."

And probably robbing her blind in the process.

The door opened and Paul and Brandon walked in together, in the midst of an animated discussion.

She nodded at them and moved away from the bar to talk to her sister.

"When were you planning on celebrating?" she asked.

"I thought a mid-afternoon party might be nice. Mom gets so tired after dinner. She doesn't want to do anything but watch television. A couple of neighbors she's still friends with said they'd stop by."

Paul and Brandon could handle the lunch crowd, even if Olivia wasn't able to show up. Sue was scheduled to come in at four, and Kiara had said she'd come in to cover the evening shift.

There was no good reason for her not to go to Butte. It was only her stubborn insistence on being in control that kept her tied to this bar.

Tomorrow was a Monday. If there was any day to risk it, that would be the day.

"I'll see what I can do," she told Sophia.

"I'll tell Mom you'll be there. She'll be so excited!"

"But …"

"Be sure to bring a gift," Sophia said. "You know how she likes to open presents. See you tomorrow!"

And with that, Sophia hung up, leaving Anna staring at her phone. With a sigh, she slid it in her back pocket.

"What do you need from the back?" she asked Brandon.

He told her, and she went to the storeroom to get the three bottles he needed.

As soon as she unlocked the door and walked into the room, she knew in her gut that someone else had been in there. Crouching down, she looked at the lock on the door. It wasn't a strong lock, more there as a deterrent than to actually keep someone out who wanted to be in. There was no evidence of any tampering with the lock, but someone skilled with picks could get it open without leaving a trace.

She checked the boxes, especially of the more expensive bottles, and found five bottles missing. One bottle here or there could be missed inventory that she could handle, but it was starting to add up. By her estimation at least ten of the most expensive bottles of liquor were missing. This included three single-malt whiskeys that ran well over a hundred dollars each.

If the thefts hadn't started before Brandon arrived, she'd suspect him. Who could it be?

The first bottle had been taken shortly after she'd hired Sue, but the newest waitress didn't have a key to the building.

Before she left for Butte tomorrow, she'd call a locksmith and get a sturdier lock put on this door.

~ ~ ~

The weather cooperated for her as she drove the two hours to Butte. She stopped at a bookstore in Bozeman to pick up a couple of the swoony romances her mother still loved. As she waited for them to be wrapped, she wondered why her mother still believed happily-ever-after was possible.

Of course, her mother had always been in denial about the reality of her situation. It was probably the only way she'd been able to get through it.

She reached the house in Butte by two-thirty. Taking a deep breath, she picked up the gift and the case of La Croix she'd purchased in Bozeman as well, and walked up the steps to her mother's house.

As before, Sophia opened the door.

"Oh! You did make it."

"I texted you I was coming."

"I know, but I wasn't sure you would really leave your precious bar behind."

Anna didn't bother to answer. Sometimes—most of the time—it didn't pay to attempt to deal with snark. Her sister had always been disgruntled about one thing or another. Whether she was using or not, it never mattered.

Sophia's eyes looked clear today. Maybe she was attempting to get clean again.

With her own background, she shouldn't be angry with her sister, but she couldn't help but feel it was time for Sophia to make a change for the better. But her mother's birthday wasn't the time to get into it with her sister.

"I brought a gift," she said as she stepped into the house.

"Mom will be pleased. Thank you."

And just like that, her sister became charming.

Her mother emerged from the hallway, dressed in her best dress, fake pearls around her neck, and lipstick.

"Anna!" she cried. "You made it!" Then she threw her arms around Anna and hugged her close. When she released Anna, she looked pointedly at the gift. "Is that for me?"

"Of course," Anna said. "You're the birthday girl."

"I am, aren't I?" Her mother beamed. "Come into the kitchen. My friends should be here any second and then we can celebrate!"

Anna followed her mother into the kitchen where a store-bought cake proclaiming Happy Birthday sat on the same wooden kitchen table where they'd eaten countless meals. Two big candles announcing seventy were in the middle of the cake. Coffee was already brewed. Anna put her offering in the fridge.

The doorbell rang, and Sophia went to get it, coming back with two women who looked somewhat familiar.

"Well, Anna Wells, look at you!" one of them said. "It's been ages since we've seen you, hasn't it, Phyllis?"

"Yes, we always say it is such a shame you don't visit your mother more often," Phyllis said.

"She must be very busy," the other woman said. "You know, owning a bar and all that."

"It's a bar and restaurant," Anna said. "And you're right, it keeps me very busy." She put a smile on her face. "But I'm here now. Would either of you like a cup of coffee?"

"That would be lovely," Phyllis said. She handed the package she was carrying to Anna's mother. "Here you go. Happy birthday!"

Her mother fluttered over the gift, and thanked the other woman for hers as well.

"This looks like a party!" Sophia said. "Are you ready to cut the cake?" she asked her mother.

"Oh, yes." Her mother clapped her hands.

Sophia produced a lighter for the candles. Once they were

blown out, she cut the cake and put the pieces on plates Anna handed to her.

The small party continued for about an hour. Her mother was happy with her gifts, and the three women kept up a constant chatter, mainly about things Anna had forgotten and people she didn't know. She smiled anyway. It was great to see her mother happy.

Once the two women left, Anna helped Sophia clean up, then said she had to get back to Willow Creek.

"Why do you have to work so hard?" her mother said. "Can't you stay a little longer?"

"I can't, Mom. I'm sorry. I'll be back again soon," she said, knowing even as she said it that she probably wouldn't be back for a while. Maybe the January thaw would really occur this year.

Maybe it wouldn't.

"Thanks for making the effort," Sophia said as they walked to the door. "Mom appreciates it."

"I know she does." Unexpected affection for her sister washed over her. "Thanks for being here for her." Anna put her arms around Sophia and held her close for a few moments before turning around and heading out to her truck.

She had one more stop to make.

Threading her way to Madison's grave, she regretted not stopping for flowers, even though they would die quickly in the night's freezing temperatures.

"Oh, Maddie," she said as she stood in front of the granite headstone. "Why couldn't I save you? You had so much to give, so much love. What took it from you? What pain did you carry that you tried to erase every day?"

Tears flowed down her cheeks, and she did nothing to stop them.

Madison's descent into drugs was one of the biggest mysteries of Anna's life. Was it genetics, a perfect storm of genes received from her father and her mother? Was it because they worked too hard and were gone too long, trying to make ends meet in a business that paid people less than the minimum wage, claiming they'd make it up in tips? Was it the crowd that Maddie had run with? Her daughter had made friends with people who were going nowhere, and Anna hadn't stopped her.

All she knew was that her precious daughter had been picked up by the cops at the age of twelve. She'd been with some of her 'friends,' shoplifting so they could get the weed they wanted.

With some assistance, Anna had taken her daughter to therapy. They'd tried an alternative high school. Anna had even scraped together money for an expensive treatment program.

Every time her daughter swore she was clean.

Every time it was a lie.

Anna wiped her eyes.

"I'm sorry, Maddie. I'm sorry I couldn't stop you." Anna made her way back the way she came, the ache in her heart threatening to tear her chest apart.

Chapter Twenty-Five

Anna managed to pull herself together before she reached the Buckhorn a bit after six that evening. As she'd hoped, things were quiet when she walked in the door.

"How did it go?" she asked Kiara.

"Fine," the young woman said with a smile. "I think people are worn out from Halloween and Day of the Dead celebrations. The place was empty for a few hours in the afternoon, and the lunch crowd was small."

"Thank you for your help," Anna said.

"Any time," Kiara said. "Well, any time I'm not tending animals."

"Why don't you become a full-time vet?" Anna asked. "That would pay a lot better."

"It would take six more years of schooling," Kiara said. "I wish I could, because I really like caring for animals." She shifted the tray she was carrying. "If I could become a vet, I could go back up home to the reservation to work. They only have one vet there right now."

"One? For all those ranches and animals?' The reservation was over a million and a half acres and occupied remote land next to Glacier National Park.

Kiara nodded, then spotted a patron with his hand raised. With a smile, she went to take care of him.

It was too bad Kiara couldn't get the support she needed to finish her schooling and help her people. There must be scholarships somewhere. Heather would know how to find out.

Anna crossed to the bar where Brandon was finishing up a tray of drinks for Sue.

"How are you doing?" Anna asked the waitress.

"Good," Sue said with a bright smile. "I appreciate the extra shifts. Things are tight at home."

"They'll only be for this week," Anna warned. "Olivia

expects to be back the week after."

"Every bit helps," Sue said, still smiling. She picked up the tray and took it to one of her tables.

It was really too bad she couldn't give the woman extra hours, but there wasn't enough business over the winter months to keep all of them employed.

She was going to have to come up with some extra events, or work with some locals to bring tourists in during the winter months. There was a new inn opening up south of town in a few weeks. They were scheduling groups for events like a knit and ski weekend. Maybe she could do a few special dinners at the Buckhorn for the groups. The owners had mentioned it in passing a few months ago, but Anna hadn't followed up on it. Now was the time to do it.

"How did it go with your mother?" Brandon asked.

"How did you know that's where I was going?"

"Why else would you take that trip at this time of year? I remember her birthday was right after All Saints Day." His smile was bittersweet. "I remember lots of things from when we were together, Anna. We were good together, or have you forgotten that? I wish we'd never split up."

"Uh-huh," was all she said. This wasn't the time or place to correct his memory. "How are the receipts so far today?"

"You want a total?"

"That would be nice."

He pressed a bunch of buttons and gave it to her. It was low, but based on what Kiara had said, wasn't unexpected.

She went to the kitchen to check on Paul.

"Everything under control?" she asked.

"Sure is, boss," he said. "I like nice, slow days like this, especially after the weekend craziness."

"I can understand that," she said with a smile. "How are things going with Brandon?"

"He certainly knows his way around a bar," Paul said. "Nice guy. He seemed to keep things running smoothly."

"He wasn't in charge," she pointed out. "You were."

"It's hard to be in charge when you're working the kitchen," Paul said with a slight frown. "He offered to take over, and I didn't think it was a big deal. Everything went well, didn't it?"

"Looks like everything went just fine," she said. She didn't need to alienate her cook. "I totally get it. You're right. You can't watch the restaurant if you're in here."

Paul gave a quick nod as he moved a steak from the grill to a plate that was already set up with a baked potato and sautéed green beans.

"Can you take this to the guy at the bar?" Paul asked.

"Sure thing." Anna picked up the plate. What Paul had pointed out made sense, but it still left her with a sense of unease. She didn't need Brandon taking over the place whenever she left. When Olivia got back, she'd have a talk with her about becoming a part-time manager. It would take some training, but she trusted her long-term waitress a whole lot more than she did her ex.

She brought the plate out and set it in front of the customer Brandon indicated.

"Have a good dinner," she said.

"Nice place you have here," the man replied. "I'm headed to Chico in the morning, figured I'd get an AirBnB up here. Can't afford those resort prices."

"I know what you mean," she said with a practiced smile.

The man gestured at Brandon. "He's a good bartender. My sister owns a place in Billings, where I'm from. She says a bartender is key to making a place hum."

Anna nodded, knowing it took a whole lot more than a bartender for an establishment like the Buckhorn to work. She made another round of the tables, and everything seemed to be running smoothly. She returned to the bar. Other than the lone diner at the end, the stools were empty.

"Thanks for stepping in today," she told her ex. "I can handle it from here on out."

"I don't mind staying," he said.

"There's no need for both of us to be here," she said. "I have to watch my bottom line, remember?" She gave him a smile to keep the conversation light.

"You can go home. I won't charge you for my time after you leave," he said. "Going to your parents' house always wore you out. That's why I discouraged you from going, remember?"

She felt like there was a stone in the pit of her stomach. Her father had been alive back then. Seeing her mother emotionally cower before him had always made her angry and sad. It took several days before she could get back to being herself.

Brandon had hammered it in that she didn't owe her parents anything, that she was safer just staying with him.

After a while, she'd agreed and stopped going to Butte.

"It's better now that Dad is gone," she said.

"But …"

She shrugged. They were no longer married. There was no need to discuss anything with Brandon.

"You can tell me," Brandon said, his voice soft. "I know better than anyone what you went through."

"I don't know," she said without thinking about it too much. When he was sober, Brandon had always been easy to talk to. "She seems almost childish, as if she's reverting to being a girl, before all that stuff with my dad happened."

"Alzheimer's?" he suggested.

"Could be, but she doesn't seem confused."

"Is she living alone?"

"No, Sophia's staying with her, at least for now."

"Ah, Sophia," Brandon said.

The sharp pain returned, like a fist plunged into her gut.

"You always did like my sister," she said, picking up a bar glass and rubbing away imaginary spots. "I've got this."

"I told you," Brandon said. "Nothing ever happened between me and Sophia."

"She says it did."

"She's a drug addict. She'll say anything to get attention."

For a moment, Anna wavered. What he said was true.

"Besides," he continued, "we were all partying back then. You weren't above a little heavy flirtation either."

Guilty. There was one guy where the kiss had been a little too passionate.

But she'd never slept with him, even though Brandon was convinced she did.

"I wish I'd fought more for our relationship," Brandon said, putting his hand on her waist.

Her knuckles whitened on the glass.

"If I'd been there, Maddie wouldn't have gone down the road she did. She'd be alive today, I'm sure of it."

It took every bit of strength for Anna to keep from bursting into tears.

"Go home," she hissed. "You're done for the night." She looked down at his arm. "And take your hand off of me."

"Sure, boss," he said, raising his hands in the air. "Let me know when you need me again. I'm always ready to help you out. That's all I'm trying to do here, Anna. I want to support you like I should have before."

"I'll let you know," she said, then watched as he made his way out of the restaurant, smiling and waving to people on the way out.

Her hand relaxed on the glass, and she carefully put it down before she broke it.

Was he right? Would Maddie have made it if he'd been around? Maybe if Anna hadn't been so insistent that he'd slept with her sister or hadn't partied and flirted, he would have stayed. She was as much to blame for the breakup as he was. And she was solely responsible for Maddie's death.

Kiara came up with a drink order, so Anna stuffed all her feelings back down and went to work.

As the night progressed, she found herself remembering the times she'd spent with Quinn, especially the fly fishing. He was as close to a friend as she had. He was the only one she'd talked to about Brandon.

Too bad she didn't have her own equipment. The river called to her, simply standing in the water, nature all around her, in a competition with the fish to see who was going to be smarter. It was almost like meditating.

She could use that about now. Brandon's words had gotten under her skin. Were her memories of the past distorted? Was he actually a better man than she remembered?

When there was a lull, she took out her phone and stared at it. She'd told Quinn going out was a bad idea.

It *was* a bad idea.

Nonetheless, she texted him.

Any chance of going fishing Tuesday morning?
The message back was immediate.
Absolutely. See you at the same time, same place.
It was followed by a smiley emoji.
Her muscles relaxed.
It was going to be okay.

Chapter Twenty-Six

Becky stretched as she woke in Quinn's cabin the first week in November. It was good to be back in Montana. She'd spent the last week in Mississippi, but her plea for more cases in the Treasure State had been heard, and she was here to start prepping for a case against the U.S. Forest Service and U.S. Fish and Wildlife Service. The agencies had approved a massive logging project in the heart of the Bitterroot Forest not too far from Missoula. The effort would be bad for the bull trout and grizzly bears. It could even drive bull trout, already at the edge of extinction, from the planet.

Her husband, Brad, was back in Colorado. Their schedules hadn't allowed them to spend time together in a while.

She needed to make a decision about having a child.

Truthfully, she already had strong feelings that it was a bad idea. The only question that remained was whether she should cave to her husband and have a child anyway, or give up the marriage.

That was the impossible choice she had in front of her.

Glancing at her phone, she got up. Quinn had said he was cooking a big breakfast around eight, and she was welcome to come along with his ranch manager and anyone else who happened to be in the neighborhood.

"Starts the week off right," he'd told her.

She enjoyed the comradery of the ranch. Quinn had built a friendly coalition of people who helped keep the operation going. People floated in an out according to need, but Quinn treated every one of them with respect and made sure they were fairly compensated. He felt no need to be rich in monetary things, he'd told her once. He was already blessed to be living in the valley.

Once she'd showered, she made her way to the ranch house.

"Smells good in here," she said as she walked into the kitchen.

"Well, that's good news," Quinn said. "Grab yourself a cup

of coffee. Food'll be ready in a few minutes."

There were two people at the table. She'd met Ted, Quinn's ranch manager, several times before, but the woman was new to her.

The woman extended her hand. "I'm Maggie. I'm working here for a few weeks until we get the cattle settled into their winter range."

"Nice to meet you. I'm Becky. I work for Climate Action."

"So I've heard. Good work you're doing. Any idea when the court will give its ruling?"

"It could take some time," Becky said. "This case could have a lot of repercussions. If my clients win, they have enshrined the right to clean water into law, at least in Montana."

"Well, let's hope it goes your way," Maggie said. "I'm all for clean water."

"Me too," Quinn said as he put a platter of eggs and sausages on the table. "Dig in, folks."

As they ate, the conversation switched to ranch business and the weather. Like farmers, ranchers were dependent on the weather service to plan when they needed to provide extra feed to cattle or when the grass would do.

"Can I borrow a horse?" Becky asked as breakfast was wrapping up. "I've got some thinking to do."

"Sure thing."

"I'll get one saddled up for you," Maggie said.

"I can do it," Becky protested.

"No problem." Maggie grinned. "Gives me something fun to do before I start working for this hard-driving boss over here."

"Oh, you're definitely on stall mucking duty after that remark," Ted said with a smirk.

"Sure then," Becky said. "Anything to save you from mucking."

"You leaving tomorrow?" Quinn asked.

"Yep. I'll stop in Helena to meet with the team for our effort in the Bitterroot, then take a flight home to Ohio."

"You spend a lot of time in the air."

"That's for sure." If she and Brad divorced, they'd probably sell the house in Ohio. What then? There was no reason to stay in the Midwest. All she needed was a good airport.

"Enough of this sitting around," Ted said. "Time to get to work."

Maggie groaned.

"I'll be right down," Becky said.

"Good. I'll get the horse ready."

Once the pair left, Quinn said, "Stick to the lower elevations, okay? There's been a good amount of snowfall already in the upper ranges. We got the cattle out just in time."

She nodded and sipped her coffee.

"Anything I can help with?" Quinn asked. "I'm told I'm a pretty good listener."

It was tempting, but spilling her guts to Anna was enough for one day. She shook her head. "Thanks."

"If you ever change your mind, I'll be here."

She nodded and put her dishes in the sink. "You need help cleaning up?"

"Thanks, but I'm okay," he said. "Doing the dishes is almost meditative."

"Okay then." She went to her cottage, grabbed her boots and jacket, and made her way to the barn.

By the time she got there, Maggie had the horse ready. "Her name is Daisy," Maggie said. "She's pretty gentle with a soft mouth so try not to pull too hard on the reins."

"Got it."

Maggie led the horse to the corral and gave Becky a leg up before opening the gate.

Becky took the path outside the winter fields, gazing at the herd at the far side of the pasture, stretched out on the path where Ted was distributing feed to supplement the dying grass. Urging Daisy into a trot, Becky tried to remember not to post as she'd been taught as a kid on an English saddle.

With a Western outfit, the rider was supposed to slap around on the leather, somehow instinctively matching the rhythm so their rear end didn't become black and blue.

She was still trying to master this technique, so she pushed Daisy into a canter. The feeling was exhilarating, making her feel as if she were as free as a proverbial bird. For about ten minutes, she simply rode, not thinking of environmental destruction or the pending demise of her marriage.

Instead, the wind rushed through her hair, and her body heated from the exercise and the warmth of the horse beneath her. The sky glinted overhead, bare-limbed trees lined the road nearby, and in the distance, pines and firs clung to their dark green needles.

She slowed the horse and began to think.

By the time she turned Daisy around to go back to the ranch, she'd made her decision and knew what she had to do next.

~ ~ ~

Becky's flight to Denver, Colorado landed at four p.m. the next afternoon. She rented a car and drove the ninety miles to Estes Park, where Brad was working on challenges to proposed drilling inside Rocky Mountain National Park boundaries. When she reached town, she called him.

"I'm in town," she said.

"Really?" he said. "What a wonderful surprise!"

Her heart softened. There was a lot of love between them.

"Where are you staying?" she asked.

He told her and agreed to meet her at the hotel in half an hour. "I'll call and tell them to let you into the room."

By the time he got to the hotel, she'd taken a shower and changed into something comfortable, but less professional than the suit she'd worn to work and on the plane.

As soon as he got into the room, he pulled her into his arms and kissed her.

"It's been too long," he said. "We have to get a better schedule."

"Mmm," was all she managed to get out.

"Dinner?" he asked. "I'm starved."

"Sounds good."

"There's a cozy restaurant not far from here. If there weren't piles of snow out there, we could walk to it."

"I don't mind the snow," she said. "I'll change into my boots."

"I forgot you're used to the cold weather in Montana," he said with a chuckle.

On their walk they kept the conversation light. He told her what he was working on, and she brought him up to date on her new project.

"It never seems to end," he said.

"No, unfortunately. That's why we do what we do." She took a deep breath. "And I love what I do."

"So do I."

The waiter brought their meals, and she let the conversation drift back to his project. Soon they were in an animated discussion with the best approach to fighting the government-backed drilling leases.

It was only when they got back to the hotel that she brought up the subject they'd both been dancing around.

"I've done a lot of thinking," she said.

He nodded, but stayed silent, knowing it sometimes took a long time for her to express her feelings. All the nimble vocabulary she had in a courtroom deserted her when she dealt with personal issues.

"I love my work too much to give it up," she said. "And I don't think it's right to bring a child into the world when their parents would be too busy to give them the attention they need."

"Taking a more research-oriented role wouldn't work for you?" he asked.

"I've thought about it a lot," she said. "I need the variety. I would feel trapped by a research-only job."

Brad looked down at his hands.

"Are you sure about this decision to have a child?" she asked. "We have a lot going for us. We're good friends. We love each other. Isn't that enough?"

There was a moment of silence while the jury in Brad's head deliberated.

Then he shook his head and looked at her, his eyes shining with wetness.

"No. I want a child," he said. "I need a child."

The ache in her chest threatened to break her in two.

"Then you'll have to find someone else to give it to you," she said, rising from the chair where she'd been sitting. "I'll pack up my things and find another place to stay."

He got up from the bed where he'd perched.

"I'm sorry," he said. "I know … well … I know what we said … it's just …" He opened his palms as if to say, "What could I do?"

Up to that point, she'd felt sorry for both of them, but then anger stirred. They'd had a deal, and he'd broken it.

"I'll get a lawyer to contact you," she said, trying to keep the bitterness from her voice. "The sooner we end our marriage, the sooner you can find someone who'll give you what you want." She threw the few things she'd taken out back into her suitcase, zipped it up, and grabbed the handle. With her hand on the doorknob, she turned back one more time.

He was once again sitting on the bed, staring at the floor.

"I loved you," she said.

He nodded, but didn't look up.

She opened the door and left.

Chapter Twenty-Seven

The air whispered through the limbs of the cottonwoods as Anna got out of her truck at the fishing access point. Even without leaves, the trees had a sound as air threaded through them. The vibrations soothed her and helped calm her mind, which had been a whirlwind of thought since her conversation with Brandon on Sunday.

It had been a mistake to let him get that close. She'd worked alone Monday night and wouldn't hire him again unless absolutely necessary. Olivia was coming back by Friday. They should be able to handle the crowd until then.

If she refused to hire Brandon, how was she going to be able to take time off when she needed it? While Olivia could definitely manage the restaurant end of things, she wasn't a bartender. She could probably learn to pour drinks, but she'd also be responsible for handling bar and restaurant charges.

The thought brought her to her other problem. The numbers hadn't added up when she rang out at the end of evening on Sunday. Even given the slow afternoon, the amount in the till was lower than it should have been. The receipts tallied out, but she knew an experienced thief could get past all the electronic balancing a modern cash register had to offer. Credit cards were relatively safe for a restaurant owner, unless someone was into ID theft. But a bar was frequently a cash business, and a slip of a ten into a pocket now and again was harder to track.

Then there was the missing liquor. While she could lay the cash problem at Brandon's feet, the bottles had gone missing long before he showed up.

Quinn's truck pulled into the lot.

Then there was him. He posed the biggest threat of all. She'd sworn never to get emotionally involved with anyone again, but already he was chipping away at her defenses, seemingly without even trying.

She smiled at him as he got out of the truck.

"Thanks for doing this," she said. "I needed to get away from the business for a bit."

"No problem," he said. "You know I love fishing." He went to the back of his pickup to get their gear.

She felt more secure getting ready and treading into the water. This time, Quinn suggested she choose her own spot. "You're going to need to understand the lay of a river if you're going to enjoy this sport."

"Okay."

"It's all right if you choose wrong," he said. "That's how you learn. You'll do better the next time."

That philosophy hadn't turned out to be true in the marriage department. One mistake had cost her everything, leaving her with no desire to try again.

Walking over to the riverbank, she stood there for a few moments, trying to discern where the fish were hiding. Finally, she waded in and walked to her chosen spot. Then she looked over at Quinn.

His face was expressionless.

Big help.

She let out some line and cast, watching the fly miraculously drift to the water and land without a large plop. After letting it sit there for a few moments, she began to make it dance, teasing the fish she believed were watching its every move.

Quinn took a position upstream from her, so she couldn't see his movements. It was almost like being alone on the river, just her, nature, and the fish.

As she repeatedly cast and played with her line, the river flowed around her, determined to make its way from the cold waters of Yellowstone Lake to the warm Gulf of Mexico. Humans could dam it or try to channel it as they wished, but water was relentless, carving new routes or even disappearing into the air if overcome with heat and arid surroundings.

Idly, she gazed beyond the river to the grasslands and tree-lined road on the western side of the valley. Here and there buildings—mainly first or second homes—dotted the landscape. Her attention was snagged by a shadow that didn't fit the grass.

The shadow raised its head and became a five point mule deer.

"Be careful, guy," she whispered. "Or you'll end up in someone's freezer."

He looked directly at her, swished his tail, and went back to grazing.

She wasn't a threat to him.

Her line tugged, and she brought her attention to the river. Trying to remember what Quinn had told her, she brought the fish closer, then let it go. Closer, then let go.

There! She could see its silver back, tail thrashing back and forth as it tried to break free.

Net. She turned to alert Quinn, but he was already by her side.

"Terrific job," he said, scooping the fish as she pulled it out of the water. "Release or eat?"

It was a good sized fish.

"I don't know how to cook it," she said.

"I do. I can fillet it, and we can have an impromptu barbecue."

"I have to work," she said, once again confronted by the limitations of her life.

"I'll bring it to you, then," he said. "You have to eat dinner sometime. There's nothing better than fresh fish. Okay?"

She nodded. It was a compromise, but one that she regretted deeply. It would be nice to share a meal with a friend, have a leisurely evening and watch the moon rise over the horizon. The desire for such an evening filled her.

Quinn took the fish and dispatched it with a rock before putting it in a small cooler he'd brought to the river.

She checked her phone.

"I have to go," she said, wading to the riverbank. "Time goes so fast on the river."

"It does," he agreed, "but all the same, it feels timeless, like nothing else matters except for you, the surroundings, and the fish."

It was the perfect mirror to what she'd been feeling earlier.

She nodded as they gazed at each other with understanding.

Understanding and something else. Something she didn't want to look at too carefully.

She looked away. "I'll leave my gear in the back of your

truck."

"It's okay," he said. "I need to get going, too. I've got a call with some horse rescue people."

They started toward the truck.

"You're going to rescue horses?" she asked.

"Yep," he said. "I've been doing some research and have a pretty clear idea of what the end result should be. Now I just have to figure out how to accomplish it. I've been a lucky man in a lot of ways," he said. "I had a good career. Okay, so the marriage didn't last, but we've remained friends and raised our kids together." He fingered one of the loops on his waders. "I thought I'd be content raising a few head of cattle, but I've realized I want more." He gazed at her. "Much more." He cleared his throat. "I want to give back, make the world a better place."

"I'm sure Heather could find something for you to do." She stripped off her waders and put them in the back of his truck.

He laughed. "I'm sure you're right, but I'm looking for something a little more long term than serving on a committee or painting Dot's house."

"How's that going?" she asked. Heather had relented and released Anna from painting duty.

"It's almost done, which is good because I hear Dot's coming back next week."

Anna groaned. "That means Heather is going to want to do one of her group things. And she's going to want to do it on short notice." She looked up at Quinn. "Thanks again," she said. "I really appreciated it."

"Hopefully, it helped."

"It did. And, I really like your idea about caring for older or broken horses." Was it horses she was talking about or herself?

Then she did something that surprised herself. She leaned in and kissed his cheek.

Before he could react, she practically ran to her pickup, climbed in, and started it up. With a wave, she pulled out of the parking lot, trying not to spew gravel in her wake.

~ ~ ~

Anna got things ready at the bar, more aware than she normally was of the lack of balance in her life. Keeping busy kept her sane; she didn't have as much time to berate herself about what more she could have done to save her daughter. Being with Quinn was dangerous. She was too relaxed around him. There was a danger in being still. If she wasn't Maddie's lousy mom, who was she? Who could she become?

Could she learn to love again? Or maybe for the first time?

For a Tuesday the afternoon was busy, and she was glad when Sue was able to come in early to pick up the slack. Kiara could only do a few hours around dinner before she had to return to the vet's office to care for the animals they had.

Anna couldn't wait until Olivia returned.

Whatever calm she'd gained fishing was gone by six-thirty when she noticed Heather and Ralph come in for dinner.

Crash!

Anna immediately looked to the source of the sound.

Sue had dropped a tray of dirty dishes.

How many times had she told the woman to use a tub and not a tray? And not to pile whatever she used too high to balance correctly?

"Everyone okay?" she asked the patrons nearest to the crash.

There was a little bit of nervous laughter, but they assured her they were fine.

She helped Sue clean up, biting her tongue not to give the woman, who kept repeating she was sorry, a piece of her mind.

Anna would have that conversation later.

Things settled down for the next hour, and she was almost back to her normal, hyper-vigilant self when Heather approached the bar.

"You know Dot is coming back next week," Heather said.

"Yep."

"We've been preparing for a while for her Women's Help gathering. It's okay if we do it next Tuesday afternoon, right?"

Anna leaned her arms on the bar. "You can't always assume everyone's ready to jump on your say so. I'm running a business here. What am I supposed to do with the knitters? With anyone else who wants a drink who isn't ready for a bunch of crying women?"

Heather's eyes widened. "Wow. I didn't expect that. I thought you supported what we were doing."

"I did. I do." Anna ran her hand through her hair. "But you want too much sometimes, Heather. I'm barely scraping by this week without Olivia as it is. Snow's coming soon, and that means my business slows down. I've got to make every cent I can right now."

"Okay, then. I'll find another place."

"No, I didn't mean that," Anna said. Why was she being so difficult? "Of course you can have it here. Just give me more notice next time. Okay?"

"Sure," Heather said with an attempt at calmness, her voice anything but. "See you Tuesday, then."

Anna nodded and watched as Heather walked back to her husband. She said something to him and then glanced back at Anna as they got ready to leave the restaurant.

After pouring herself another glass of club soda, Anna went back to straightening up behind the bar, a sense of shame flooding her system. Heather was a friend who always tried to do the right thing. Anna admired her. Why had she treated her so badly?

It had to be stress. The question was what was she going to do about it short of selling the business and retreating to her lonely cabin on the hill?

Chapter Twenty-Eight

Quinn stared at the spreadsheet on his computer, but his mind was really on the kiss Anna had given him before she'd left their fishing spot that morning.

Anna wasn't given to spontaneous signs of affection. Even when she was a teen she'd been pretty buttoned up. Just last week she'd told him she didn't want to see him anymore.

But when she'd texted to go fishing, he couldn't say no.

The whole time they'd been together he'd wanted to reach out to her, to hold her, and to listen to whatever was bothering her. It had been obvious that she was troubled.

Her walls had remained up, however.

He should back off a little and focus on a project for himself. He'd made a bit of a plan, but realized that he was going to need an influx of cash on a regular basis to make it work. The initial costs were bad enough, but horses were expensive to feed, groom, and shoe. Then there were unexpected vet bills. With older and abused animals, that could mount up. Like humans, their bodies broke down and needed tending to manage them along until that final giddy-up to the great open spaces of the beyond.

The people he'd talked to about sanctuaries said they funded their projects with a combination of grants and donations. They had websites and Kickstarter accounts. It was a whole new world to him.

Before he went begging for money, though, he'd need to figure out how much he needed.

He turned back to the spreadsheet.

There was a brief knock at the kitchen door, then it opened.

"How's it going?" Caleb asked as he walked in.

"I'm crunching numbers. I hated doing budgets for the city, and this isn't much better."

"I hear you." Caleb grabbed a coffee mug from the rack and poured himself a cup from the ever-present pot.

It's the way it was in the West. Good friends and neighbors always had a pot brewing, and familiar guests knew where the cups were.

"Why are you crunching numbers?" Caleb asked as he turned a chair around and straddled it.

"I'm thinking about setting up a sanctuary for old and abused horses."

"You should also save space for the horses the out-of-staters abandon as soon as they've had enough winter."

"That's way too many animals," Quinn said. It was a problem at times. People with money bought cute ranches, planning to be gentlemen ranchers. They'd buy horses and sometimes cattle. After a few of the state's long winters, though, they'd rethink their options, sell everything off, and head for warmer climates.

Most of the time, the soon-to-be-ex-Montanans could offload their livestock, but every once in a while there were no takers, particularly for horses that weren't trained to do something useful. Some ranchers had abandoned horses to herd cattle altogether, relying more on ATVs and even pickup trucks. If they didn't have a use, horses were just another expense for a rancher.

"How many are you thinking of having at one time?" Caleb asked.

"All depends on where I can pasture them. Most of the ranchland to the south of here, up to Ralph and Heather's place, is designated for cattle and the few horses I already have. That leaves the stretch between your place and here. A lot of that is rocky with pockets of trees. Not ideal pastureland."

"Particularly not for older horses," Caleb said. "When was the last time you took a ride out there?"

"It's been a while," Quinn admitted.

"Why don't we saddle up some horses and take a look? Weatherman is predicting snow to reach the valley in a few days. It's a beautiful day; let's take advantage of it."

It sure beat crunching numbers on a spreadsheet. Quinn closed out the program and shut down the computer.

"Let's go," he said as he stood.

~ ~ ~

A half hour later they were headed north toward Caleb's place. Caleb had been right; it was going to be one of the last good days for riding with any kind of comfort. As it was, Quinn had bundled up in a heavy Carhartt jacket, work gloves in the pockets, and a felt cowboy hat on his head.

The land closest to his house was strewn with rocks, and the trees that climbed the mountain grew in patches.

"Almost looks like an avalanche or two came through here," Caleb said, pulling up his horse and pointing to what looked like a chute climbing the steep slope.

"That would account for the large amount of rocks here," Quinn said.

"Not the best place for a herd or even a building to shelter them," Caleb said.

"Wonder when the last one occurred here."

"They should have records at the forest service office. If not, Virginia will know."

"That woman knows everything about this valley."

"Pretty much."

They rode past the avalanche chute and were confronted by a thick grove of aspens, leaves long gone, that ran from the mountaintop to the valley below. The blue of the sky sharply outlined their black and white trunks. Overhead, the thin branches whispered against each other. Quinn paused his horse to take a few moments to study the valley laid out below them. It was a beautiful place to live, what his dad would have called "God's Country."

Quinn urged his horse forward through a natural break in the trees.

Caleb followed behind him.

There was something holy about an aspen grove. The root system lay beneath them, connecting each trunk to the rest, enveloping whoever, or whatever, walked through their embrace. It would be nice if he could build a corral for the rescues near this place.

When they emerged from the other end of the grove, he paused again. This side wasn't as rocky as the land they'd left behind. Parts of it were thick with brown grass that would turn green once winter was through. Why hadn't his memory of this direction included this place? Sometimes he was far too willing to view the rocks of life instead of the smooth patches.

Caleb pulled up next to him. "This could work," he said. "You'd need to do a bit of clearing, bring in some water, and build a fence, but you could pasture a dozen horses here easily."

"And a barn, or some kind of shelter," Quinn said. He looked back to the aspens. "Getting here might be an issue. I'd hate to cut a road through that grove."

Caleb pointed down the hill to where pavement was visible. "The road curves into the land here. Run a road up from there."

Quinn nodded, envisioning the setup. "Let's ride where the perimeter would be."

"Good idea."

They rode the circumference of the space in front of them, discussing the best place for shelter and water, as well as what would need to be done to level out the area to eliminate the chances of an older horse stepping wrong and breaking a leg. As they rode, Quinn scrawled in a notebook he always carried. Possibilities emerged, and Quinn could almost see the completed project, filled with animals getting a second chance.

Everyone and everything needed to be given a second chance once in a while.

"Thanks," he said to Caleb. "This was a good idea."

"No problem. How's it going with Anna?"

"So-so."

"What's that supposed to mean?"

"You knew her in Butte, didn't you?" Caleb asked.

"Yeah. She was about fourteen, and I was an oh-so-mature eighteen."

"Don't you wish we knew now what we knew then?"

"All that macho confidence," Quinn said with a laugh. "I think she had a crush on me way back then, but I thought of her as one more sister."

"And now?"

"Definitely not thinking of her as a sister." Quinn scanned the valley again. "For some reason I'm feeling very protective of her these days. She needs to stop working so hard."

"I think everyone in town agrees with that sentiment."

"It's almost like she's desperate to keep working because if she doesn't, something bad will happen."

"She'll run out of money?"

"That could be part of it, but I think it's more." Quinn shook his head. "I get the feeling she's running from something … maybe even running from herself."

"That never works."

"No, but we've all tried it once in our lifetimes. It's only when we stand still and face our demons that they lose their power over us." He pulled a water bottle from his saddlebag and took a sip. "We went riding a few times, and then I took her fly fishing."

"How'd that go?" Caleb had pulled out his own water.

"Really well. She took to it … well … like a duck to water." He chuckled. "But then, when I asked her to go riding again, she turned me down flat. Said she didn't want a relationship of any kind. A few days later she texts me and wants to go fly fishing again. Haven't heard from her since."

"C'mere, c'mere, c'mere, go away, go away, go away."

"Pretty much."

"Do you think it could be her ex that's making her blow hot and cold?"

"Could be," Quinn admitted. "I don't trust him."

"Me either," Caleb said. "Maybe we should have Jake check him out."

"Already did that. Jake did a cursory search but couldn't find anything on him. If I ever have cause, though, he'll be able to go deeper."

Caleb nodded, capped his water, and put it back in the bag. "But don't give up on Anna. She's not going to be easy, but she needs someone like you in her life."

"Even if she doesn't want me?"

"Especially if."

Quinn contemplated his friend's advice. Caleb was right. Quinn wasn't ready to give up on a relationship with Anna, no matter how hard she fought him. He wanted to get past her defenses, to let her know he was there for her. If she finally felt safe, maybe she'd be able to love again.

Chapter Twenty-Nine

Once dinner hour was finished around seven, the bar began to empty out. It was unusual for a Wednesday night, but snow was predicted for overnight. People tended to believe the weather forecast when it came to snow.

"What do you think, boss," Paul asked Anna as he surveyed the empty space.

"It may be an early night," she answered. She'd already sent Kiara home. "You set in the kitchen?" she asked.

"Yep. All cleaned up and ready for tomorrow."

"Why don't you head home, then? Olivia and I will get the rest."

"I can help you finish up. That way, you can go home early, too," Paul said.

Holding a cowboy hat, Olivia came over to the bar. "Someone left this. Probably Caleb, Quinn, or Jake because I found it where they were sitting." The three men had a standing get-together for dinner every Wednesday night. Sometimes Destiny and Laura joined them, but it was usually just the three ex-cops from Detroit.

Anna took the hat from her. It was Quinn's. She ran her fingers over the worn brim. "Odd that he didn't remember it, especially given the forecast."

"Those three were still talking when they left tonight," Olivia said. "They weren't thinking about much besides what had them all worked up."

Anna nodded. If she closed the bar early, she could take Quinn's hat back to him before she went home. Ever since their last fishing trip, she'd felt a need to see him.

A dangerous need.

It would be good to get her employees home before the snow hit.

"Yeah, let's clean up and call it a night," she said, flicking off the switches behind the bar that turned off the open sign.

The three of them made short work of cleaning.

As she locked the door behind Paul and Olivia, Anna wondered at the wisdom of taking Quinn's hat to him. It hadn't started snowing yet, but when she'd opened the door, she'd smelled its closeness in the air. It was odd that snow had a smell, but anyone who lived in a place like Montana definitely knew when it was coming.

Going over there was a bad idea. Why did she have this yearning to see him?

Her life, the one it had taken her years to construct, felt like it was falling apart. Another expensive bottle was missing. The register had been short again last night, and Brandon had been nowhere around. To top it off, Sophia had drunk-called her saying she couldn't handle their mother anymore.

When Anna had asked why Sophia thought their mother needed tending, her sister had gone off on a rant so foul, rambling, and full of victimhood that Anna had finally hung up on her.

If her mother needed help, then Anna was going to need to take time off to find out what was what. That meant either hiring Brandon to bartend or closing the bar.

With a sigh, she started to text Quinn to let him know she was dropping off his hat.

She deleted it before she even sent it.

Grabbing the hat and her purse, she left the Buckhorn, making sure to lock the front door, and walked to her truck. Once she left the parking lot, she turned toward Quinn's place.

The roads were dark, with clouds covering whatever moonlight there was. She kept an eye out for moving shadows as she drove. The bare limbs of the trees were motionless, as they often were when temperatures headed toward zero.

Would it get that cold this early? Freezing, zero, and even below zero temperatures were usually reserved for February, but winter had her own moods that weren't dependable.

A large shadow stepped onto the road, and she hit the brakes. In front of her a good-sized black bear ambled across the road, paying her no heed.

"You should be in your den right now," she told the fat and furry animal. "All safe and snug before this snow hits."

It was exactly where she should be, too. Safe at home instead of on this fool's errand.

She watched the bear lumber up the slope on the far side of the road, then took her foot off the brake and continued down the road to Quinn's driveway.

As she reached the spacious level area that contained the house, barn, and other outbuildings, she was relieved to see warm lights glowing from the house's windows. It was only eight-thirty at night, a borderline reasonable hour for someone to make an unexpected visit.

It always amazed her, at least according to books she read and movies she watched, that the majority of Americans made plans to see each other. They "penciled each other in" and had elaborate back and forths about when and where they'd meet.

In Willow Creek, people dropped by when the mood struck. If their quarry wasn't home, they might leave a note. Or during the height of summer, a bag full of unwanted zucchini.

She preferred it this way.

After parking, she got out of the truck. Hat in hand, she climbed the steps to the front door. As she did, snowflakes began to drift down from the sky.

"Anna!" Quinn exclaimed after opening the door to her knock. His face broke into a happy smile. "What are you doing here?"

"I brought your hat back," she said. "You left it at the bar."

"Thank you. Come in. Do you have time for a coffee? It's decaf."

"I shouldn't." She gestured at the snow.

"It's not coming down hard. Please. I think I have some cookies left, too."

"For a little while," she said and stepped inside.

She shed her boots to avoid tracking moisture on the polished floors and followed him into the kitchen, trying to figure out how long she had to stay to be polite.

This had been one of her worst ideas in the last few weeks.

The worst had been hiring Brandon.

Quinn poured a mug of coffee and handed it to her. Then he pulled a plate from the cabinet and cookies from a jar.

The kitchen was spacious with modern, but not sleek and expensive-looking, appliances. There was a good-sized table on one side surrounded by a half-dozen chairs. The lack of curtains or other coordinated table linens or towels announced it was a man's kitchen.

She started to take one of the chairs.

"No," he said. "Let's go into the living room. I've got a fire going."

He led her past the door and into a room of comfortable-looking chairs and a soft sofa. The furniture didn't have the stiff leather of classic Western décor, but the invitation of well-constructed and well-used pieces. The artwork on the walls, mostly western scenes, was the only thing that looked pricey.

She paused in front of one and found the tell-tale signature.

"A Charlie Russell?" she asked.

"One of two. I bought them during my visits here from Detroit. I wanted something in my apartment back there to remind me of the valley and values that mean a lot to me."

She nodded. Russell was Montana's artist. He'd been a cowboy during the brief period that was captured in television shows and movies as the "real" Old West. His paintings had captured the winter of 1886-1887, the worst for ranchers in the history of Montana, as well as the last herds of buffalo, the cowboy life, and the lives of Native Americans.

She'd always coveted one of his paintings or sculptures, but the prices were beyond her budget. The closest she had come was a postcard she'd bought in the museum in Great Falls when she went there on a trip with Quinn's parents. She'd had it framed and it still hung on her wall.

She settled in the armchair next to the small table where Quinn had set the cookies. After picking up one, she took a bite, then swiftly ate the whole thing.

"These are amazing," she said. "Where'd you get them?"

"I made them," he said.

"You?"

"I happen to like homemade cookies. I've been a bachelor for a long time. If I want homemade, it's up to me to make them."

She snagged another one, this time eating it more slowly as

she watched the flames dance in the fireplace. Shifting in her seat, she relaxed a bit into its comfortable arms.

Nearby, Quinn sipped his coffee in quiet.

The silence between them was easy … too easy.

Anxiety made her shift again.

"Thanks for the coffee and cookies," she said.

"No problem. It's a little early for you to be done with the bar, isn't it?"

"It was dead. With the storm coming, I wanted to let Paul and Olivia get a head start home. He's got a bit of a distance to drive because his house is closer to Livingston."

"His mom lives up there, doesn't she?" Quinn asked.

"Yes. Assisted living of some sort. She's got dementia."

"Hard getting old," he said.

At almost fifty, she didn't consider herself old, but her sixties and seventies were right around the corner. With the way time seemed to whizz past these days, it wouldn't take long to get there.

"It's not for the faint of heart," she said.

"No." He let silence fall again.

She stared at the fire again. This was peaceful. Some of the tension she'd been feeling since her mother's birthday party began to ease.

"I wonder if my mother is starting to have some form of it," she said.

"Why's that?"

"We had her birthday party last week. It was my sister's idea. Mom was … I don't know … almost like a child. I don't know how to describe it. She got excited at everything that happened—the small gifts, the cake …"

"Doesn't sound bad to me," he said. "We should all enjoy the little things in life more than we do."

"It wasn't just enjoyment. It was—I don't know—other than to say it was childish."

"Your mother had a hard life," he said. "I don't know everything that went on in your house. All I knew was that you were constantly at ours. I overheard my parents once or twice talking about your dad, and it didn't sound good. Perhaps your mom had the same thing growing up, then she married your dad because it was familiar. Maybe she never had the chance to be a child and is making up for lost time."

"Could be." Sophia seemed to think it was more than that, but her sister's views were skewed by her own addiction problems.

Memories flooded her brain, and she sighed.

"Want to talk about it?" he asked.

Sitting here in this warm house, with a man she'd known most of her life, she wanted to release all that misery that formed one of the hard knots in her chest. But if she let that go, what else would she wind up saying?

Was it time to start letting it go?

There was no one safer to talk to than Quinn.

She began to talk.

Chapter Thirty

Quinn put down his coffee cup and focused entirely on Anna. Her eyes were unfocused, as people's eyes often were when they were reliving a memory.

"When I was little," she said, "I was Daddy's little girl. I always wanted to be with him. Mom and Dad seemed happy, so I suppose they were. He was a plumber and always had steady work. I remember he'd frequently have a beer in his hand, but it was no big deal. And then Mom got pregnant with Bethany."

Quinn waited for her to collect her thoughts.

"Bethany wasn't planned. I'm not sure if Dad ever wanted more than one. Somehow he ended up with four of us. Bethany was a cranky kid, very demanding." A slight smile came across Anna's face. "She still is. It's a good thing her husband is happy catering to her.

"Dad began to drink more as each kid came along. There wasn't a lot of room in the house. We were two to a room before puberty hit. Then Richard got his own room, and the three of us were crammed together. By that time, Dad was drinking all the time he wasn't working. He fought with Mom all the time until she just gave up. I think he hit her. No, that's not right." She shook her head. "I *know* he hit her."

Anna looked at him with shiny eyes full of tears. "Your place was safe. Your mom and dad loved each other. I could see that. It gave me hope that two people could love each other and raise kids who thought they were wanted and loved."

A tear spilled down her cheek.

He wasn't sure whether to sit tight or get up and take her in his arms and comfort her.

She swiped at her face, then picked up her mug. After taking a drink, she shrugged. "Some of us get lucky, and some of us don't." A mask dropped over her features. "And some find bad luck no matter what they do, or how good they are."

Was she talking about herself? Or someone else?

She snagged another cookie and munched on it.

He got up and stirred the fire, more for something to do than the need of the fire.

"Can't one of your siblings help with your mother? Or maybe all of them? Take turns?" he asked.

"Doubt it," she said. "Bethany begged off from Mom's birthday because the drive was too long. She sent a pricy gift though, some kind of doodah for the kitchen Mom will never use. She's still cooking the same meals she made when we were all growing up. Easy stuff. You know: meatloaf, spaghetti, stuffed peppers. My dad always required beef for every meal. No need for fancy gadgets.

"As for Richard, once he left for college, he swore he'd never come back. He's kept that promise. He sent Mom a card. And Sophia? Sophia is a mess. She's been an alcoholic and addict since high school. She's gone to rehab numerous times and is always sober for a long time after that, but eventually she reverts. She keeps saying she's sober now and swears it's for good, but since she just called me sounding very drunk ..." Another shrug.

"So you're the responsible one."

"Not really. I'm the one left standing." She stared toward the fire. "It's time for me to step up. And that means figuring out something to do with the bar."

He hated to ask, but forced himself to. "What about your ex? Can't he help?"

"He's capable and willing, but ..." More staring.

Quinn kept quiet. While he wasn't interrogating a suspect, the practice had taught him how valuable a tool silence was when listening to someone.

She turned to face him.

"I don't want this leaving the room."

"No problem," he said.

"For the last few months someone has been stealing liquor bottles, the most expensive ones. And lately, someone has been taking money from the till."

"Brandon?"

She shook her head. "The thefts started before he showed up.

He could be responsible for the shortages, but it would be odd to have two thieves working at my place, wouldn't it?"

"It's not unheard of," he said. "But, I agree, it's rare."

"I'm not sure I trust anyone to run the place while I'm gone," she said. Straightening up, she added, "I'm going to close on Mondays. It's a slow day. Most of the time Paul and I handle it."

"Won't Paul miss the income?" Quinn asked.

"I'll give him a raise to cover it and add a little extra."

"That's good of you." His admiration for Anna rose.

"I know what it's like to live on a restaurant income. The waitresses share their tips with him, but no one is getting rich at the Buckhorn."

"Not even you?"

"Especially not me."

Like many people, Anna worked hard for her money, but things seemed stacked against the everyday people these days. For the richest nation in the world, there were a lot of barely-making-it folks. The money was going somewhere, but it wasn't going into the pockets of most of the people he'd met in his life.

He was one of the lucky ones with a strong union while he was working, and a solid pension now that he was done.

There must be some way he could help her, but she was proud, so he needed to be careful. Fortunately, there was something he could do that she would probably accept.

"Do you want me to look into your thefts?" he asked. "I may be able to see things you can't."

She hesitated.

"People shouldn't be getting away with stealing," he said.

"But what if they are poor and need the money?"

"Steal some bread, and you'd have a chance at convincing me. But not booze and money from a till. It's not like you're loaded. What's more, you treat employees and customers fairly. You're a good person, Anna. You don't deserve this."

She looked at him as if no one had ever told her she had merit before.

If her father was still alive, Quinn would have a hard time not beating him within an inch of his life.

Brandon was still within reach. He'd better not be the one

stealing.

"Okay," she finally said. "But be as discreet as you can. I haven't told anyone else about this."

"Not even Jake?"

"No. I mean, what if I was wrong, miscounted inventory or something?"

"Now you're sure it's theft," he said.

"Yes."

"How about you lend me a key and the first Monday you're closed, I'll go in and take a look."

"Okay," she said. "I don't know how to thank you."

"I do," he said. "If you have a few more minutes, I'd love to go over my plans to develop a horse sanctuary. You're a good businesswoman. Your input would be appreciated before I begin trying to raise money."

"Sure. But I don't know anything about horses, other than riding," she said.

"No problem. More coffee?"

She looked into her empty cup and nodded.

When he returned with coffee, she had her head against the back of the chair, and her eyes were closed. She looked so tired he wanted to swoop her up and tuck her into the guest bedroom.

He put the mug on the table next to her, and her eyes flew open.

"Maybe I should have requested the high-test stuff," she said with a smile.

"You're tired. We can have this discussion another time."

"No, let's talk. I'll pretend this is the real stuff and wake up enough to drive home."

"You sure?" he asked.

"Yep. Now tell me about this rescue plan of yours."

He told her his plan, the area of the ranch he wanted to dedicate to the operation, and the grant applications he'd need to write to get support for the venture. She asked some good questions, and he grabbed a pad of paper from his nearby office and took notes.

"Have you ever heard of equine therapy?" she asked.

"Vaguely. Isn't it where horses help humans?"

"Basically. By working with the horse, grooming, riding, feeding, and leading it around, a person can develop self-awareness, trust, and confidence. All kinds of people can use the help, including addicts. If you're going to work with abandoned horses and horses that are too old to do much more than stand around, you might have an ideal situation."

"But I'm not a therapist."

"No, but I bet you could work a deal with one. That would help pay for some of your expenses, and you'd be doing a good service as well."

"I'll have to look into it. It's a great idea. Has your sister done that kind of program?" he asked, wondering how Anna knew about it.

"No," she said, looking away. "I did."

Anna hadn't escaped unscathed from her father's abuse.

"I've been sober about ten years now." She turned back to him. "You don't seem surprised."

"I wondered," he said. "You always have club soda at the bar, and at community gatherings, there's usually a soda in your hand instead of a beer."

"Observant."

"A cop has to be," he said. "And I care about you."

"You do?" She seemed to shrink back.

"Well, I've known you since you were a kid. Seems only right to look out for you."

"Oh," she said. "I thought you meant something else."

He had, but chose not to tell her.

She put her cup down. "Now I need to get back home."

"I'll walk you out and help you clean off the truck."

"I can take care of it."

"Stop being so stubborn," he said. "Let me help."

"Okay."

He grabbed the broom he kept on the porch for exactly this purpose and rapidly cleared the two inches of snow that had piled on top of her windshield and hood.

"You okay to drive home?" he asked. "I've got a guest room."

"I'm a Montanan," she said with a grin. "Four wheel drive and good tires. I'm set. I've driven in worse conditions than this."

The schoolgirl she'd been shone through her at that moment. The snow falling all around them made it feel like time had stopped.

He took a step closer.

She looked up at him, her grin slowly fading.

Slowly, he leaned down and laid his lips on hers.

There was no resistance, so he deepened the kiss.

She leaned into him and explored his lips with her own.

He put his arms around her and pulled her closer. Their bulky jackets were a hindrance to the heat that rose within him.

Too fast, his brain warned him.

Suddenly she broke away, her eyes wide with conflicting emotions.

"I have to go," she said, climbing into the cab.

Within moments all he could see were her taillights as she drove down to the road.

Chapter Thirty-One

The memory of Quinn's kiss made Anna toss and turn all night. In spite of the snow, her sheets were damp when she awoke.

For a while she lay there, unable to rouse the energy to get up.

If someone had asked her what was the worst thing that could happen to her, she would have said to fall in love again.

She'd have been wrong.

The worst thing was to fall in love *with Michael Quinn* again.

If she'd had doubts about her growing feelings, the kiss had erased them. He'd initiated it, but she'd fully participated until she'd come to her senses.

The kiss was one she'd been waiting for her entire life. It was as if she'd never been kissed before.

Truth was, she hadn't. Teenage boys had been as inexperienced as she was, leading to sloppy, if sincere, results. And Brandon? His reason for kissing her was to get her into bed so he could satisfy himself. That stayed true even after they'd married.

Although he hadn't really cared whether or not she had an orgasm, he'd berated her for not letting go enough to have one. Eventually, she started faking them just to avoid the verbal abuse.

Since Brandon, she'd tried dating now and again. Kisses were perfunctory, obligations.

But last night? It was the stuff of romance novels. He'd been tentative at first, checking for her acceptance. As soon as she leaned in, he delivered the passion she'd been waiting for, without the crushing need to ramp up fast to move onto the next step.

Instead, she'd sensed the next step was up to her. His purpose wasn't immediate sex, but an exploration of the best way to love her.

Oh, how could she have been so foolish!

She wasn't good enough for the likes of Michael Quinn.

Not only was she twisted from growing up with an alcoholic

father and compliant mother, but her marriage to Brandon had been volatile. She couldn't totally blame him; her drinking had been as out of hand as his. Their fights were spectacular, more equal than their love-making had ever been. More than once, one of them had cleared the dining room table in frustration, leaving a pile of broken crockery.

It was only when she'd found she was carrying another life that she stopped cold. It hadn't been easy, but she wasn't going to do anything to hurt her child. As soon as Maddie was born, though, the siren song of alcohol had returned. It had taken a lot of time and effort to learn the difference between not drinking and being sober.

Brandon had seemed sympathetic, but more than once he disappeared for an evening, coming home in the wee hours of the morning, stinking of booze. He'd fumble for her, but pass out before anything could happen.

One time a cop had followed him home, and she'd woken to blue lights flashing in her window. Memories of the same thing happening when she was a child slammed into her heart.

It had been her first inkling that the marriage couldn't last.

But she stayed another seven years. When she found her five-year-old finishing off her father's whisky glass, she'd confronted Brandon about leaving the drink around. He'd told her she was overprotective and a little booze never hurt anyone.

When the cops finally cracked down and he had to go to jail for a weekend because he'd driven drunk, she listened to his complaints about overzealous cops.

She'd finally had enough the day she came home from shopping and found him giving Maddie a hard spanking for messing with his things.

"She has to learn!" he'd screamed.

"You need to leave!" she'd yelled back, holding her shivering child close.

He'd raised his fists, and she'd fled to her mother's without any belongings of her own. God must have been with her because Bethany was home and forced the story from her. Once her sister had gotten done with her "I never liked him anyway" speech, Bethany demanded Anna go to a lawyer. She hadn't let up until

Anna actually went.

A few weeks later she was back in her house—alone—and several months after that, she'd been divorced.

With a sigh, Anna pushed aside the covers and got up.

~ ~ ~

A few hours later, Anna pushed open the door to the Buckhorn Bar and Grill. For a few moments she stood there, taking in the space around her. Little of what she'd originally purchased was left. Tables were clean and polished, old beer and liquor signs were crack-free and gleaming, and no cobwebs grew between the antlers and horns of the game trophies.

The memories that clung to the walls were better, too. Instead of people lining the bar, destroying themselves and their relationships, holiday parties, knitters, baby and wedding showers, as well as Heather's Women Help meetings lingered in the air.

Anna had done a good thing. She'd sunk every penny she had into this place and given it hours of elbow grease. In the process she'd created a center for community.

As solid as the establishment looked, she knew from looking at the books on a constant basis, she was one mistake away from disaster. No matter how hard she worked, she didn't feel secure. Someone—anyone—could take it away from her. All they had to do was raise her taxes, her insurance, or file a lawsuit.

Was closing on Mondays going to be that disaster?

She shook the idea from her brain. Helping take care of her mother and maybe even supporting Sophia if she ever truly wanted to get sober were non-negotiable. They were family, and she felt an obligation.

It was the only move that made sense. She walked to the bar and began to set up.

Within the next half hour, Olivia and Paul came in. She got them together and said, "I hate to do this, but I need to close the bar on Mondays."

"Thank goodness," Paul said.

"It's about time," Olivia added.

"Closing one day a week doesn't bother you?" Anna asked.

"Nope," Paul said. "I've been dying for a day off."

"I'm rarely here on Mondays. Neither are the other waitresses. It won't really affect us." Olivia put her hand on Anna's arm. "You need the time off, too."

"Thanks," Anna said.

"That it?" Paul asked.

"Other than telling you both how valuable you are to me? Yes." She'd tell Paul about the raise when they were alone.

"Well, then, let's get to work," Paul said. "A day off a week! Woohoo!" he yelled out as he walked back to the kitchen.

Olivia gave her a grin and started pulling chairs off tables.

That had gone a lot easier than Anna had anticipated.

Soon people came in for lunch. The roads had been cleared early that morning, and the sun had done the rest to eradicate whatever leftover there was on the pavement. Even that brief snow must have reminded people what winter was like because there were more people in for lunch than a Thursday in mid-November warranted.

Jake came in for his usual burger. He often stopped in for lunch when he was on patrol. Anna had been counting on seeing him sometime soon.

She laid two keys next to the cup of coffee she'd poured for him. "Can you get these to Quinn?"

"Sure." Jake picked them up and pocketed them. "What's up?"

"Nothing much. I'm missing some inventory, and Quinn said he'd look into it."

"Is it something I should look into, too?"

Anna shook her head. "I want to keep it unofficial now. If it's someone who works here, I want to give them a chance to explain."

"You're a nice person," Jake said. "Just don't let them snowball you. You've worked too hard to let someone else take advantage."

"Got it," she said. "Let's see what Quinn finds and then go from there."

"Good."

Anna went down the bar to help another customer.

Once the lunch rush ended, she told Olivia she would be back in the kitchen helping Paul prep for dinner.

"Do you think we'll have the same rush?" he asked.

"Hard to tell, but from past years, this season is unpredictable. It's so dependent on the weather. A long stretch of nice days can suppress customers because people think they have time before winter sets in. A snowstorm like we had last night reminds them winter will be here soon."

"If you could get a bunch of salads ready and parse out coleslaw and potato salad into their plastic dishes, I'll get on the phone to the supplier. We're getting low on burgers and steak. I'll get as many chicken breasts as I can, but the supply is low and prices high."

"Because of the bird flu," she said.

He nodded.

"Let's limit the number of chicken dinners we serve each night. We can let the waitresses know when we've hit that limit."

"That should help."

Paul opened the walk-in freezer and took inventory while she took care of side dishes.

In less than an hour, they were all prepped.

As she went back to the bar, her phone rang.

"Hello, Brandon," she said. In spite of the years, her body always tensed when he called.

Why had she let him back into her life again? Because she'd thought she was beyond his power.

"Do you have any more hours for me?" he asked. "I could really use them. It would sure help with my sobriety."

"Don't you have another job?"

"Yeah," he said. "I stock shelves at Walmart. They are keeping me part-time. Most of us here are part-time."

It was how the service industry worked. Some companies worked the part-time angle more than others.

"I don't think I have anything coming up," she said. "I'm going to close on Mondays, and we're entering our slow season." *And I don't really trust you.*

"That's too bad. We worked together well once. It was partly my fault things got so bad, but you could dish it out, too."

"Agreed. But that's ancient history now."

"Even Maddie?"

Grief snuck up behind her and stabbed her in the back, the tip pushing right into her heart.

"You weren't around for Maddie, so you don't get to talk about her."

"I would have been if you hadn't thrown me out. It's your fault she took the path she did. She needed more discipline."

She gasped. How dare he?

"I'm sorry," he said. "I overstepped. You did a wonderful job with Maddie, I'm sure. I'm just mad at myself for not being there. I took it out on you. I shouldn't have."

She didn't know what to say next. The pain was too great.

"I know you have a business to run, but you know I could help you out. I'd even wait tables or grill burgers if that's what you need. I want to show you I've changed. I want to make up for the times I wasn't there for you and our daughter. Please give me a chance."

The door opened and a group of six people walked in.

"I've got to go," she said, grateful for the interruption. "I'll let you know. Talk to you later."

She hung up the phone and, with a smile on her face, went to greet the arrivals.

Chapter Thirty-Two

When Quinn woke up Friday morning, his first thought, as it had been a lot lately, was to wonder how Anna was doing. He hadn't heard from her since he'd seen her on Wednesday evening.

After the kiss that rocked his life.

Before then, he'd thought he was in control of his emotions. If all she wanted was friendship, then she could have it, no problem. She was his kid sister's best friend, even if decades had passed. His desire to protect had been a tradition handed down from his parents to always take care of those who needed it.

Now everything had changed. As soon as he'd touched her, he knew he'd been lying to himself. Ever since he'd moved back to Montana, he'd been aware of Anna. It was he who'd suggested that Caleb and Jake join him for weekly dinners at the Buckhorn. He'd told himself it was to keep their friendship close, but he'd always been aware of Anna's every movement around the establishment.

There'd been a half flirtation between them, but he'd always claimed it was friendship.

He could no longer lie to himself. He wanted a no-holds-barred relationship with her, to take long rides, and spend days fly fishing with her. He desired to make long slow love to her, finding out what made her feel good. He wanted to listen to her talk about her day.

Most of all, he wanted to erase the pain he saw in her eyes every time he looked at her.

He got out of bed and strode to the shower. Ted would be in soon to discuss the day. That meant Quinn had to get moving on breakfast. Maybe he'd switch it up and make a frittata this morning.

Whistling, he got in the shower and soaped up. Once the ranch chores were done, he'd investigate what was going on at the bar. Maybe he could call Anna and ask her to go to dinner with him that night to report her findings. It was going to be great now that she'd agreed to one day a week off. If she needed help with her mom, he'd drive to Butte with her.

About forty-five minutes later, he was showered, shaved, dressed, and the frittata was done. He pulled the cast-iron skillet from the oven and put it on the burner to cool.

As timely as ever, Ted came into the kitchen.

"Smells good in here," the ranch manager said as he walked inside.

"Hope it tastes good, too," Quinn said.

"You've never served me something that didn't," Ted said with a grin, pouring himself a mug of coffee.

Quinn smiled as he dished out the frittata. As a long-term bachelor, he'd learned to enjoy cooking, first for his kids when he had them, and then for friends. Feeding others built community and strengthened friendships.

"How's the grass holding up in the winter pasture?" he asked Ted once they'd each taken their first bite.

"It's strong. The snow greened it up a little. But it's not going to last forever."

The two of them hashed out the best time to add to the current supplemental hay the cattle were getting. Like his uncle before him, Quinn sold his cattle as "grass-fed," which meant the animals could only eat grass and hay. Having enough hay to last the entire winter was a judgement game. So far, he and Ted had been successful in getting enough—almost too much—hay for the winter.

Once Ted left, Quinn cleaned his kitchen, then walked down to the stables to let the horses into their corral and muck out the stalls. In effort to keep costs down, they didn't hire much help during the winter months. While the work was often hard and not always pleasant, Quinn knew that keeping active was going to keep him healthy as he moved into his later years.

It took him a few hours to complete his chores, including a pat and a carrot for Champion. He should take the horse for a ride again soon. Hopefully, Anna would come with him.

He went back to the house, cleaned up, and settled down to do some office work for an hour. Some government agency or another always needed some form filled out. At first he'd resented the constant bureaucracy, but then he'd realized they needed the information to make the right decisions for rules, regulations, and funding, including the Farm Bill.

After lunch, he'd do some more research into how to get grants for his horse sanctuary—more paperwork!—and look into the equine therapy that Anna had mentioned.

A glance at the clock told him she should be at the bar setting up by now. It wasn't the best time to ask for a date, but it wasn't the worst, either. If he didn't call now, he'd have to wait until tomorrow.

He called her number.

"Buckhorn Bar and Grill," she answered as she often did.

"It's me, Quinn," he said.

"Oh, hi."

"How are you?"

"Fine."

Fine did not bode well.

"You're still taking Monday off?" he asked.

"Yes. Oh, I sent the keys to the bar and the storeroom with Jake. He said he'd get them to you."

"I'm sure he will," Quinn said. "I'll come in on Monday and take a look around."

"Good. Anything else? It's almost time to open up."

"Actually, there is. Can I take you to dinner on Monday evening? Not everything is open in Livingston, but there are a few good restaurants. Or we could go down to Pray and eat at the lodge. The view is great from there if we get there early enough."

"I'm afraid not," she said.

"Why not?"

"Because I don't want a relationship, not with you, not with anyone. Riding and fishing are one thing. The thing the other night; that was a mistake. I'm not open to dating anyone, and dinner feels like a date."

"Yes," he said. "Dinner would be a date. I want to date you, Anna. There's something between us. You can't deny that. Not after that kiss. And it wasn't a mistake."

"That's exactly why I'm turning you down. Like I said, I

don't need anyone else in my life. I'm fine just the way I am."

"Need or want?"

"Same difference. Now, is there anything else? I really have to finish up."

"No," he said, a hollow in the pit of his stomach. "I'll let you know what I find on Monday. If you change your mind—"

"I won't. Talk to you later, Quinn." The phone went dead.

~ ~ ~

It was difficult for Quinn to concentrate on his research. Pulling the information together for a grant proposal seemed tedious at best. In addition, there seemed to be an art to writing one. Doing fancy things with words had never been his strong suit. He'd done okay as a lieutenant, but had never wanted to go higher in rank because the paperwork only seemed to increase.

Finally closing his computer, he went to the stable, saddled up Champion, and took a ride.

The bare trees, overcast skies, and slight chill suited his mood. How could she have turned him down? Was she involved with her ex? Was that what was going on?

No, she'd said she didn't want *any* relationship.

Still, he had a feeling that her reluctance had to do with Brandon. Had seeing him again made her remember how bad a relationship could be? Was that what haunted her?

She also had a child she never talked about. Were they estranged? Had the kid run away from home and Anna unable to find her? That would kill him. But if that were true, he could use his connections to help Anna find them.

Unless the child was dead.

His mind wouldn't even go there. There wasn't anything harder in the world than a parent whose child had died.

He came to an open stretch of the trail he was on and let Champion have his head. The hard gallop invigorated Quinn and lifted the cobwebs from his mind.

Whether or not Anna was open to a relationship, he needed to tend to his own life. He couldn't control her emotions. All he could do was show up and do what he'd promised to do.

As he turned back to the ranch, he let his mind wander over the information he'd read before coming out here. Slowly, he began to sort through it and formulate a plan of how to tackle the situation. If worse came to worst, he'd hire a grant writer to put things in their final format. First, he'd make a plan of how to build and maintain the sanctuary, then he'd assemble all the numbers and check them multiple times.

He could do this.

~ ~ ~

Jake showed up as Quinn was putting a steak on the grill.

"Want one?" he asked. "I've got an extra potato, too."

His friend shook his head. "Laura's got something cooking. Something healthy, she says. She's been on me about my diet. Too much red meat."

Quinn looked at his steak. "Probably. But it is Montana."

Jake laughed. He fished something out of his pocket.

"Anna said to give these to you," he said. "Something about doing some investigating. Anything I should know about?"

"What did she tell you?"

"The bare bones. She said she didn't want to involve the cops until she uncovered who was doing what."

"Probably wants to protect her ex."

Jake shook his head. "I didn't get that impression. I think if he's stealing, she'd be happy to toss him in jail."

"We'll see," Quinn said.

"How are things going between you and her?"

"They aren't. We had some good times, then, well, I asked her to dinner, and she turned me down flat. Said she didn't want to get involved in a relationship with anybody."

"That's all that happened?" Jake asked.

He'd never been able to hide much from the former detective.

"I may have kissed her."

"Yeah. That has a tendency to scare a skittish woman."

"She responded."

"Probably worse," Jake said.

"Well, what am I supposed to do?"

"I take it this means you're finally admitting you have feelings for her."

"Uh … yeah," Quinn admitted.

"Then you're just going to have to wait her out. Help her solve her theft problems and keep talking to her. No guarantees. Laura has mentioned she's always felt Anna had a lot weighing her down."

"And Laura knows this how?"

"She's an actress. She's always studying people, trying to figure out what makes them tick. I've learned to trust her judgement."

"So I can try, but I may well be doomed."

"Yep. That's about the size of it."

Quinn cursed to himself. Why did he have to love the one woman who was unavailable?

Because that's how he really felt. It was love.

Chapter Thirty-Three

By nine o'clock on Monday morning, Anna was restless. She wasn't used to having a day full of nothing streaming ahead of her. What she should do is go see her mother, but having time to do whatever she wanted had appealed so much she'd decided to postpone a trip to Butte for a week.

Now she was faced with the reality. She was an organized person, so there was no cleaning or laundry to be done. A series of freezing nights had eliminated garden chores.

She couldn't sit here all day. There was too much going on in her head.

It was only a few hours to Billings. She picked up her phone and texted Bethany. Her sister could easily ignore phone calls, but was addicted to texting.

What are you doing today? Anna typed.

Not much.

Up for a visit?

You took a day off?

Miracles occur.

Sure. Love to see you.

Anna put her phone in her back pocket, slid on a heavy jacket, and took off for Billings.

~ ~ ~

Around one o'clock, Anna pulled into the driveway of her sister's place. It was a lovely two-story home in one of the developments that had been built up on the Rimrocks. The dominant geological feature in the area, the cliffs had been carved over the centuries by the Yellowstone River. The airport stood close to the edge that overlooked the older section and downtown. Beyond the airport, newer developments had been built on what was once ranchland.

This was where Bethany and her husband, Ron, had settled and raised their two boys. One was finishing up his senior year at Billings Catholic High School, while the oldest was in his sophomore year at Eastern Montana University.

Anna carried the flowers and carrot cake she'd picked up at the Safeway on the way up to the Rimrocks. It had been a while— years—since she'd visited Bethany, and she hoped the gifts would smooth the way.

"Hi, Bethany," she said when her sister opened the door.

Bethany pushed the screen door open and practically dragged Anna inside.

"Oh my! It's so good to see you! And you brought flowers? And cake?"

"It seemed right."

Bethany shook her head. "Just having you here is enough."

Whatever reaction she thought she'd get from her sister, this wasn't it.

"Come into the kitchen." Bethany took the flowers and led the way through the modern-looking—and spotless—living room to the kitchen beyond.

"Excuse the mess, I decided to bake some bread after you called. I figured I'd send some home with you. I also have canned tomatoes, pickled green beans, and some garlic. Now put that cake down and let me give you a proper greeting."

Somewhat numb from the unexpected warmth of Bethany's welcome, Anna did as she was told. Seconds later, Bethany enveloped her in a big hug. At first Anna stiffened, then she tried her utmost to relax.

"I'm guessing you're no longer a hugger," Bethany said.

Anna shrugged. "It's not something I'm comfortable doing."

Bethany tilted her head. "I seem to remember you used to hug me, Sophia, and Richard—at least as long as he'd let you."

"Yeah. That was then."

Bethany seemed ready to ask another question, but clapped her mouth shut.

"Tea or coffee?" Bethany asked. "I have some sodas, too, if you want."

"Coffee's fine."

Bethany nodded and prepared the coffee in a gleaming stainless steel contraption. Then she pulled out a cake plate and slid the carrot cake onto it before cutting precise wedges and putting them on matching dessert plates.

"This looks wonderful. I'm going to have to work out an extra half hour tomorrow morning to make up for it."

"What gym do you belong to?" Anna asked, feeling at sea in this world so different from her own. She'd never had to worry about weight. Waitressing or owning a bar had kept her figure in line. Maddie had been an active child as well. Even if it had been a problem, what did it matter? She had no interest in impressing a man.

"None," Bethany replied. "We have exercise equipment in the basement, along with a big screen TV. There are a lot of exercise programs that we can get online. Ron's really dedicated to keeping himself fit, which makes it easier for me to pay attention to myself."

Anna nodded and picked up her fork. If she stuffed her mouth with food, she wouldn't inadvertently say something stupid or rude.

"What made you take a day off?" Bethany asked. "Who's taking care of the bar while you're here?"

"I decided to close on Mondays. Mom's getting a little vague, and Sophia wanted some help. There's no one else who can manage the business, and Mondays are slow, so it made sense to close then."

"Meaning you couldn't find anyone you could trust."

"It's hard for me to hand over my business to someone else."

Bethany got up to pour two mugs of coffee.

"Mom appreciated your birthday card," Anna said.

"I'm glad."

Taking the mug from her sister, Anna sipped her coffee, trying to figure out how to continue the conversation without stepping on any landmines.

"Sorry I couldn't get up for the party," Bethany said. "I was really busy, and it's a long drive."

"No problem," Anna said. "It was a short party. Some of her friends came over. They were cute." The party had been a little strange, but her sister didn't need to know that.

Bethany picked up her coffee mug, looked into it, then put it back down.

"No," she said. "That's not the truth. I didn't want to go to the party. I can't stand being around Mom, and Sophia's not much better."

"I get Sophia, but why Mom? She was always nice to us."

"She was … still is … weak. She's really good at playing the victim. She never hurt us, but she didn't help us either. And she stayed with him. Even though Dad wasn't nice to her, she stayed."

"I don't think she had much choice," Anna said, her emotions developing a slow burn of anger. "There were four of us, and she had no marketable skills that I knew of." She paused. "And it wasn't just that Dad wasn't nice to her. He belittled her and hit her."

"And she let him."

Anna started to speak, but Bethany held up a hand.

"I know," Bethany said. "Victims of domestic abuse have a hard time getting out from under it. Their confidence has been undermined. They're afraid. Heck, after you three left, *I* was afraid."

Anna hadn't thought at all about her youngest sister being left alone in that household. Guilt made her nerves tingle.

"By that time, though, Dad changed. He settled into the recliner most nights, and that was that. On Saturday mornings, he used to take me out for breakfast. We'd talk about a lot of things, especially his life when he was younger, before marrying Mom. I got the impression he hadn't expected to become a father as soon as he did."

"That's not an excuse,"

"I know it isn't. People should step up to their responsibilities. And he did what he could. We were never hungry."

"Sorry," Anna said. "I don't have quite the same picture as you do."

"That's because you were the oldest. In your own ways, you each protected me, but we were never close, the four of us."

"Too much turmoil," Anna said.

"You escaped to the Quinns, Richard withdrew to his studies, and Sophia disappeared into drugs."

"What did you do?"

"I made lists of the qualifications I needed from any man I would ever marry. I was really, really careful. I know you think I married Ron for his earning potential, and that was part of it. But we genuinely love each other. We just do it without all the drama our family is used to."

Anna looked around the kitchen. To have this stability as well as a man who loved her must be heaven. For the first time, she was jealous.

"What would happen if he died, or left you? I know you don't think that can happen, but I've seen it too much."

"First of all, he has a great life insurance policy," Bethany said, seemingly unperturbed by the question. "Second, he knows I'd cut him into narrow ribbons if he ever looked at another woman that way. Third, I have my own income, almost as much as Ron's."

"You do? How?"

"I write cozy mysteries," Bethany said with a grin.

"And that makes you a lot of money?"

Bethany nodded, her grin spreading across her face. "I've got a very popular character who helps seniors downsize, and solves mysteries on the side."

"Good for you!" Anna had had no idea her sister was that talented.

"I started when the boys were small, just to keep myself sane. It was just pin money in the beginning, but they took off."

"I really am glad for you."

"Thanks."

They sat in silence for a few moments.

"That means I have some extra money to pitch into taking care of Mom," Bethany said.

"I thought you didn't like her," Anna said.

"I don't, but that doesn't mean I'm going to walk away from my responsibility. I'm sure Mom's enabling Sophia the same way she did Dad. I'm afraid I can't deal with that. I'd do more harm than good if I were there. But I can, and I will, provide financial support so she can get the care she needs. Plus, I know how to navigate social security and Medicare. Ron's dad had dementia for years before he passed. I handled a lot of the phone calls and arrangements while Ron worked."

It sounded like Bethany and her husband had a good partnership along with everything else. Was this what love was supposed to look like? Her relationship with Brandon had never gotten close to this idea.

"I'm sure Richard will help, too."

"Why do you say that? I barely get a Christmas card," Anna said.

"We text a lot," Bethany confessed. "One time when Ron and I were in San Francisco, we stopped by his apartment." She gave Anna a strange look. "You know he's gay, don't you?"

What?

"Gay?" Anna repeated.

"You were in your own little world. Richard had some problems in high school because some of the bullies tormented him. Dad didn't help. They used to have knock-down arguments with Dad yelling that no son of his … Well, you get the gist."

"I had no idea."

"I understand. I've had a bunch of therapy over my life. We did what we had to do to survive. I'm glad you had the Quinns. Do you hear from them anymore?"

Now there was a question.

"Michael lives in the same town as my bar," Anna said, hoping to sound casual. "His uncle died a few years back and left him his ranch. Michael had retired from the Detroit Police Force by then and decided to move to Montana. He brought a couple of friends with him."

"Still have that crush on him?"

"How did you know about that?"

"Oh, please. You didn't say much, but when you did talk about the Quinns, he was always the main topic of conversation."

"That was a long time ago. We're just friends now. He and his buddies come into the Buckhorn once a week to have dinner."

"And that's it?"

Anna took another bite of her cake.

Bethany laughed. "That is so not it. Spill. What's going on?"

"Nothing."

"Liar."

How did this sibling, the one she'd spent the least amount of time with, know her so well?

"We took a couple of horseback rides," Anna said. "And he taught me to fly fish. But that's all over now."

"For heaven's sake, why?"

"I don't want a relationship, and I think he does."

"You're not still pining over Brandon are you? If so, you need to get your head examined. He was bad news."

"Brandon's working for me now," Anna said. She was so anxious to change the topic away from Quinn she didn't think about the landmine she was stepping into. "Well, not all the time. Just when I need him."

"You don't need him in any way, shape, or form," Bethany said. "He never treated you well, even in the beginning. It reminded me of Mom and Dad. Brandon would put you down, and you'd go along with it."

"I was young and in love," Anna said.

"You were young and damaged," Bethany said. "Instead of finding a marriage like the one Quinn's parents had, you took the one that was most comfortable because it was familiar. You never gave yourself the time to figure out who you were and what you wanted."

"Like you?" Even though what Bethany said might have been right, it was annoying.

"I was lucky," Bethany said. "There was an innovative program that put a therapist into the school. She spent a long time talking to me. She'd seen the three of you go through school and figured out there was something going on at home that wasn't good. She encouraged me to keep a journal, and she'd point out that Mom and Dad had a whole lot of dysfunction going on."

Anna didn't know what to say to that. Bethany seemed intent on picking apart Anna's life, and she wasn't comfortable with it.

"I'm sorry," Bethany said, surprising her. "I just hate to see you hurting, or letting an opportunity for happiness pass you by. I'll let it drop, but if you ever want to talk, I'm here."

"Thanks." Anna grasped the safest topic at hand. "How are

the boys?"

Bethany happily talked about her kids, both of whom were doing well. They were involved in lots of activities. Then she talked about the vacation they were all taking to Hawaii in February.

"By February, I need a break from the cold and snow."

Anna nodded. Flying to the tropics seemed like a dream to her. She'd be in Willow Creek, shoveling snow.

They finished their cake and coffee. After they cleaned up, Anna found herself agreeing to keep in touch, and Bethany reiterated her commitment to help out financially.

When she went to leave, Anna leaned into the hug her sister demanded.

Bethany had turned into a much better person than Anna had thought she was.

The chill hit Anna as soon as she stepped out the door. It had a bite to it that usually meant snow. She looked up at the sky, the clouds confirming her hypothesis.

No snow had been in the forecast when she'd set out.

She got in her truck and pulled up her weather app. Sure enough, a significant chance of snow had suddenly appeared, high winds pushing the cold down the Rocky Mountain Front to mix with the moist air that had settled onto the plains the week before. The forecasters were predicting several inches and the wind had already picked up across the plains.

She turned on the car and pulled out. Hopefully, she'd make it to Willow Creek before the storm got too bad.

Snowflakes began to fall even before she got on I-90. Normally, she enjoyed this drive where the highway wound next to dramatic earth sculptures carved by the Yellowstone River. Now, as she watched the flakes begin to stick to the grasses along the side of the road, her nerves became taut.

She'd been driving in Montana all her life, in good weather and bad. Her tires were good and she had four-wheel drive. There were no mountain passes to speak of between here and home. Everything should be just fine.

Then why did she have this feeling of foreboding?

~ ~ ~

For the next hour the snow increased in intensity as she gained altitude, adding inches to the highway and deeper snow in the fields that lined the road. The wind speed increased, blowing the flakes into a kaleidoscope of swirling white. Traffic slowed. Like every other Montana driver, she was grateful for the tall reflectors that lined both sides of the road.

Most people moved to the right lane of the interstate, staying a healthy distance behind the car or truck in front of them. Every once in a while, a sleek car would pass, the driver thinking themselves invincible against Mother Nature.

More than one of them ended up in a ditch.

She should pull off in Big Timber and get a room.

Hotels were expensive. So was eating out. No, better to keep pushing forward. As long as she kept at it slow and steady, she'd be okay.

She was about ten miles from the Big Timber exit when it happened.

A few vehicles in front of her, a semi began to swerve, its rear end slipping from one side of the lane to the other, the arc increasing with each rotation.

Immediately, she took her foot off the gas to increase the distance between her and the small red car in front of her. The driver in front of her must be blind because he kept to his too narrow distance behind the semi.

She wouldn't follow any vehicle that close even in good weather.

Maybe the semi driver would get it under control.

It took another mile, but the inevitable happened. The truck jackknifed, bending around both ends of the highway to land on its side, blocking both lanes.

The red car slammed on its brakes, before beginning the slide toward the truck's wheels, still spinning darkly in the white snow.

She'd been able to pull back, but not enough. Even if the red car managed to avoid totaling itself on the overturned vehicle, she didn't have enough runway to stop. If she hit him, the driver would die or at least be seriously injured.

She swung the wheel hard to the right managing to keep the truck straight as she plowed off the highway, slamming into a hidden boulder, and landing in a high drift. The snow around her immediately crumbled, almost covering her truck. The windshield wipers did little good, so she turned them off with trembling hands.

She could have died. Worse, she could have been responsible for other people being seriously hurt or dying. She'd never be able to bear that. No one needed their lives ended like that, especially not if she was to blame.

Part of her knew she wasn't the cause of the accident, but her mind kept replaying all the horrible things that could have gone wrong. She took in a long, shuddering breath. When she let it out, tears spilled out of her eyes. She let herself cry for a while, knowing it was shock driving the emotion.

Her stomach twisted with nausea.

She had to get ahold of herself.

Stupid red car driver. He could have gotten them both killed. Had he made it?

Would she make it? Could anyone see her here?

She grabbed her cell phone. Good, she had bars.

Someone had probably already called 911.

She shivered as the cold began to seep in through the windows and seams of the truck. With any luck, she wouldn't freeze out here. Like every good Montana driver, she had things stowed in the back part of her cab just for situations like this.

But first, she needed to get out and look things over.

With a shove, she managed to get the door open and jumped down into a few feet of snow, some of which found its way into the tops of her boots. She shivered. She'd dressed for a cool fall day, not winter. A down jacket would be nice about now, but she'd left it at home.

Coming to the back of the truck, she could see a few people standing on the edge of the road. One of them was looking her way. She started trudging up the slope, curiosity overriding common sense. A man in a Carhartt coat—now there was someone dressed for the weather—waved at her and shook his head.

Making a megaphone with his hands, he yelled, "Keep warm in your truck. Emergency vehicles are on their way! We'll let them know you're down there."

She nodded and yelled back, "Thanks!"

After making sure her tailpipe was clear of snow, she got back into her truck and turned the engine on for a few minutes to help warm it up while she pulled a blanket, snacks, and some water from where they were stowed in the back seat. When the cab had heated, she wrapped the blanket around her and turned off the truck.

Then she waited.

Not planning a stop, she hadn't brought a book with her. No point in turning on the radio, it would only drain the battery. The same for watching videos or listening to music on her phone.

No, she was good and stuck here with only her thoughts to keep her company.

She had to admire Bethany's determination to do what was best for herself.

What would her life have been like if she'd given her relationship with Brandon an ounce of critical thought? Looking back, she could see what Bethany meant about him. He'd always gotten his little digs in, and she'd always excused him. There were times she thought he must be right, other times when she decided he was tired from working too hard, or had had a little too much to drink.

Problem was he'd always had a little too much to drink, or too many drugs, or too much something.

She'd never stood up for herself, and she'd never gone after the thing that she'd told herself she wanted most when she was a kid: a steady, secure family like the Quinns.

Decades later, Michael Quinn was offering her a second chance, and she'd turned him down. Why exactly? Because she was too afraid to take a chance? Or was Brandon doing his work again, somehow undermining her belief in herself.

Was she going to spend the rest of her life alone?

If she did, it was going to be her own fault.

Someone rapped on her window.

Startled, she turned to find a man in a firefighter's suit

standing there. She rolled down the window.

"We're here to get you out," he said. "I'll take you up there and have the EMTs check you out. Once the tow truck gets here, we'll tow you back to the road. Sound good?"

"Sounds wonderful."

Chapter Thirty-Four

"There's a rumor going around that you're creating a sanctuary for old and abused horses," Jose Diaz said to Quinn.

Quinn was at the Diaz house that Wednesday evening for a meeting to make sure everyone in town had a place to go or enough food for a true Thanksgiving event. The group had been in existence for a few years before he'd moved back to Montana. Until he'd joined, he hadn't realized how pervasive poverty was.

"The rumor's true," Quinn said. "I've been working on estimates and grant applications."

"If you ever need any help with that, I know someone who works on grants for non-profits," Jose said. "It would cost you some money, but she knows the right way to craft the final result."

"Sounds wonderful," Quinn said. "Let me have her info. Writing wasn't ever my strong suit, and when I try to follow what they're asking, I keep having the feeling I'm missing something."

"Or someone?" Ken Greenbriar joined them. "What's up with you and Anna?"

"Nothing," Quinn said. "We're old friends, nothing more than that."

"She'll be here later," Jose said. "She told me she wanted to make sure whoever is filling in for her was set before she left the bar."

Quinn had to keep from scowling. The person filling in had to be Anna's ex. Quinn had spent a chunk of time at the bar on Monday but hadn't uncovered any clues to point to who was stealing from Anna. His gut instinct told him it had to be her ex, but he didn't have the proof.

Yet.

The front door opened, letting in Heather and Riley.

"It looks like everyone's here," Jose said. "Let's get started, okay?"

As they settled around the spacious dining table, Elana, Jose's wife, came into the room, bearing several glasses of iced tea on a tray.

"I figure you will all be talking so much, you'll need something to drink," she said with a smile as she set the tray on the table.

"Thank you," Ken said. He helped her pass out glasses.

"I'll bring out a snack in a little while," she said, then left the room.

Jose's gaze followed his wife's graceful figure as she walked away.

The love in that gaze made Quinn's heart ache.

"Let's get started," Jose said.

There were nods around the table. Heather took out a notebook and pen. "I'll be happy to take down some notes," she said.

"Thanks," Jose said. "Anna has always offered her establishment to lonely friends and acquaintances. This year, I think we should also have a dinner at the community center in the new housing development."

The small grouping of tiny homes and multi-unit buildings, included a multi-purpose building with offices for mental health workers, substance abuse counselors, and financial advisors, as well as space for a subsidized day-care center. While many of the older residents had disabilities of some sort that impeded them from getting a job, some of the younger families had simply fallen on hard times and needed a hand up.

"That sounds good," Riley said. "We might be able to have room to get some people who don't think the community is for them. You know the people who are barely hanging on, but too proud to admit there's a problem."

"Good idea," Ken said. "I'll provide the turkeys you need, as well as soft drinks, tea, and coffee. The attendees can fill in with side dishes and desserts. That will make them feel like it's their Thanksgiving and they aren't getting a handout."

"How about a sign-up sheet so we don't get five sides of mashed potatoes and no green bean casseroles?" Heather asked.

"Someone *always* brings a green bean casserole," Quinn said. "Just like there's that one person who brings a Jello salad."

The group chuckled.

"What about the group that shows up at Anna's?" Riley asked.

"She usually covers that," Jose said. "I think she supplies the turkey and drinks. The rest is potluck."

"She won't accept any other help," Heather said. "We've offered in the past, but she turns us down. Most of the people who show up there are lonely more than they are poor."

A wave of sorrow hit Quinn. Being lonely was its own type of poverty.

"It's her major give-back to people," Heather said. "Even though she does so much for the community already."

That was true. Anna was always as generous as she could be to everyone … except herself.

Once again, he wondered what she was punishing herself for.

"I'll talk to her," Ken said. "I think she does a sign-up list for the dishes people are bringing. I'll let her know I'll help fill in what's missing."

"You can try," Heather said. "But she's pretty stubborn about the whole thing."

"Hear you." Ken's smile stretched across his face. "I'll be my most charming self for her."

"That leaves the people who have families or places to go in town, but don't really have much money to splurge on extra groceries."

"Food is getting so expensive," Jose said. "At least, that's what Elana keeps telling me."

"With most of the county working service jobs or on ranches, a lot of them aren't making much more than minimum wage," Quinn said. "I don't know how they make that work."

"Somehow they do," Jose said. "That's why we need to give them a helping hand for the extras."

Quinn suddenly felt far wealthier than he'd ever felt before. A lot of what he took for granted, like his pension, retirement fund, and the gift of a fully-paid off ranch, were beyond the reach of most of the people he knew.

He needed to stop taking it for granted.

There was a knock on the front door before it opened.

"Hello!" Anna called out.

"In here," Jose yelled back.

"Sorry I'm late," she said, her gaze immediately landing on Quinn before circling around the group. "What did I miss?"

As she sat next to Riley, Jose caught her up to speed.

"Ken's offered to help fill in things you need for the meal you host at your place," Jose said.

"I'm—" Anna interrupted herself, then took a deep breath. "Let me think about that," she said. "It's very generous."

"No problem. We're doing well. Winnie and I agree sharing our abundance with the community is the right thing to do."

"Thank you," Anna said.

"We were about to talk about getting extra food to those who may not have enough to have a big feast with lots of leftovers," Jose said.

"I can put a donation can on the bar," Anna said.

"That's a great idea," Riley said. "I can do it at the coffee shop, too."

"I bet if you ask the other shops to do the same, they would," Heather said.

"I'll do that," Riley said.

Heather made a notation in her book.

"My manager, Ted, and a few others go turkey hunting this time of year," Quinn said. "I wonder if they'd be willing to donate a few birds to the effort."

"Wild turkey is really good," Jose said. "I should go out, too. Of course, I'll have to do everything I can to make it look like it came from Ken's place before Elana will accept it."

Laughter greeted the statement.

"I've got several big pots for brining at my place," Quinn said. "That's supposed to be really good for wild turkeys. I can be in charge of making them look as supermarket ready as possible." He grinned, glad to find a niche where he could contribute.

"How do we know who needs what?" Jose asked.

"I can handle that," Heather said. "I've got spies everywhere."

"Delivery?" Ken prompted.

"Like zucchini," Heather said. "Put the stuff on the porch,

ring the bell, and run as fast as you can. No one ever leaves food, even zucchini, on the porch."

Everyone at the table grinned.

Like Quinn, he'd bet every one of them had gotten vegetable leftovers from people's gardens.

After a little more discussion, the meeting broke up.

Quinn made his way over to Anna.

"Hi," he said.

"Hi, yourself," she said back. She picked up her jacket.

Without thinking, he helped her get it on.

Briefly, she stiffened, then let him assist her.

"I was wondering," he said, "if I could get a seat at your Thanksgiving table. Jake and Laura are going to her folks in Iowa, and Caleb and Destiny are heading to their families in Detroit."

"No problem," she said. "Love to have you."

He gave her a glance. Her tone was a far cry from how she'd treated him when he'd asked her to dinner.

They left the house together.

"Did you find anything at the Buckhorn?" she asked.

"Nothing that points to who might be stealing from you. I did find scratches on the back door that looked like someone jimmied the lock. And the lock you have on the storeroom is so flimsy it could be opened by a credit card. I suggest you replace that lock and add a deadbolt to the back."

"That makes sense. So it could be an outside job? It might not involve anyone working for me?"

"Hard to tell at this point. Someone had to know where you kept the liquor. As for the shortages at the till, I don't see how that can be anything but an inside job."

Her shoulders slumped.

"Sorry," he said. "I know that wasn't what you wanted to hear."

He let a few moments of silence pass as they walked toward her pickup.

"Can you write down a list of everything that's gone missing and when it happened?" he asked her.

"I think I can. I didn't take notes right at the beginning, thinking I'd forgotten what I did with a bottle, but as it continued,

I started to keep track."

"Good." He frowned. "Was your bumper bent like that before?"

"No. I had an accident on the way back from seeing my sister in Billings on Monday."

"Are you okay? What happened?" It was hard to resist the urge to check her over and make sure she wasn't injured.

"Yes. I was able to avoid the worst of it." She told him about the truck jackknifing and a small car that had smashed into the truck, as well as her efforts to avoid it that landed her in a snowbank.

"The pickup hit a boulder on the way down, but it only slowed me down. They got me out pretty quickly. The wait was for them to clear enough space around the trailer for the traffic to go around the wreck."

"Any injuries?"

"Truck driver and the guy in the red car. Thankfully, no one died and the injuries weren't too severe."

"I'm glad you're all right," he said.

"So am I." She looked at him and touched his arm. "It gave me time to think, and really take stock of what I'm doing."

"And?"

"And I'm sorry I was so rude to you. Frankly, I'm a mess. I … well … I don't know if I can really have a relationship, or why anyone would want me. But if you wanted to ask me out again, I wouldn't say no."

The air in his lungs expanded, and lightness filled him.

"How about tonight? Come to my house, and I'll grill up some of the trout I've caught."

"I shouldn't." She took a deep breath. "But since Brandon's already at the bar, and he's begging me for more hours, I'm going to say yes."

He smiled.

"Six o'clock?" he asked.

"Sounds good. Should I bring anything?"

"Just yourself. That will be enough."

It would be more than enough.

Chapter Thirty-Five

Anna drove to the bar to make sure everything was still running smoothly. She was taking her hands off the steering wheel, and she wasn't sure the other people could drive. Wednesday evenings were an unknown. Mondays were always slow, and Tuesdays were when groups had meetings at the Buckhorn. It was also the day women came in to knit, plan showers, or have lunch.

Thursdays were the ramp-up to the weekend.

But Wednesdays? They were always a mystery. They could be as dead as a Monday or as crazy as a Friday night.

In her time alone in the truck on the snowy side of the highway, she'd had plenty of time to think. If she hadn't managed to avoid the accident, the man in the red car would definitely have died. There was also a good chance she'd have been critically injured, or worse.

What would she have to show for her life? A failed marriage, a dead child, a business, and no one who loved her. That wasn't a life; it was an obit.

She'd determined she had to change her ways. That meant releasing her clutch on the business and maybe opening her heart a little bit.

Tonight she was going to try to do both.

She pulled into her space at the Buckhorn and walked around to the back. No one would be expecting her to come in that way.

Surprisingly, there were fresh tracks in the lingering snow by the back door. Crouching down, she saw they were large footprints. Definitely a man's shoe. Paul's feet were small—she'd noted it on more than one occasion.

That left Brandon … or someone else.

The door was locked, and she opened it. On the other side she could see small puddles on the floor. As she walked toward the front, she checked the storage room door. It wasn't locked.

Maybe someone had simply come in the back way. It would make sense except no one else had a back door key. On an impulse, she opened the storage room door.

"Oh, it's you," Brandon said.

"Who else would it be?" she asked. She gestured for him to leave the storage area, closed and locked the door, but not before noting the damp spots on the floor of the storage room.

"Well, you're the one who keeps saying things are missing," he said. "I thought it might be the robber. I know I didn't take anything, and I doubt the waitresses have time. So that leaves an outsider."

"How's business this afternoon?" she countered.

"C'mon, Anna. You can trust me. I wouldn't steal from you. You're working too hard. Everyone agrees on that. Maybe you're only imagining things are missing."

She'd thought the same thing herself at times. Maybe he was right.

Except Michael thought someone had been in there.

She looked at Brandon's shoes.

The tops were dry as a bone. How long had he been in the storage area before she arrived? Long enough for his shoes to dry?

Or maybe it wasn't him at all.

"How's business?" she repeated, brushing past him to get to the bar area. On her way past the kitchen, she stuck her head in and asked Paul, "Things going okay?"

"Nice, steady crowd," he said. "Everyone's glad the snow is over."

"For now," she said.

"Right." He flipped a couple of burgers.

She continued to the bar, crossed to the register, and ran a total.

Not bad, but she'd expected more from the number of customers in the place.

Brandon and Olivia were the only two authorized to work the register.

She should stay and figure out what was going on, but she'd promised Quinn—and herself—that she'd have dinner with him.

"Can you finish up the night?" she asked Brandon.

"Sure. Where are you going?"

"Having dinner with a friend," she said.

"A male friend?"

"Not any of your business."

"Definitely a man. While I'm happy you're having fun, I … well … I'd hoped there might be a second chance for us."

What?

"No one knows you like I do," Brandon said. "We could be happy again. Get over the past, and finally bury Maddie together, like we should have."

She stabbed her finger in his chest. "Don't you ever mention her name again to me. You hear that? You weren't around when she died, so you have nothing to say. Just do your job here, make sure you're not slipping any bills from the till, and we'll be fine."

She spun away and walked down the hallway to the back door.

How dare he?

~ ~ ~

By the time Anna got to Quinn's, her rage had reduced its grip on her muscles, but left her feeling drained. The image of Maddie, the last time she'd seen her at the morgue, had resurfaced from where Anna thought she'd buried it.

She thought about calling Quinn and cancelling, but was driven by a need to see him, an urge she didn't understand, but decided to trust. He had always treated her with respect and kindness. She could use a little of that now.

He'd told her to come to the kitchen door and walk in when she arrived. In the mudroom, she kicked off her shoes and padded into the kitchen.

He looked up from the vegetables he was sautéing and turned off the flame. Striding to her, he placed his hands on her arms.

"What's wrong?" he asked. "Did someone hurt you?"

She was horrified to feel a tear trickle down her cheek.

He gently tugged her to him.

She was stiff at first, but once the tears started, she couldn't turn them off. It was comforting to simply lay her head on his chest and cry.

His arms surrounded her, and he rocked her like a mother would a young child who'd scraped her knee.

The image of Maddie resurfaced, followed by others, snippets of a life cut too short. It was her fault her daughter was dead. If only she'd done more, known more. If only she'd had the right tools or the words to say that would have turned Maddie from her destructive path.

She sobbed until Michael's shirt was wet beneath her cheek.

When she began to quiet, he led her to a chair and fetched a cup of coffee for her. When he placed it in front of her, he said, "It's decaf. Or, if you like, I have club soda, or some non-alcoholic beer."

"I thought you drank the real thing," she said.

"I got it for you," he said.

If she hadn't been all cried out, she would have started again. "Coffee's fine," she said.

He nodded, poured them both a cup, and sat down next to her.

"It might be good if you talked about it," he said.

"I never have before."

"This is as good a time as ever." His smile was sweet as he placed his hand over hers. "It's a safe space. No judgements. Promise."

She looked into his eyes to gauge his truthfulness.

Kindness and concern was all she could read.

"Maddie was my daughter," she began. "She was the sweetest thing. We'd cuddle together and watch old movies. She had trouble reading, so we'd lay in bed and go over her letters and sounds. She'd help in the kitchen. But she was also Daddy's little girl and thought the moon and sun hung on Brandon."

She broke for a sip of coffee, and Michael let the silence linger.

"His alcoholism got worse. I no longer partied with him—someone had to stay home with our daughter. I know he had affairs, although he denied it. He also started dealing drugs—low level—but we argued about it. Finally, I told him to leave. Maddie was about seven at the time. She was devastated."

Michael gave her hand a squeeze, but still didn't say anything.

Anna drew in a deep breath.

"Somehow I made it work. I got as many lunch shifts as I could. Brandon threw some money my way when he was flush, but there wasn't anything regular about it. A friend took Maddie when I had to work evenings—usually Fridays and Saturdays. That's where the big money was."

"I was a good mother … at least I thought I was."

She drank more of the coffee.

"Maddie got into trouble for the first time when she was about twelve. She was caught with some older girls shoplifting in a drugstore. I had to go to the police station to get her. I don't know how to describe it … humiliation? Fear? It scarred something in my soul." She looked up at him. "Of course, you're used to bars and locks. I felt like I couldn't breathe."

"I'm sorry," he said. "Even though I was around jails, I know what you're talking about. It's supposed to invoke those feelings. It's when people don't have those feelings, when they become used to it, then they keep winding up back with us because it becomes the only home they've known."

"That's sad."

"Yep." He picked up her cup, refilled it, and brought it back to her. "What happened next? Did she learn?"

Anna shook her head. "She got into marijuana first, and started skipping school. I spent a lot of time on the phone with administrators, but they didn't seem too invested in helping her. If she wasn't there, she wasn't causing them problems. It was my headache. I tried everything I could—tough love, letting her know how much I loved her, getting a tutor, therapy." She tried to smile. "I even went to church."

"Nothing helped," he said.

"No. I think she was doomed from the start. She had parents with alcoholic bloodlines, and drugs are just too easy for kids to get their hands on. But I continued to try: programs, alternative schools, more therapy. Nothing changed her trajectory. My beautiful little girl became gaunt, her skin blotchy, and her eyes bloodshot." Anna's throat closed with grief, and she drank more coffee.

"She ran away from home at around sixteen," Anna

continued. "By that time, I was so exhausted, I just let her go. My spirits would go up whenever she called, but besides praying to whatever god was listening, I couldn't do much. I didn't have money to hire a private detective." Guilt flooded her. "It was almost a relief not to have her around, not to have to watch her throw a wrecking ball at her life. Somewhere around eighteen, she did a stretch in Deer Lodge for theft, but even that didn't turn her around."

Anna's heart ached so much, she didn't think she could continue.

Michael squeezed her hand. "Tell me the rest. It's time to let it all out."

She looked down at her hands. Somehow they'd started to age--a few spots, roughened knuckles. At best guess she was past the mid-point of her life. Michael was right. She needed to let go of this burden. She could no longer carry it alone.

"I hadn't heard from her in a while. She'd gotten into heavier drugs. I'd heard she was in a shelter in Billings, panhandling, and doing who knows what to get her fix. I went to find her. It took a while, but as big as it is, Billings is a small town. She was in this horrible apartment. Half the walls were gone, leaving only studs, sleeping bags on the floor, dishes in the sink. Her face was drawn and her eyes wouldn't focus. She seemed to be in a great deal of pain."

Anna had to take a deep breath. It felt like she had no air left.

"She wouldn't come home with me. Didn't want to go to rehab. She claimed she was happy." Anna shook her head. "I didn't understand the power of drugs until I saw her like that. They had taken her away from me. There was nothing I could do. Nothing."

Michael held her hand, but didn't say anything.

She took another deep breath.

"A few weeks later a policeman called me. She'd been found dead in that apartment. I … I had to go identify her. There was my baby girl, lying in a morgue. She was gone. And she was so young, so very young."

There were no tears left. Anna was empty.

They sat there silently for a few moments.

"I'm so sorry," Michael said. "No mother deserves to go through that."

"I should have found a way … It's all my fault."

"No." Michael shook his head. "You did everything you could. I've seen this scenario play out before. As you just said yourself, there was nothing you could do. Until the person decides they want a different life, nothing will change for them."

"It's those people who bring drugs into the country."

"Yes, that's a big part of the problem, just like the ease of getting alcohol fuels alcoholics. I'm not saying we give up the fight to make things better than they are right now and give young people more of a chance to make sure they don't get hooked in the first place." He paused. "All I'm telling you is it isn't your fault. You did the best you could. I know you. You aren't someone who gives up easily. It's time to let go, to forgive yourself, and maybe forgive her."

A little bit of the stone she'd carried for so long cracked off, giving her hope that someday, maybe not too far away, she could do exactly as Michael was asking and forgive herself, and Maddie.

Chapter Thirty-Six

Anna's alarm went off early Thanksgiving morning. Ice etched the corners of the windows in her bedroom, so she hid under the blankets for a few more minutes.

Her world had changed since the night she'd told Quinn about her daughter. Impossibly, she felt lighter. Although she hadn't completely absolved herself, the guilt had lessened.

He'd come in several afternoons when the bar was slow, to have a cup of coffee with her and talk. They didn't discuss anything earth-shattering, but told tales that helped them know each other even better. She understood how much effort he'd put into his job as a police officer, and she'd told him how much sacrifice she'd had to make to save for an establishment like the Buckhorn. It had been perfect, run-down enough with a tired owner who was willing to sell for a bargain price and a percentage of profits for the first two years of her ownership.

Sometimes they talked of the town, gossiping like two old biddies.

Always, she felt at ease around him.

On Monday he'd gone to Butte with her, dropping her at her mother's while he ran some errands and checked in with his siblings who still lived in the city.

She'd had lunch with her mother and Sophia, who appeared to be back on the wagon. After lunch, as their mother dozed in a living room chair, she and her sister had coffee in the kitchen and talked about options for their mother's care. Sophia had good ideas and was willing to do the legwork. She was pleased when Anna told her Bethany was willing to kick in some money to help insure their mother had adequate care.

If only Sophia could be like that all the time.

When Anna had finished with her visit, Quinn had picked her up and taken her home, stopping for a pleasant dinner in Livingston.

This intense time together had left her torn.

All the feelings she'd ever had for Michael Quinn returned, only with a more mature feeling than a school-girl crush. She didn't quite dare to call it love. That was a word she'd used too easily with Brandon. That love had been crazy-making.

What she felt for Quinn was anything but. She felt safe with him, wanting to be his friend and make him happy, but not at a huge cost to herself.

It would take someone smarter than she was to figure out if that was love.

Taking a deep breath, she tossed off the covers and raced to the bathroom to start her day.

~ ~ ~

By eight o'clock, she, Chloe, and Kiara were hard at work. Sue and Olivia were with their families. Chloe's family lived in Pennsylvania. Kiara's folks had gone to Browning, a town on the Blackfeet Reservation, to have dinner with family, but Kiara was on call for the vet and couldn't go with them.

"How many are coming?" Chloe asked.

"About twenty-five if everyone shows up."

"One turkey isn't going to be enough," Kiara said.

"Maribel is cooking one," Anna said. "And Virginia promised to bring one."

"Virginia's coming?" Chloe asked.

"She called me last week and wanted to come. The friend she usually visits passed away last year. She offered to do anything we needed, so I asked her to bring a turkey."

Chloe chuckled.

"What? When Virginia offers, you take her up on it."

"Is the hardware manager coming?" Kiara asked.

"Robert is, yes," Anna said.

"Won't that be awkward? If he and Maribel are no longer together?" Kiara asked.

"They're mature adults," Anna said. "Maribel told me the breakup was a mutual decision. It'll be fine. Now, while the turkey's cooking, let's get the tables set up for drinks and coffee."

Quinn and Paul arrived about ten to help set up the tables and chairs. They made a long buffet table, then set up another set for potluck dishes. A third table would hold desserts. Once that was set up, the pair helped her arrange tablecloths and place the centerpieces the florist had donated.

"I think that's as good as it's going to get," Anna said.

"You're set until everyone's scheduled to be here?" Paul asked.

"Yep. Thanks for the help, guys."

Paul waved and left.

As soon as the cook was out the door, Quinn put his arms around Anna. "Mind if I give you a Thanksgiving kiss?"

"Um …" She looked up at him. "Not at all."

He pressed his lips against hers, and she softened her mouth. This kiss went on long enough to leave her weak-kneed.

~ ~ ~

Chloe and Kiara came back at one-thirty, along with a few of their friends. They placed their dishes on the side table, then made sure the refreshment table was set with soda, several pitchers of water, and a space for wine. Anna had already put out a couple of bottles.

While they started the coffee, Anna pulled the turkey from the oven and set the timer for it to rest before she began carving. When Maribel staggered in with her bird, Quinn took it from her and brought it to the kitchen area.

"Getting crowded in here," he said.

"Always does," she said.

"How can I help?"

"Any good at carving up turkey?"

"I'm your man." He grinned and set to work on Maribel's offering.

Once he had the bird dissected and placed on a platter, he leaned over to give Anna another kiss.

Just at that moment Virginia walked in, all rhinestones and glitter.

Quinn stepped back.

Virginia grinned. "All I can say is it's about time. You two have been dancing around each other for years now. I thought you'd never figure it out."

Anna felt her cheeks flame.

"Oh, don't go getting all embarrassed," Virginia admonished. "You deserve a good man like Quinn, not like that last yahoo you married." Virginia looked around. "He's not coming here today, is he?"

"No," Anna said. Brandon had asked, and she'd almost let her guard down, before realizing she didn't want her holiday ruined by the tension he would bring.

"Good for you." The older woman grinned. "Now I'm going to get me a glass of wine so you two can go back to your smooching. Then you can send someone to get the turkey that's in the back of my SUV." She strode from the kitchen, light glittering on her rhinestone pockets.

Anna and Quinn looked at each other and laughed.

"What's so funny?" Paul asked as he walked in.

"Nothing," Anna said.

"If you say so. Looks like you have everything covered in here." He pointed to the platter. "Want me to take that out there?"

"Good idea. Put it in the center of the long table," Anna said. "That way we'll encourage people to sit in the center and work toward the edges."

"Got it." Paul picked up the platter and left.

"Let's go out and see how folks are doing," Anna said.

As she went through the bar area, she flicked on the stereo system to provide background music, then grabbed a glass of club soda, adding a splash of grenadine to celebrate the occasion.

Fifteen people mingled by the drinks table. Robert had arrived and was chatting with Virginia. Maribel had taken Dot under her wing, and the pair were chatting with two older men Anna only saw at Thanksgiving. They were outfitters of some sort and pretty much kept to themselves.

The door opened and a few more people trickled in.

"I think I'm going to go back and carve a second turkey," Quinn said.

"Good idea. I'll help"

"You can't 'help' carve a turkey," he said with a chuckle. "Stay here and mingle. It'll be good for you."

He walked back to the kitchen.

She took a deep breath and plunged into the crowd.

~ ~ ~

The afternoon was filled with laughter, stories, and good food. No one argued, each person on their best behavior. Early in the meal, Virginia proposed a toast.

"To Anna, the instigator of this feast. Thanksgiving is a time for people to gather, enjoy each other, and appreciate what we have. Anna provides a space for those of us who would otherwise be alone. Thank you." Virginia raised her glass. "To Anna."

Everyone raised their glass and echoed, "To Anna."

"Don't you dare say you don't deserve it," Quinn whispered in her ear. "Just take it in. They're your friends, and they love you."

She raised her glass. "Thank you."

Everyone cheered, and she let their affection fill her.

The food was top-notch. Everyone had brought their A game to the meal. By the time she was finished eating, she felt every corner of her stomach had been stuffed as completely as one of the turkeys.

As if by some unseen signal, everyone started moving at once, gathering plates, putting away casseroles, and generally cleaning up.

Within a half hour, the table was cleared, desserts were cut, and someone turned down the stereo and put a quarter in the jukebox.

The party lasted another hour before people started gathering their dishes and heading home. Soon only she and Quinn were left.

"You throw a nice Thanksgiving," he said.

"Thanks."

"I've had a great time with you this last week, but I don't think I've been as clear as I need to be." He sat on one of the bar stools.

"What do you mean?" She sat next to him.

"I never thought I'd be seriously interested in anyone again once my marriage broke up. I figured I'd be fine with friends and the occasional friend with benefits." He smiled. "I even thought I could keep you in the friend zone. But there's something about you …" He brushed a lock of her hair behind her ear. "I want more. I want an us. Do you think that's possible? I know you've been hurt, and hurt badly, but I'm hoping you can get past that, because …" He took a deep breath. "It's already too late for me."

She should say no. Her internal walls had crumbled a bit over the last week and begged to be reassembled. But if she said no, she'd lose her chance to experience what having a relationship with a good guy would be like.

A familiar voice in her head said, "But you don't deserve that."

Why didn't she? Brandon hadn't been the only one to screw up their marriage. And Maddie?

Maybe Anna had done the best she could with a bad situation. Short of locking her daughter in a room, she had had very little control over Maddie once she became a teenager. She'd provided the tools to her daughter. It had been up to Maddie to pick them up.

"Yes," she finally said to Quinn. "I'd like that. I have no guarantees that anything could work out, but I'd like to try."

"Thank you." He smiled, leaned over, and kissed her.

Chapter Thirty-Seven

Anna woke the next day with a light heart. She and Quinn had talked for another hour, finding their way to a new level of intimacy and possibility. He'd walked her to her truck where they'd kissed before she left.

It was nice to have someone care for her.

After breakfast and tending to a few chores, she left for the bar early to make sure everything was cleaned up from the Thanksgiving feast and to prep for one of the busiest weekends in the year. All hands were on deck, except for Brandon, although she'd let him know she may need him if things got too busy.

Humming a tune, she climbed the steps to the front door, opened it, and walked inside.

As soon as she did, she knew something was off. At first glance, nothing looked to be disturbed, but there was something in the air that felt out of place.

She walked closer to the bar. Something was scrawled across the back mirror, and bottles were missing from the shelves. Behind the bar, disaster loomed.

Shards of glass and smashed bottles carpeted the narrow space. Someone had launched their rage at her. The word scrawled across the mirror read: *Bitch.*

Who had this much anger toward her?

She walked back to the kitchen, dreading what she might find. The damage there was milder. A few packages of hamburger buns were stomped on. With trepidation, she opened the walk-in fridge, but it seemed untouched. So did the freezer inside it.

Her office lock had been jimmied, and there was paper strewn everywhere. Fortunately, it was her habit to take her laptop home with her at night. She hadn't even brought it to work yesterday.

Anxiety increasing, she walked to the storage room. The door was wide open.

Here the miscreant had limited themselves to theft. Her most expensive liquors were gone, whole boxes removed, but nothing had been broken.

She sank to the floor. Her business, which had been filled with happiness only the day before, had been terrorized while she was gone.

How was she even going to open? She always counted on this weekend to bring her a good amount of business as people joined their families. Friday and Saturday nights were always filled with young people eager to reconnect. Families came for dinner to recover from all the cooking on Thanksgiving.

Who would do such a thing? Who had access?

Who hated her this much?

While she would suspect Brandon of petty theft, this seemed over the top for him. He preferred to use more passive-aggressive means to try to get to her. She didn't have any competition in town to speak of. Riley's coffee shop took care of breakfast. The Buckhorn handled the rest. For anything else, a person had to go to Livingston.

There hadn't been any other people who'd tried to buy the Buckhorn. The owner had been grateful when she came along.

Olivia had been with her since the beginning. Kiara had a sweet soul. Although she'd suspected Sue of the thefts originally, Anna couldn't see her exhibiting this kind of rage.

Paul?

No. She just couldn't see him doing something like this.

She pushed herself to standing to check out the back door.

It was still partially open. She went to shut it, but stopped herself. If she wanted any shot at getting insurance to pay for any of this, she'd need a police report. It was time to call Xavier, the sheriff who had taken over after Jake decided to become a part-time deputy.

But first she went into the office and searched until she found a piece of cardboard. In black magic marker she wrote, "Opening Late. Sorry."

After attaching it to the front door with a piece of duct tape, she called Paul and Olivia and told them briefly what she'd found when she came to work.

"How terrible!" Olivia exclaimed.

"Do you need help cleaning up?" Paul offered.

She told them both to come to work in a few hours. Hopefully, Xavier would be done by then, and she'd be able to get most of the damage cleaned. She made the call to the sheriff.

Then, with a sense of relief she hadn't experienced in a long time—if ever—she called Quinn. He was in Bozeman, but said he'd get there as fast as he could.

Xavier and a second officer arrived a few minutes after she'd hung up with Quinn. Xavier introduced the woman with him as someone who was taking forensic classes. She knew how to dust for fingerprints.

"Thanks for coming," Anna said. "Let me show you what I found."

"You didn't touch anything, did you?" Xavier asked.

"A few things, and I'll point them out to you."

Anna showed them the vandalism.

"I know it's a pain," Xavier said. "But can you make an inventory of what's missing and what was destroyed? Your insurance company is going to want that, too."

"I can do that. I'll start in the office."

"Let my officer get in there and take pictures first," Xavier said.

Once the officer was done, it didn't take Anna long to realize that the office looked worse than it was. Her desk had been ransacked, with papers all over the place, but nothing looked damaged, and the papers all seemed intact.

"Are you finished with the storeroom?" she asked Xavier.

"Yep. And just about done with the mess behind the bar."

"Did you find anything?"

Xavier shook his head. "Whoever did this wore gloves. Do you have any idea who would do something like this?"

"Not really," she said. "I've been wracking my brain to figure out who … or why … someone would want to do this to my business."

"Like I know Quinn told you, the back door lock was easy to jimmy. Same with the storeroom and your office."

"How do you know what Quinn said?"

Xavier gave her a look that said, "Do you really need to ask that?"

"Jake."

Xavier nodded. "There's not much to go on. Unless we catch this person in the act, or you can think of someone who might have it in for you, I wouldn't expect anything."

"That's frustrating."

"I understand. We'll do the best we can. I'm trying to set your expectations, that's all."

"Got it," Anna said.

In another half hour they were gone. She'd done the inventory on the storage room, a number that was depressingly high. She was staring at the glass on the floor when her phone rang.

"What's up, Brandon?" she asked.

"I wanted to wish you a belated Happy Thanksgiving," he said. "I missed you yesterday. I remember all those great holiday meals we used to have."

She didn't remember them as fondly as he did. There was always a delicate balance to walk as the evening wore on and the drinking increased.

"Happy Thanksgiving to you, too."

"So, do you need me to come in today? I remember how busy this weekend always was. I'm sure you could use a helping hand, cleaning up and all."

A buzz started in her brain.

"We cleaned up really well last night. Many hands make light work, as my mother used to say."

"I meant—" He cut himself off.

She looked at the mess on the floor. Could he really be that angry?

"I'd be happy to help out, even if for a little while. You work really hard. Let me give you a hand. Give me a chance to prove how much I've changed. You don't need that cowboy. We're much more alike than you and he are."

So that's what this was really about. Brandon was jealous of Quinn.

No, that didn't make sense. Brandon had been out of her life for a long time. Why now?

She needed answers.

"Sure. Come on in. I don't know how long I'll need you, but there are some things I need to attend to."

"When do you need me?"

"Whenever you can get here."

After she ended the call, she pulled a chair off a table and sat down. Her gut told her he'd been stealing from her all along, even before he showed up to ask for a job. He knew how to pick a lock; she'd seen him do it, telling her he'd forgotten his keys.

As for the rage … he might be what they call a "dry drunk," someone who'd stopped drinking but who hadn't done the work to uncover why they drank in the first place. The residual anger and pain was still in play, just as unpredictable as ever.

When he finally got there, she watched him carefully as he took in the damage. He'd always been a good actor, turning on the charm when he needed to get out of one tight place or another.

"What happened here?" he asked.

"I'm not sure."

"Sure looks like someone was angry."

"Yep," she said. "I've been racking my brain, but I can't think of anyone angry enough at me to do something like this."

"You must have made an enemy somehow."

"It's not that kind of community," she said. "People here are more interested in lending a helping hand to another person, not tearing them down."

"That's Pollyanna of you. Every community has some bad apples. It might be someone down on their luck who decided to rob you because he thought you were rich."

"Who told you I was robbed?"

"You did. You told me someone was stealing expensive liquor from the storeroom."

"I did? I don't remember that. And I'm not rich." She knew she'd never told him she was robbed. He was trying to gaslight her again.

"You must have forgotten," he said. "You never could remember everything even though you thought you could. Especially when you're drinking."

"I don't drink anymore," she spat back. "Do you?"

"No, I told you. I've been in recovery for a while now." His expression softened. "I wanted to work for you so you could see, so you could remember how good we were together." He took a step toward her. "We could make this place so much more than it is. All you need to do is trust me and let me in."

"I wouldn't trust you if you were the last person on earth," she said.

"But you trust that cowboy."

"Michael Quinn has never gaslit me or yelled at me." She drew herself up as tall as she could. "He never, ever hit me."

"Probably because you never pushed him to it."

"You're so full of it," she said. "I know. I know from the marrow of my bones that you're the one responsible for this."

He smirked at her. "If I did, you'll never be able to prove it. But I didn't. Work with me, Anna. It will be much better. You'll see. I'll even forgive you for letting Maddie die."

"You ..." She lunged toward him.

The front door opened, and Quinn walked in.

Chapter Thirty-Eight

It took thirty seconds for Quinn to figure out what was going on. He rushed toward Anna and Brandon, but she stopped in her tracks, turned toward him, and held up her hand in a "stop" motion.

Brandon smirked.

"Thanks for coming," she told Quinn. "But I've got this handled."

Quinn nodded and sat in a nearby chair. It was important that she own her strength. She really was formidable.

Brandon's expression of triumph faded.

Anna squared off with her ex again.

"Why?" she asked Brandon in a low voice, but still loud enough for Quinn to hear. "Why do something like this?" She gestured toward the bar.

Quinn looked over, his muscles tensing in anger as he took in the missing bottles and the word written on the mirror.

"You keep saying you love me, that we were good together once," Anna said. "But it looks like you're really angry with me, too."

"If I ever did something like that—which I'm not saying I did—how can you blame me? You pushed me from the relationship and kept me from my little girl. She died on your watch, not mine."

Anna stiffened, but didn't say anything.

Quinn got ready to punch the man in the face. He knew Anna could take care of herself, but Brandon was pushing the limit.

"Then—somehow—you managed to scrape together enough money to buy this place. Who'd- you steal from to do that, Anna? You'd never make enough money to do it on your own. You must have done something. Or did you sell yourself to someone like him." Brandon nodded in Quinn's direction.

It took everything in Quinn's power not to stand up and deck the man.

But it was not what Anna wanted. She wanted—needed—to face down her ex on her own.

So he satisfied himself with cracking his knuckles.

The sound reverberated in the empty room.

"You're angry because I didn't follow you into the gutter," Anna said. "And now you want a piece of the action. When I wouldn't give it to you, you decided to get revenge, first by stealing from me, and then doing more destructive things."

"You're just making things up to justify yourself," Brandon said. "I'm fine. I don't need to steal from you." He flicked a gaze at Quinn, a dark look that said he'd take care of Quinn later. "Or anyone else."

"I don't believe you." Anna walked over to the bar and examined the damage again. She looked at the bottles left on the back wall. She frowned and walked around back of the bar, the sound of broken glass crunching under her feet.

She selected one of the remaining bottles and brought it back to where Brandon was standing.

"Isn't Bookers Bourbon your favorite brand?"

He shrugged. "Lots of people like it."

"Yes. But I remember. With you it was almost an obsession."

"So what? That's a pricy bottle. The thief obviously has good taste." Brandon said, his smirk of defiance returning.

Quinn cursed quietly. He'd seen men like Brandon before, always so cocky and sure of themselves. Even when he'd had them dead to rights, they'd deny everything pointing to them, keeping up the act right until the time the judge sentenced them.

"Interesting," she said. "There were several boxes missing today, including two of Bookers Bourbon. In fact the theft wiped out my entire supply. Except for this bottle." She swung it back and forth by its neck, Brandon's eyes tracking it like a ping pong ball. What stopped you? Couldn't destroy your favorite swill?"

"You know that's not swill. Besides, like I said, lots of people drink that stuff."

"But lots of people don't have the combination of drinking Bookers and wanting revenge."

"You have it all wrong, Anna," Brandon said.

Quinn pulled out his phone, hoping Brandon was too occupied to notice. Quinn texted Xavier the information about the Bookers Bourbon and suggested they get a warrant for Brandon's car. Quinn doubted the man had had a chance to move it to another location.

Got it, Xavier texted back. *Where is he?*

Buckhorn.

"The only thing I got wrong was letting you back into my life," Anna said. "You're fired. Don't expect anything from me ever again."

"But Anna—"

"Leave. Now."

Quinn started to rise from his chair.

Brandon caught the movement and stepped back.

"Have it your way," he said to Anna. "Enjoy life with your cowboy until he finds out what a skank you are."

He started for the door, but paused to lobby one more shot. "Have you told him how you killed your own daughter?"

Anna whitened.

Quinn stood and walked to Brandon. "I think the lady told you to leave," he said.

Brandon laughed and walked out the door.

Quinn followed to make sure he actually left.

With a rude gesture, Brandon got in his car and sped out of the lot, spraying gravel everywhere.

A minute later the sound of sirens pierced the air.

Quinn grinned and walked back inside.

Anna was standing where he'd left her.

He went to her and pulled her into his arms. "It's over. You can let it go now."

"He's right," she said. "If you knew how I'd behaved when we were together … and I let Maddie down, too. You'd leave if you knew the real me."

Quinn led her to the chair she'd made him sit in and got her seated. Then he pulled down another chair, pulled it close to her, and took her hands in his.

"Whatever happened, it's in the past," he said. "I knew you when you were young, and I know you now. You're a strong woman, Anna. When you told me the story of Maddie, all I could think about was the fortitude you needed to keep going, keep trying. Addiction isn't easy. I saw more than one mother give up when I was a cop. You never did. Even if you hadn't told me, I'd know that's what you would have done. It's who you are. You do the best you can at the time, but you never give up. Never."

Her eyes were luminescent with tears when she looked up at him.

"Do you really believe that?"

"With all my soul."

She stared at him.

"And I'm not the only one," he said. "People in this town like and respect you. You're one of them. Their only complaint is that you don't let them help you as much as you'd like."

"It's hard for me to accept help."

"I get that. But how about we start right now? Show me what he did and we'll come up with a plan to get this place open. There are a lot of young adults who'd like to get away from their parents about now."

She smiled. "That's true enough. Follow me."

The devastation behind the bar made him angry all over again. "Are you going to have enough glasses to make it through the night?" he asked.

"I'm not sure."

"How about the missing liquor bottles?"

She scanned the back bar. "I think we'll get through the night without them. I sell mostly beer and wine with enough martinis and mules to round out the night. There's enough here to cover that."

"Okay."

Following her to the back, he asked if she needed more buns, and she nodded.

After examining the lock on the back door, he said, "Like I told you, this needs to be replaced. It's been lock picked too many times, and it's just about useless."

Her shoulders slumped. "I should have done it last week."

"Shoulda, coulda, woulda," he said. "Do you have anyone you can get to help clean up?"

"Paul and Olivia should be here soon. But I'd hoped it would be all cleaned up by the time they got here."

"You don't have do it alone, Anna. You really don't." He pulled her in for a hug and kissed her lips. "I'm going to enjoy getting used to that," he said with a smile. "Don't you see? People want to help you. They like you. Let them give you a hand. We're here for you. *I'm* here for you." He leaned over and kissed her again. "And I'm here for the long haul."

"You heard what he said."

"And I know what kind of person he is." Quinn pulled her into a hug. "You're important to me. I care about you. I'm not letting a two-bit hustler scare me off." He held her closely, wanting to tell her how he really felt, but knowing it wasn't the time. Not quite. But soon.

"I'm going to go to the hardware store, get some new locks, pick up my tools, and change these locks. I think I saw some plastic cups in their kitchen section. I'll pick some of those up, too. They're not classy, but they'll do in a pinch."

"Thank you," she said. "Keep track of what you spend. I'll get the money from the insurance company eventually."

He had one more thing he had to tell her, but wasn't sure of her reaction. But it needed to be out in the open. Nothing destroyed a relationship faster than secrets.

"I texted Xavier what Brandon said about the case of bourbon. I had the feeling he was lying. He couldn't have gotten far with it. I suggested Xavier get a warrant. "

"You shouldn't have done that," she said with a scowl. "That's my business. I'll take care of it."

Quinn shook his head. "I'm a cop. I couldn't let it go. If he's innocent, Xavier won't be able to find the box. But we both know it was Brandon who did all this. He broke the law. No one is above the law in this country. No one."

She stayed silent for a few beats and then nodded.

"Okay," she finally said. "I don't like it, but I understand."

"Thank you," he said. "Now let me get going while you make those calls."

"Will do," she said. "And Quinn?"

"Yes?"

"Thanks."

"Anytime. See you in a bit."

~ ~ ~

Once Quinn got to town, he put in a call to Xavier.

"Did you get the warrant?"

"Better than that," Xavier said. "I went out to a spot by the Buckhorn to wait, hoping I could nail him for some kind of violation which would give me reason to search his car. Luck was with us. He spun out of that parking lot so fast that he was over the speed limit right after he hit the pavement. Moving violation."

"And?"

"The box was in the trunk, along with several other bottles of upscale liquor. We also found lock picks on him and a pair of gloves. Our officer found a few fibers in the storeroom, and we're betting it's a match. All of this gives us enough to apply for a warrant to search his place."

"Well done," Quinn said.

"I thought so." Xavier chuckled. "I'll keep you posted."

"Thanks."

Quinn hung up and walked toward the hardware store, stopping by a sign in an empty storefront announcing: "Willow Creek Fiber Coming Soon!!!"

The knitting ladies would be happy about that.

He quickly found what he needed in the hardware store and brought them to the front.

"That for Anna?" Robert asked.

Quinn nodded.

"Then I don't need your money. Tell her anything else she needs it's on the house." He held up a finger. "As long as it's not something big like a Weber grill or something."

Quinn smiled. "Thanks, man."

"She's good people and done a lot for this town. It feels good to give back."

"I'll let her know."

"And I'll make sure to get there this weekend and spend some of my money there."

"She'd appreciate that."

When he got back to the Buckhorn, the parking lot was almost full. He trotted up the steps and opened the front door.

It looked like the entire town had turned out. The music was going and people were working and chatting. As usual Heather seemed to be in charge.

Anna spotted him and rushed over.

"I didn't do anything," she said. "They just showed up." Then she burst into tears.

Michael Quinn pulled the love of his life into his arms and held her until she was all cried out.

Chapter Thirty-Nine

By mid-afternoon Sunday, Anna was ready for the long weekend to be over, but she was pleased with the revenue. Even with the late opening on Friday, she'd exceeded what she'd made the year before.

It seemed like the entire town streamed through the bar in the last three days, some of them coming in every day. People she knew well, like Riley and Heather, had made a point to offer their sympathy and to ask if she needed any help. Those community members she didn't know personally made sure to let her know they were rooting for the Buckhorn.

More than one person sitting at the bar had over-tipped, telling her to get new glassware with the extra.

Her heart was overflowing with their good wishes.

The only damper on her emotions was that Brandon was in jail. She'd never wished that on him. She'd loved him once.

But it was where he belonged. She'd survived her parents' dysfunction, she'd had the strength to leave a bad marriage, and maybe, someday soon, she'd be able to fully forgive herself for Maddie's death.

With Quinn all things were possible.

The door opened, and her potential future walked in.

She gave Quinn a big smile. He'd been there every day of the long weekend, usually coming in just before the busiest time of the day. He'd stepped in to bartend so she could check on tables, clean up, and relieve her waitresses for a break.

"How's it going?" he asked as she poured him the glass of soda he normally drank at this time of day.

"It was a decent lunch crowd," she said. "A fair number of people returning from cabins and stays at inns south of here. Some had gone into Yellowstone, reporting on a lot more wildlife out and about. Snow's already covering most of the park."

"I'd love to do a winter tour there sometime," Quinn said. "I hear it's a totally different place, fewer people and more animals."

"Plus the stillness that winter brings."

He nodded. "All I have to do is persuade the woman I'm seeing to take a few days off."

"In February, that could probably be arranged," she said with a smile.

This camaraderie was totally different from the angst and drama of her relationship with any man in her life, and she was beginning to appreciate it.

"Good," he said, matching her smile. "I'll look into it. My treat, of course."

"I should be able to buy a meal or two," she said, not wanting to be totally beholden to him.

"We'll talk about it. Anything else interesting going on?"

"Riley and Sean and their two hellions were here for lunch. I don't know how they do it. Those boys are on the go all the time. And they're into things they shouldn't be before anyone realizes. Today, it was cue balls. They were trying to figure out why they didn't bounce."

"Ouch. On the bright side, their curiosity could lead them to make great discoveries later in life."

"Could be … if they survive childhood. Oh, and Heather was in with a few other women, no doubt dreaming up her latest scheme. I'm sure I'll know about it as soon as she finds something for me to do."

"Apparently, there's a new knitting store coming to town," he said. "I meant to tell you a few days ago, but it slipped my mind."

"The woman who will be running it was in, too," Anna said. "She's about my age, very warm. She'll do well, I think."

"Hope so. We need a few more small businesses."

"Yep." Anna excused herself to tend to the two other customers at the bar.

They chatted a while longer, but parted ways when Sue came in for her shift. Shortly after that, Caleb and Destiny came in. They challenged Quinn to a game of pool.

Soon the soothing sound of cues smacking balls filled the bar. Anna adjusted the volume on the sound system so it could still be heard over the game.

While it was quiet, she restocked as best she could. Although she'd notified the insurance company, she wouldn't be able to talk to a claims adjuster until Monday. She wasn't looking forward to filling out all that paperwork.

Paul came back in for his second shift.

"Everything cool?" he asked.

"Everything's cool," she responded.

"Good," he said, heading to his kitchen domain.

She relaxed into a feeling of well-being.

~ ~ ~

Surprisingly, the Sunday dinner hour was more crowded than she'd anticipated. Ken and Winnie Greenbriar were there, as was Robert with a woman Anna didn't know. At another table Maribel laughed with one of the ranchers who had a place southwest of town. It looked like the pair were really over each other and had moved on.

Chloe came in with a girlfriend. Both were smiling. Once they'd gotten their drinks, they challenged Caleb and Quinn to a game of pool. Destiny was sitting with the mayor, who'd come in to have dinner as well.

There was no doubt in Anna's mind. They were here to support her in the best way they knew how. She was one of them.

Virginia came in and sat at the bar.

"So," she said, once Anna served her the top-shelf bourbon she'd requested. "Are you going to get over whatever's holding you back and start dating that fine man?" She nodded toward the pool table.

"Could be," was all Anna would commit to saying.

"Are you out of your mind, woman?" Virginia asked. "You still don't have hopes for that idiot you married last time, do you?"

"Oh, no. I'm past that."

"Good thing, 'cause I hear he's in jail."

Anna nodded.

"I know you have feelings for Quinn," Virginia said. "And what he feels for you is written all over his face. Life is too short to keep ignoring what's in front of you."

Her statement made Anna smile. Virginia was right. Life was way too short. Anna was already more than halfway through hers. Maddie had died too young, before she'd discovered what love really meant.

The tragedy of her daughter's life still tugged at her, but wasn't it time to move on? She didn't have to forget Maddie, but it didn't mean she had to punish herself for the rest of her life, either.

Now was the time to take down all her walls and step into the future

She nodded at Virginia, then turned to refill a glass for a man at the other end of the bar.

After all these years, Anna still had a huge crush on Michael Quinn. Now was the time to tell him she still did.

~ ~ ~

People cleared out early, realizing Monday morning brought a return to reality. For her, it was a day off. If the weather cooperated, she could take a drive to Butte. Maybe Quinn would come. It was time to re-introduce him to her mother.

Anna smiled at the image of her mother gushing all over a new man in her daughter's life.

"What's got you in good spirits?" Quinn asked as he brought a bunch of empty glasses to the bar.

"All of this." She gestured around the entire restaurant and included him in the sweep of her arm.

He grinned at her.

"Let me help clean up, and then, maybe we can have a nightcap?"

"I don't drink."

"I know, but we can still cap the night, can't we?"

His smile was infectious.

"Sure," she said. "If you want to help, Sue and Kiara could use some help clearing tables and setting up chairs. I'll clean glasses."

"On it," he said.

Before starting the barware, she checked in with Paul to see how he was doing.

"It shouldn't take me long," he said. "I was able to keep up with most of the dishes throughout the night. It wouldn't be a bad idea to hire a dishwasher-slash-busboy. Give some teenager a chance to learn what work really means."

"Could another person fit in here?"

"Hire a skinny teen," Paul said, chuckling.

"I'll think on it."

It was a good idea.

By the time another hour had passed, the restaurant was cleaned and set for its re-opening on Tuesday. Quinn and Anna sat at the bar, he with a long-neck beer, her with her traditional club soda.

A long time ago she might have envied him his beer, but she'd accepted it wasn't for her. Besides, she'd found a lot of the benefits of being sober.

They chatted about everything and nothing. She talked about hiring a busboy and maybe asking Olivia if she wanted to learn how to tend bar.

He told her how his grant proposals were going. Jose's friend had helped him put them into the best shape for submission. With any luck, he'd be able to break ground for a corral and shelter in the spring.

During a lull in the conversation, Whitney Houston's clear voice sang out the first words of "I Will Always Love You."

"I love this song," Anna said.

"Me too." Quinn slid off his stool and held his hand out. "Dance with me."

She stepped into his arms, and they began to move together to the slow beat of the song. Within a few measures, she shifted to get closer to him, feeling like she'd finally found where she belonged.

Silently, they moved to the music. When it was over, and the last notes died away, they still stood together.

"It's true," Quinn said. "I will always love you."

She lifted her head. "Are you in love with me?"

"I have been, for a while."

She swallowed, willing herself to say the words she'd always wanted to tell him.

"That's good," she said. "Because I've been in love with you my whole life. And I still am."

"Then it will all work out," he said.

"Yes."

She lifted her face to his and put her arms around his neck, tugging him close.

He obliged by lowering his lips to hers.

"I love you," he whispered against her lips before pressing his mouth against hers.

I love you, too, her soul whispered back.

Author's Note

The case that Becky Oakland argued is based on a real lawsuit that was brought against Lucky Minerals by Earth Justice. The company was planning to do gold mining that would have affected the clean water of the Paradise Valley north of Yellowstone National Park. In 2020 the Montana Supreme Court ruled against Lucky Minerals because, among other things, it went against the state's constitution protecting the public's environmental rights.

The other two lawsuits mentioned (Mississippi and the Bitterroot Valley) are also based on real cases.

We have only one planet, and I believe it is up to us to care for it. At the same time, we have to tend to human needs. It's one of the reasons I like the Nature Conservancy. They work with all the stakeholders in any project they develop, from fishermen who depend on the oceans for food, to ranchers in Montana who want to protect their livelihood for future generations.

This story also has a lot of personal elements for me. I have an addicted child. It can be heart-breaking. Fortunately, she is still among us.

I hope you've enjoyed visiting Willow Creek. Let me know if you'd like to read more stories set in this small town by emailing me at casey@caseydawes.com.

About the Author

Casey Dawes writes non-steamy contemporary romance and inspirational women's fiction with romantic elements.

Her women's fiction series, Rocky Mountain Front, explores the five siblings from a ranching family living in Montana, the people who love them, and the characters in the small town in which they live. Previous to that she wrote a 5-book contemporary romance series about friends and family on the Central Coast. Her latest series features love between "seasoned" heroes and heroines in a small Montana town.

Currently, she and her husband are traveling the US in a small trailer with the cat who owns them. When not writing or editing, she is exploring national parks, haunting independent bookstores, and lurking in spinning and yarn stores trying not to get caught fondling the fiber!

Like short, heartwarming stories? Go to my website, www.CaseyDawes.com, to get your copy of *Sweet Shorts,* only available to members of my newsletter mailing list: *On the Road to Your Next Read ...*

Other Books by Casey Dawes

Promise Cove
Return to Promise Cove
Spring in Promise Cove
Hope in Promise Cove
Winter in Promise Cove
Promise Cove Wedding
Summer in Promise Cove
Away from Promise Cove

Willow Creek Series
Clean, small-town, later-in-life romance with a little bit of suspense.

The Sheriff of Willow Creek
The Wrangler of Willow Creek
The Rancher of Willow Creek

Beck Family Saga
This series revolves around a Montana ranching family—women's fiction with a touch of romance!

Home Is Where the Heart Is
Finding Home
Leaving Home
Coming Home
Starting for Home
Finally Home

Coharie Beach Café
Clean women's fiction with romantic elements

Coharie Beach Café (Complete Series)

Grown-Up Second Chance RV Park Romance Series
Romantic comedy series!

Grown-Up Second Chance
Her Son's Secret Father
Her Texas Cowboy

California Romance Series
Two mothers, two daughters, and one friend explore
contemporary romance on the California coast.

California Sunset
California Wine
California Homecoming
California Thyme
California Sunrise

Montana Christmas Series
A new adult contemporary romance series set in Missoula
Montana—just right for the holidays!

Sweet Montana Christmas
Montana Christmas Magic
Second Chance Christmas